IMAGE COMICS, INC.
Robert Kirkman – Chief Operating Officer
Erik Larsen – Chief Financial Officer
Todd McFarlane – President
Marc Silvestri – Chief Executive Officer
Jim Valentino – Vice-President

Eric Stephenson – Publisher
Corey Murphy – Director of Sales
Jeremy Sullivan – Director of Digital Sales
Kat Salazar – Director of PR & Marketing
Emily Miller – Director of Operations
Branwyn Bigglestone – Senior Accounts Manager
Drew Gill – Art Director
Jonathan Chan – Production Manager
Meredith Wallace – Print Manager
Randy Okamura – Marketing Production Designer
David Brothers – Content Manager
Addison Duke – Production Artist
Vincent Kukua – Production Artist
Sasha Head – Production Artist
Tricia Ramos – Production Artist
Emilio Bautista – Sales Assistant
Jessica Ambriz – Administrative Assistant
IMAGECOMICS.COM

JONATHAN HICKMAN
WRITER

NICK DRAGOTTA
ARTIST

FRANK MARTIN
COLORS

RUS WOOTON
LETTERS

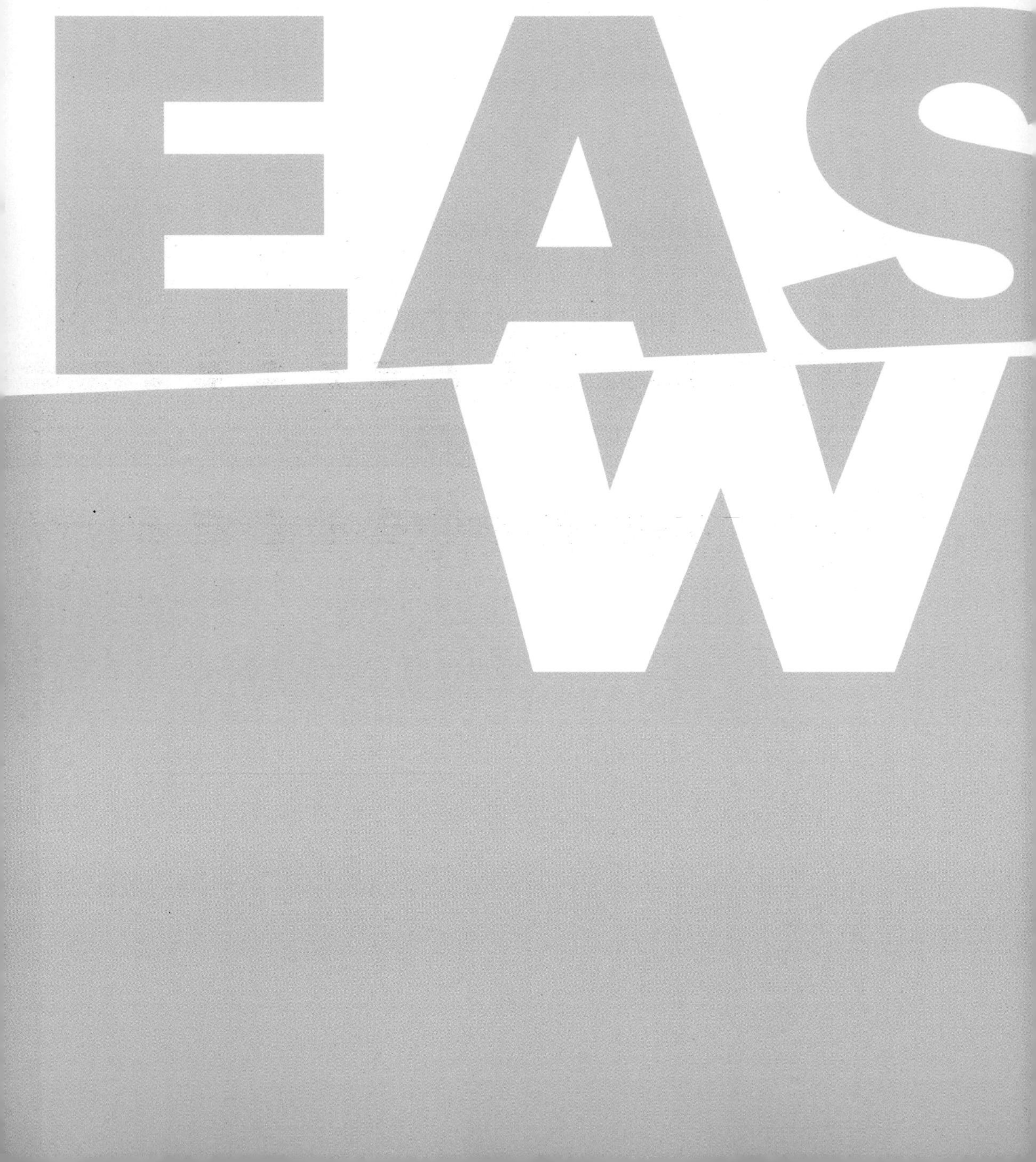
EAS
W

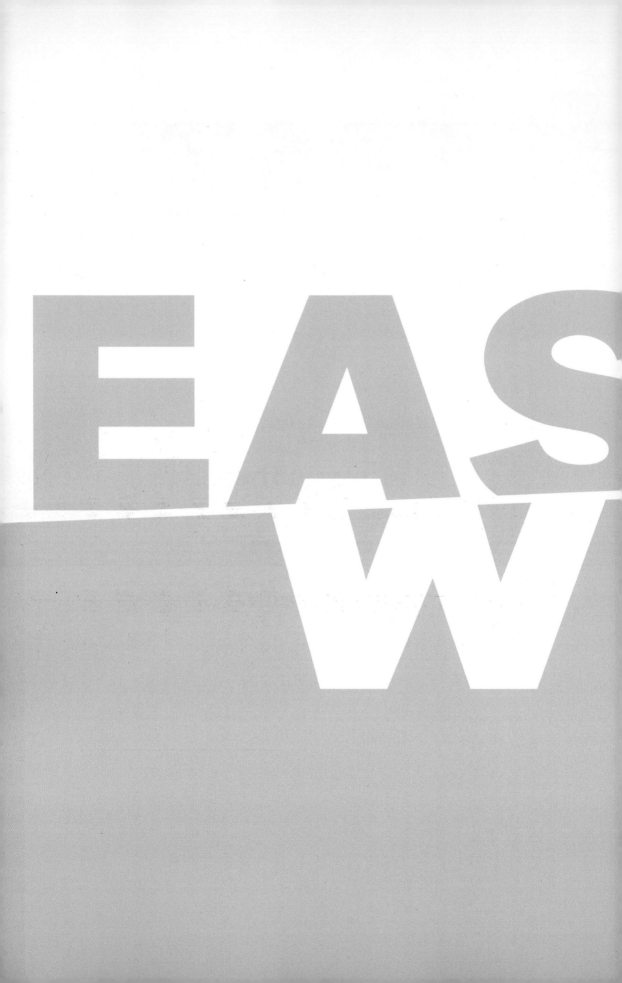

T
OF
EST

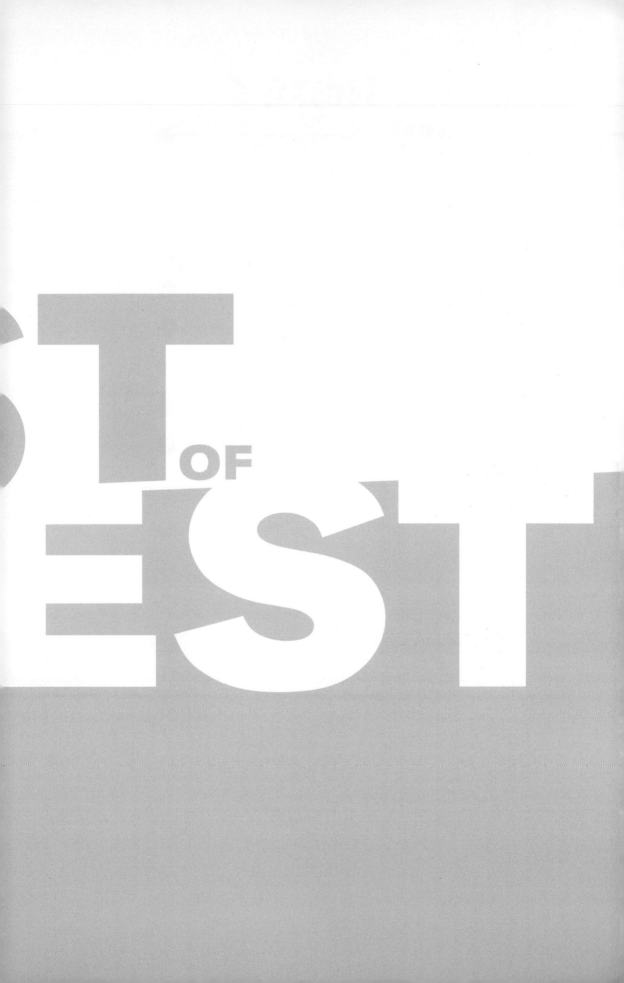

INDEX

THE **WORLD**

SOURCEBOOK | ATLAS |
ENCYCLOPEDIA | TIMELINES |
APOCRYPHA

THE RIDE.

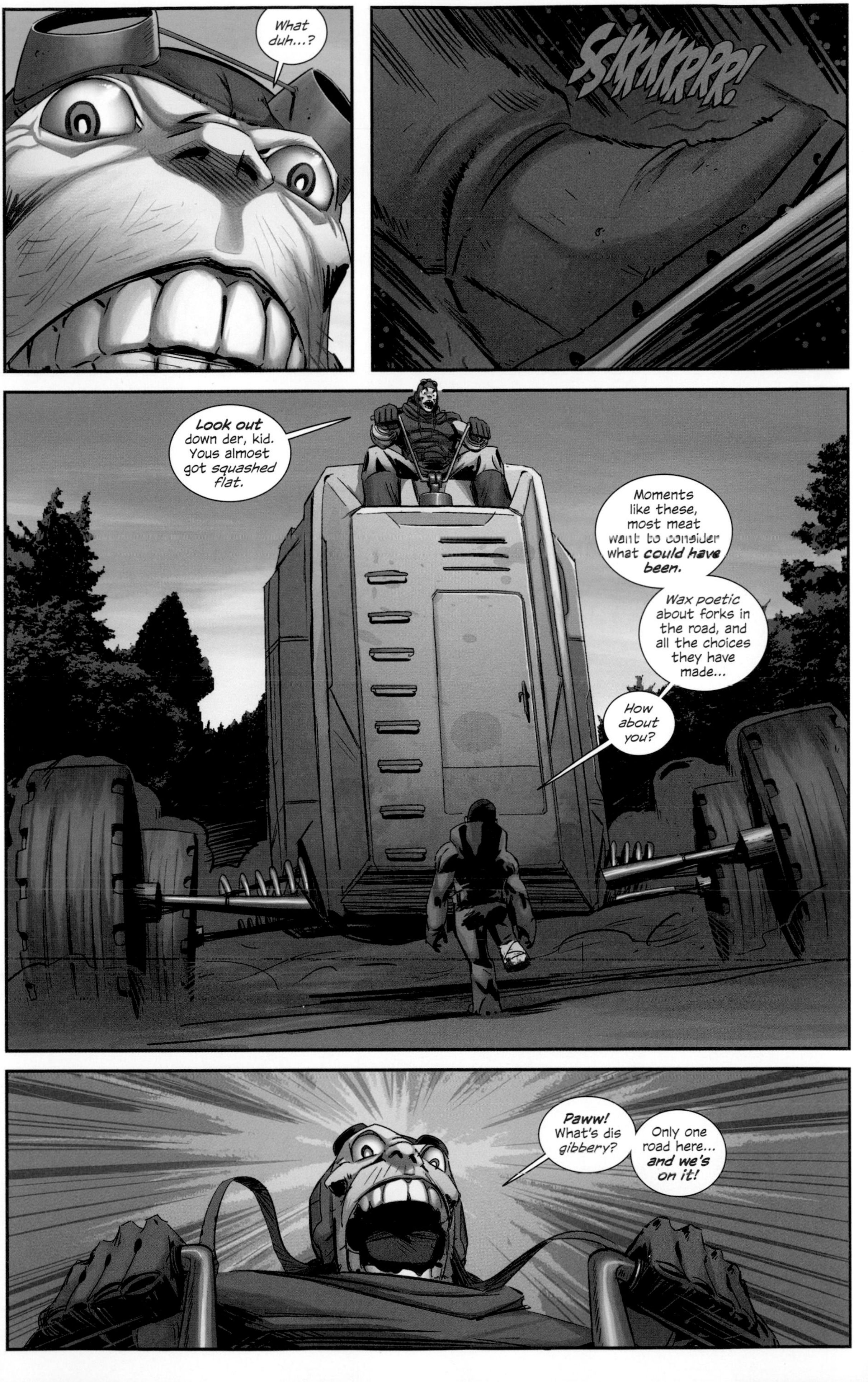
What duh...?
SKRKKRRR!
Look out down der, kid. Yous almost got *squashed* flat.
Moments like these, most meat want to consider what ***could have been.***
Wax poetic about forks in the road, and all the choices they have made...
How about you?
Paww! What's dis *gibbery?*
Only one road here... ***and we's on it!***

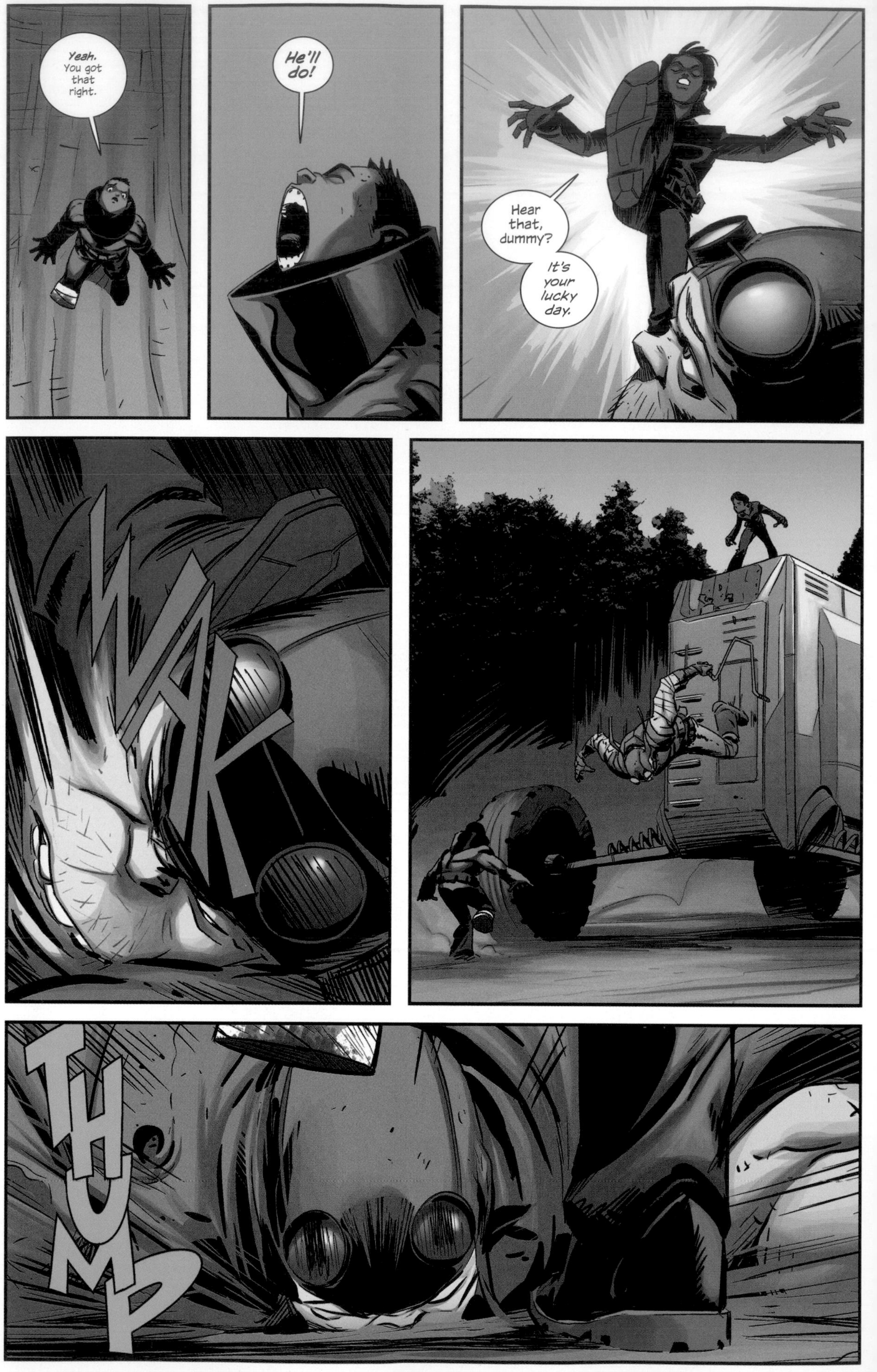
Yeah. You got that right.
He'll do!
Hear that, dummy?
It's your lucky day.
WAK
THUMP

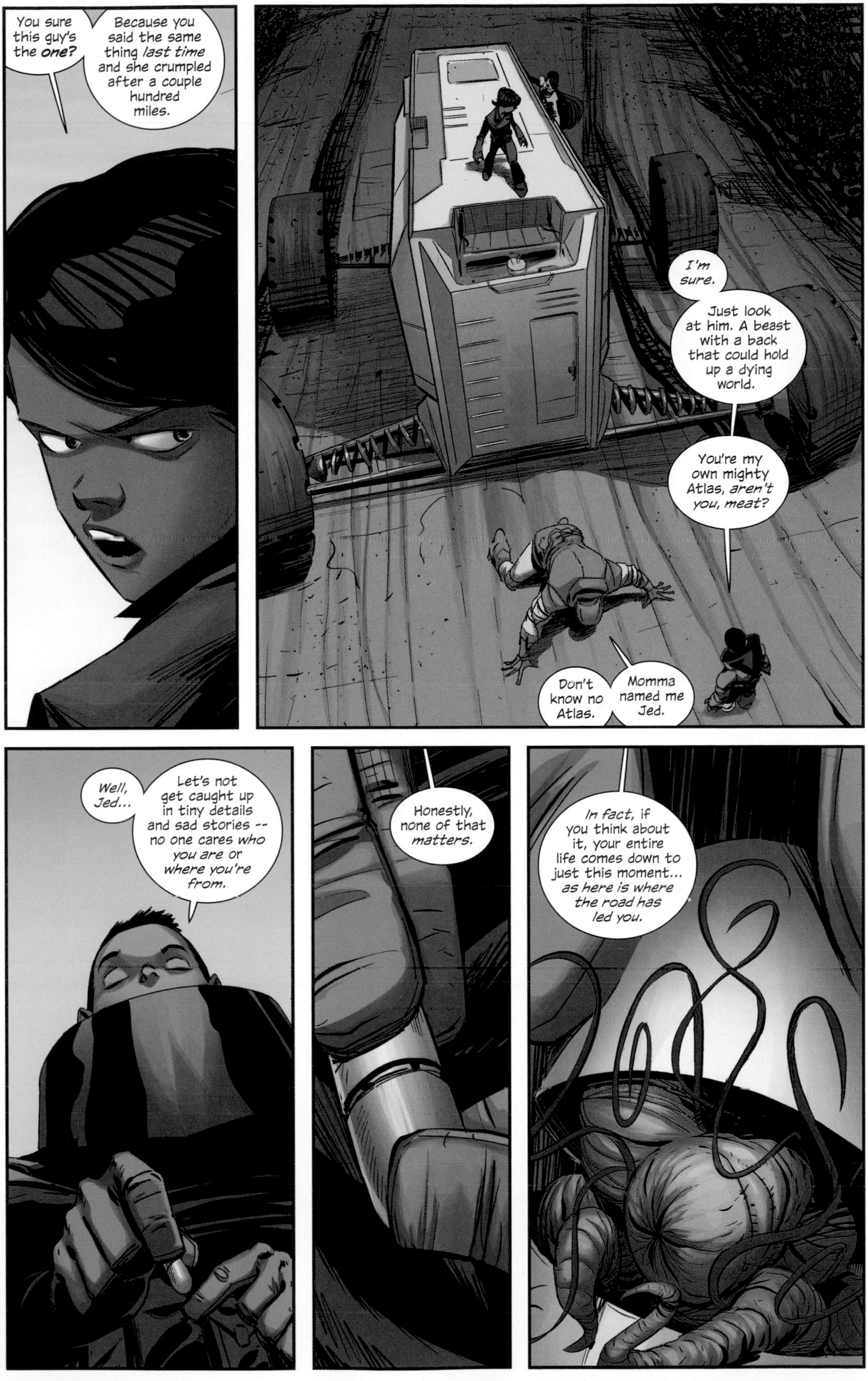
You sure this guy's the *one?*
Because you said the same thing *last time* and she crumpled after a couple hundred miles.
I'm sure.
Just look at him. A beast with a back that could hold up a dying world.
You're my own mighty Atlas, *aren't you, meat?*
Don't know no Atlas.
Momma named me Jed.
Well, Jed...
Let's not get caught up in tiny details and sad stories -- no one cares *who you are* or *where you're from.*
Honestly, none of that *matters.*
In fact, if you think about it, your entire life comes down to just this moment... *as here is where the road has led you.*

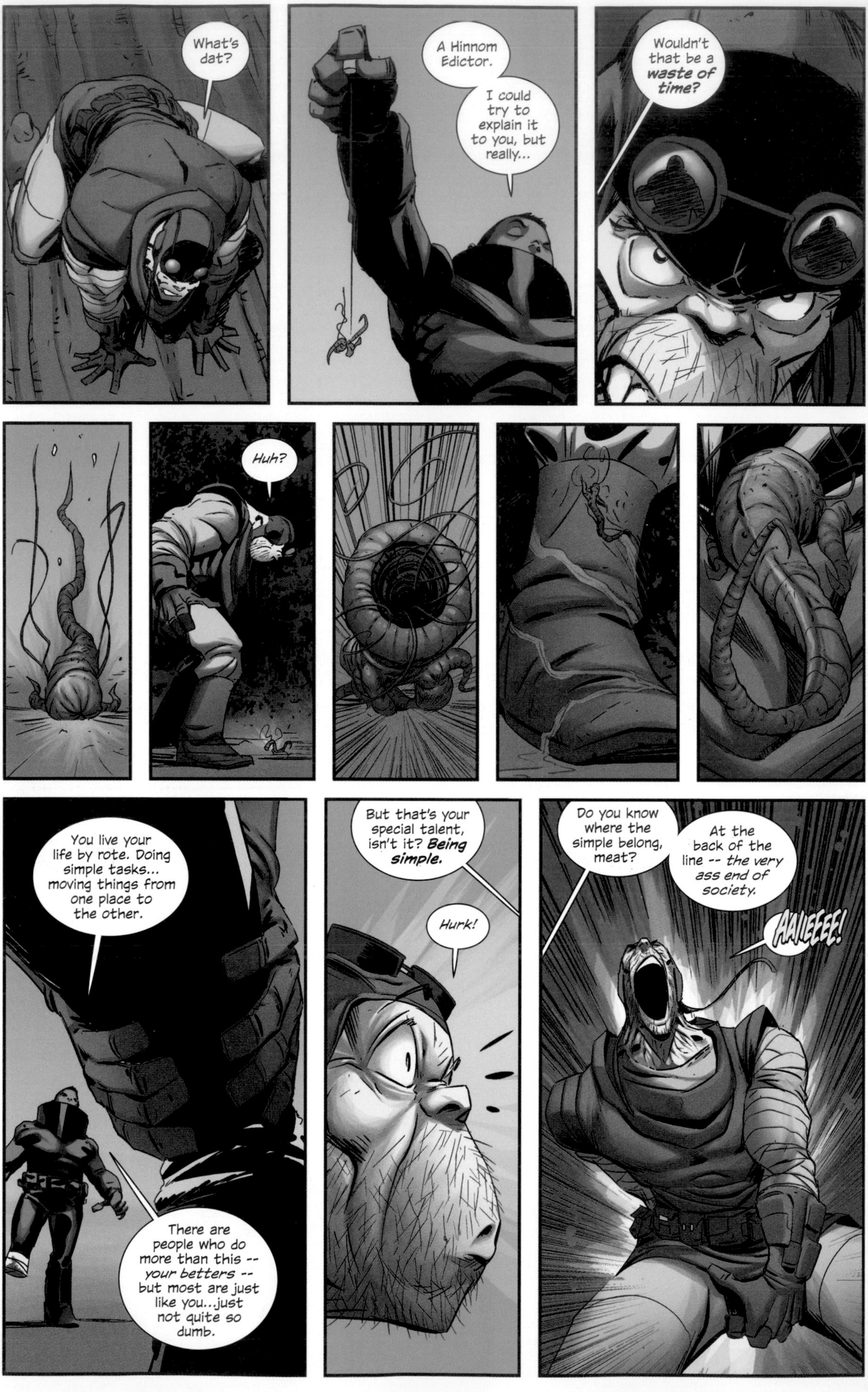
What's dat?
A Hinnom Edictor.
I could try to explain it to you, but really...
Wouldn't that be a *waste of time?*
Huh?
You live your life by rote. Doing simple tasks... moving things from one place to the other.
There are people who do more than this -- *your betters* -- but most are just like you...just not quite so dumb.
But that's your special talent, isn't it? ***Being simple.***
Hurk!
Do you know where the simple belong, meat?
At the back of the line -- *the very ass end of society.*
AAIIEEEE!

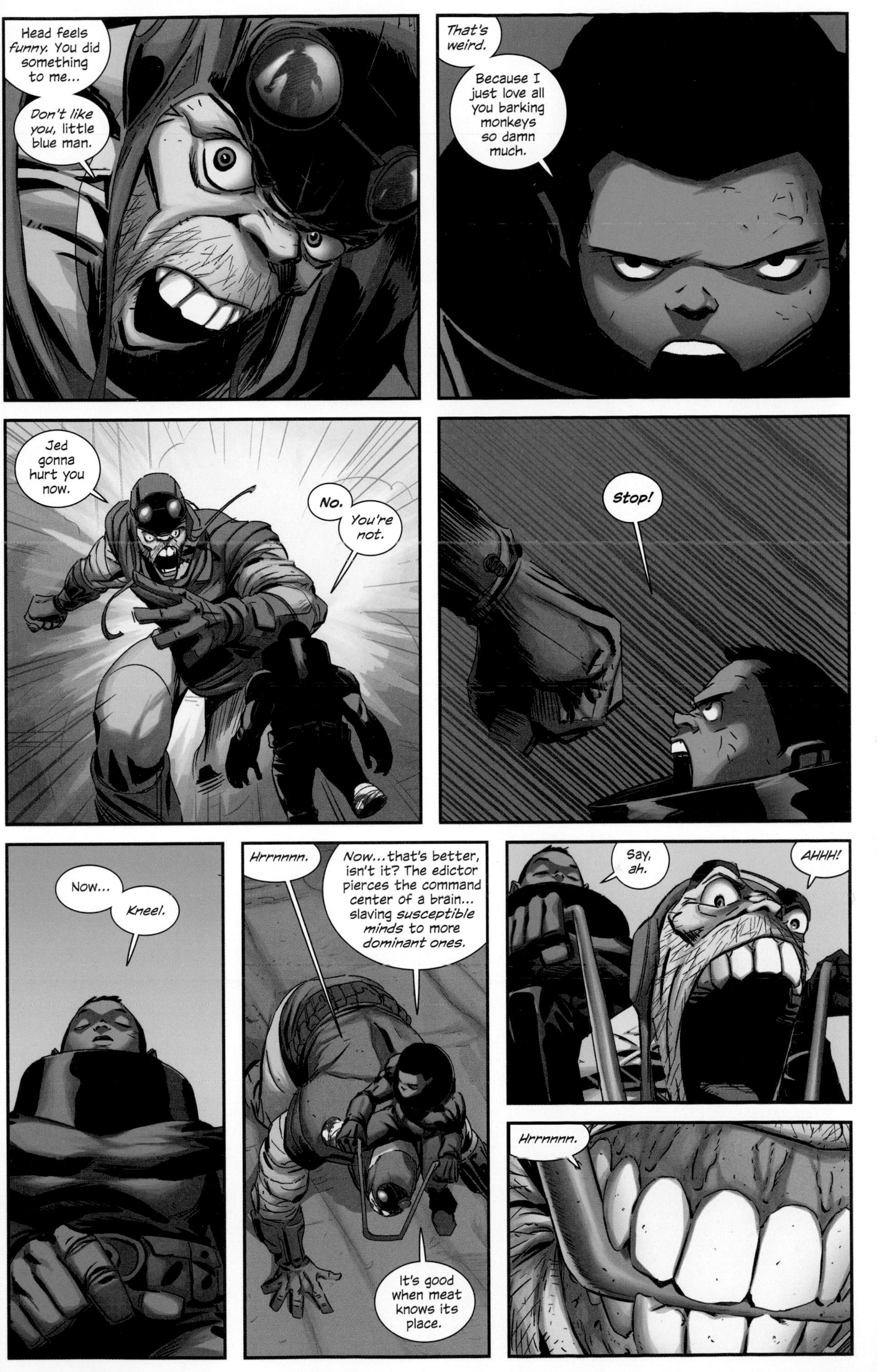

Head feels funny. You did something to me...
Don't like you, little blue man.
That's weird.
Because I just love all you barking monkeys so damn much.
Jed gonna hurt you now.
No.
You're not.
Stop!
Now...
Kneel.
Hrrnnnn.
Now...that's better, isn't it? The edictor pierces the command center of a brain... slaving susceptible minds to more dominant ones.
It's good when meat knows its place.
Say, ah.
AHHH!
Hrrnnnn.

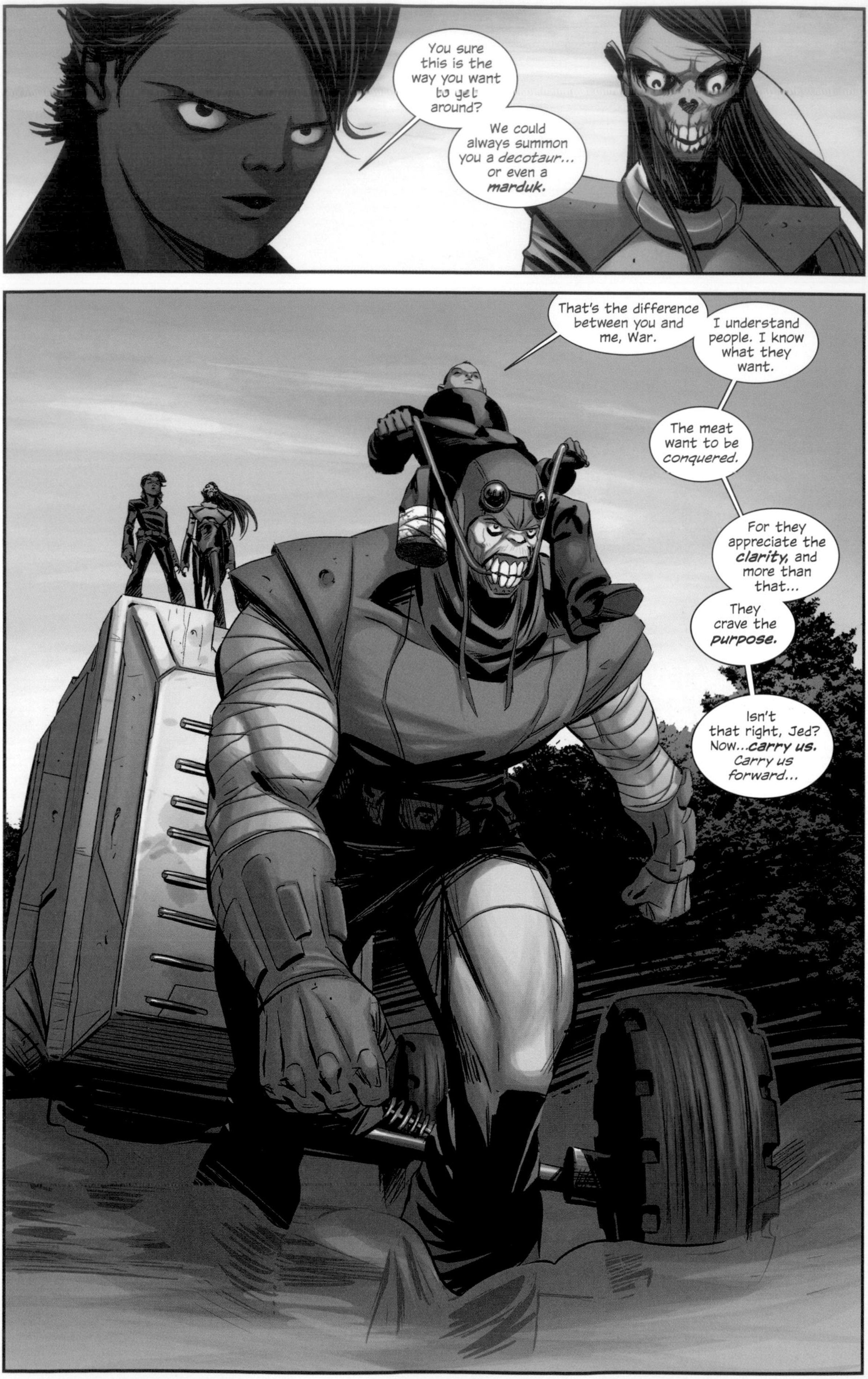
You sure this is the way you want to get around?
We could always summon you a *decotaur*... or even a ***marduk.***
That's the difference between you and me, War.
I understand people. I know what they want.
The meat want to be *conquered.*
For they appreciate the ***clarity,*** and more than that...
They crave the ***purpose.***
Isn't that right, Jed? Now...***carry us.*** *Carry us forward...*

FORWARD
TO **BABYLON.**

[01] THE UNION

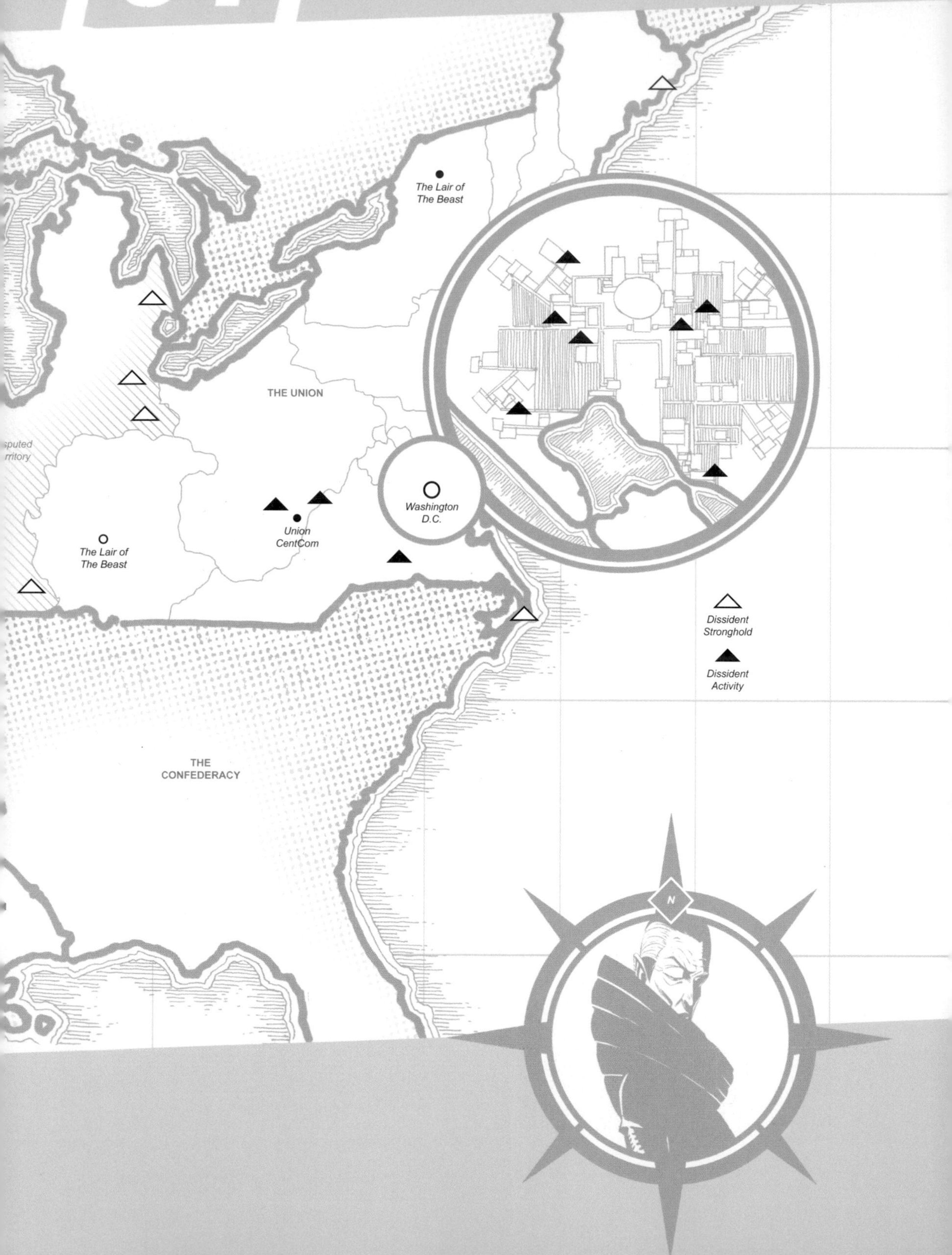

The Lair of The Beast
THE UNION
puted
rritory
Washington D.C.
Union CentCom
The Lair of The Beast
Dissident Stronghold
Dissident Activity
THE CONFEDERACY
N

THE UNION
OF THE UNITED STATES OF AMERICA

MOTTO:
"In God We Trust"

Capital:	Washington, D.C.
Language:	English
Government:	Federal presidential Constitutional republic
Current leadership:	President Antonia LeVay Chief of Staff Doma Lux
Independence:	1910
Area:	422,973 sq mi
Population:	103,648,330
GDP:	$1.568 trillion
Currency:	dollar
Military strength:	
Economic strength:	
Political stability:	
Long term viability:	

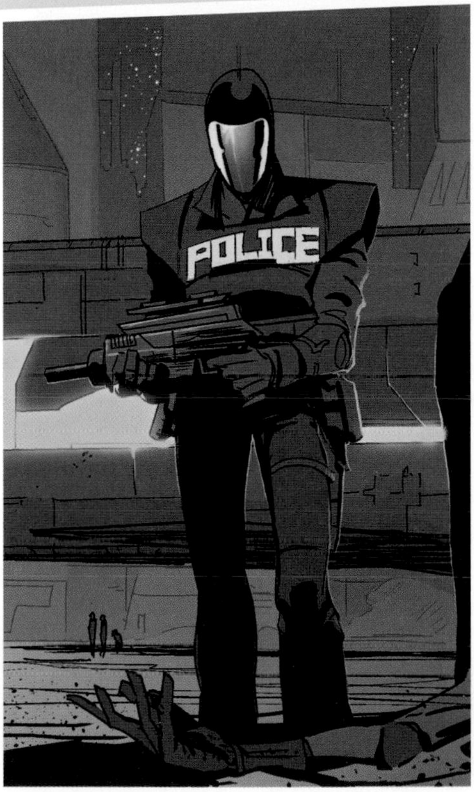
POLICE

POLITICAL UNREST

Discord. Turmoil. Anarchy. The current political and economic climate in the Union has led to massive unrest by the general population with rallies and protests occurring daily and numbering in the hundreds of thousands.

Beyond the controversial events that led to the present administration, the questionable collapse of the Union economy has lead to unparalleled stratification and the rapid emergence of a class system.

In today's Union, there is no denying that there are those who eat well, and those who do not eat at all. It can be argued that the only thing preventing the total collapse of the Union is the current state of martial law.

The heavy hand of control has resulted in the disappearance of a number of dissidents. Rumors of a forced conscription service are rampant and questions regarding the validity of such speculation remain unanswered.

[02] THE CONFEDERACY

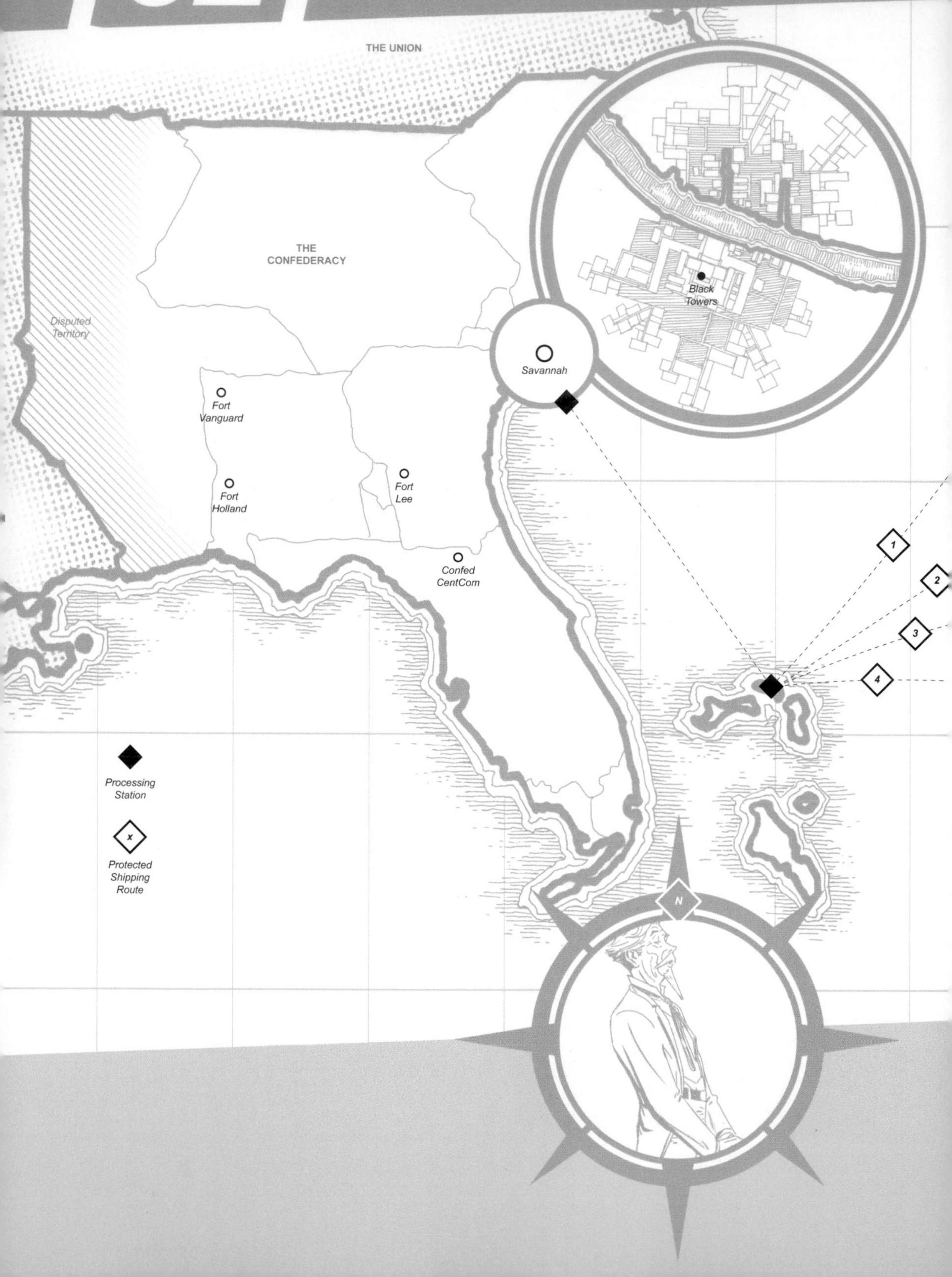

THE UNION
THE CONFEDERACY
Disputed Territory
Black Towers
Savannah
Fort Vanguard
Fort Holland
Fort Lee
Confed CentCom
1
2
3
4
Processing Station
x
Protected Shipping Route
N

CONFEDERATE
STATES OF AMERICA

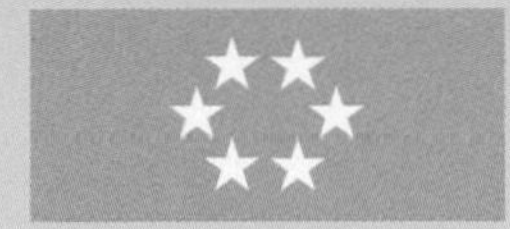

MOTTO:
"Liberty, Equality, Prosperity"

Capital:	Savannah
Language:	English
Government:	Presidential
	Council of Regents
Current leadership:	President Archibald Chamberlain
	Cheif of Staff Winston Wallace
	Warmaster Caroline Van Buren
Independence:	1910
Area:	643,712 sq mi
Population:	86,634,008
GDP:	$4.218 trillion
Currency:	dollar
Military strength:	■■■■■■■□□□
Economic strength:	■■■■■■■■□□
Political stability:	■■■■■■■■□□
Long term viability:	■■■■■■■□□□

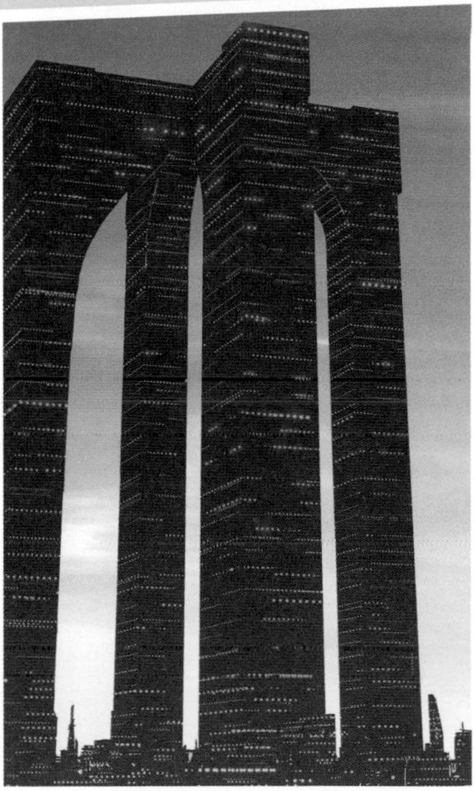

TRADE
THE GATEWAY TO THE WORLD

Stretching from the province of Charleston to the Black Towers themselves, the port megacity Savannah is the gateway to the world.

Contrary to the other North American isolationist states, the vast majority of annual Confederacy revenue is gained from the exporting of state-manufactured goods and the monopolized continental distribution of imported items.

Enjoying favored trade status with most local nations has provided the Confederacy with both a stable economy and a prolonged peaceful period. This has resulted in what many call the South's two nation policy. The first is an external, diplomacy-first strategy, and the second is a hyper-secretive, internal system of long-term planning.

It has been suggested that the monetary reserves of the Confederacy are intentionally underreported, and that the current military operational strength has been massively understated.

[03] TEXAS

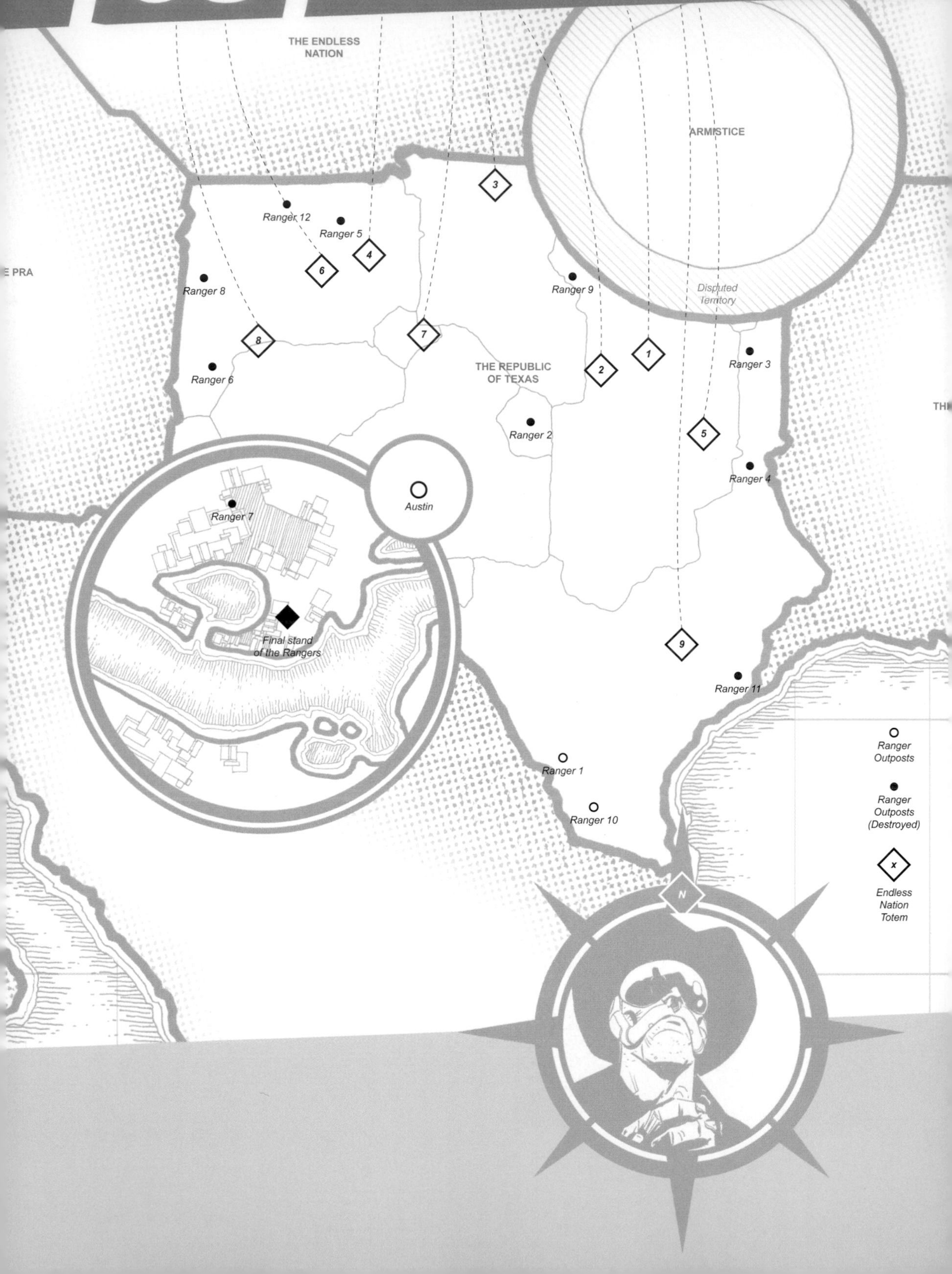

THE ENDLESS NATION
ARMISTICE
Ranger 12
Ranger 5
Ranger 8
Ranger 9
Disputed Territory
Ranger 6
THE REPUBLIC OF TEXAS
Ranger 3
Ranger 2
Ranger 4
Austin
Ranger 7
Final stand of the Rangers
Ranger 11
Ranger 1
Ranger 10
Ranger Outposts
Ranger Outposts (Destroyed)
Endless Nation Totem
N

THE REPUBLIC

OF THE UNITED STATES OF TEXAS

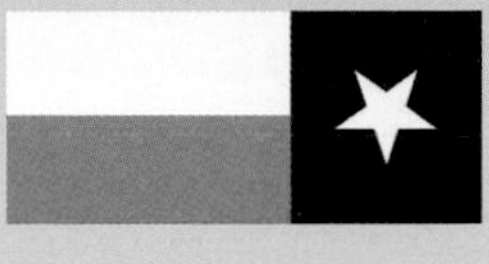

MOTTO:
"The Lone Star of freedom"

Capital:	Austin
Language:	English, Lakota
Government:	Conquered state
	Subjugated protectorate
Current leadership:	None
	(Caretaker government)
Independence:	1910 (no longer independent)
Area:	723,974 sq mi
Population:	19,456,973
GDP:	$3.568 trillion (seized assets)
Currency:	dollar
Military strength:	■□□□□□□□□□
Economic strength:	■□□□□□□□□□
Political stability:	■□□□□□□□□□
Long term viability:	■■□□□□□□□□

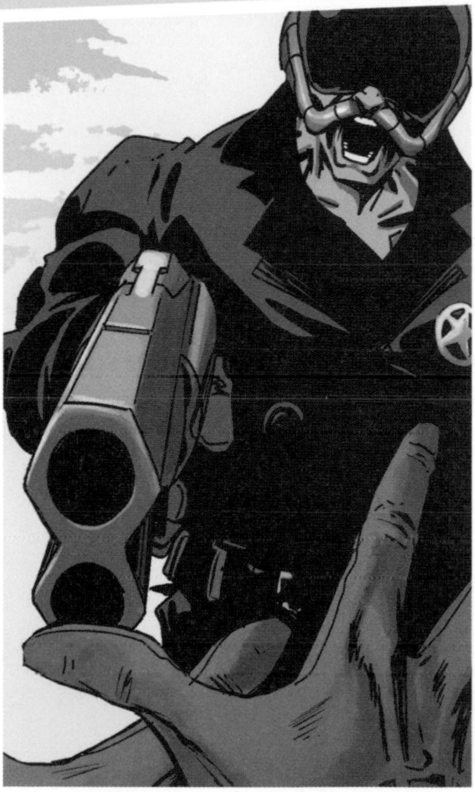

THE REPUBLIC

HAS FALLEN

The unilateral surrender of the Republic of Texas to the Endless Nation came on the fifth month of the last war of the Apocalypse.

Retreating from the devastating campaign of the Nation, the final holdout was the capital city of Austin, where Governor Bel Solomon, under the specter of a no-confidence vote from his Senate, eventually surrendered after suffering heavy losses.

This was the last stand of the Rangers, and the public executions that followed marked the end of Texas law.

The Republic has fallen. Long live the conquered state of Texas.

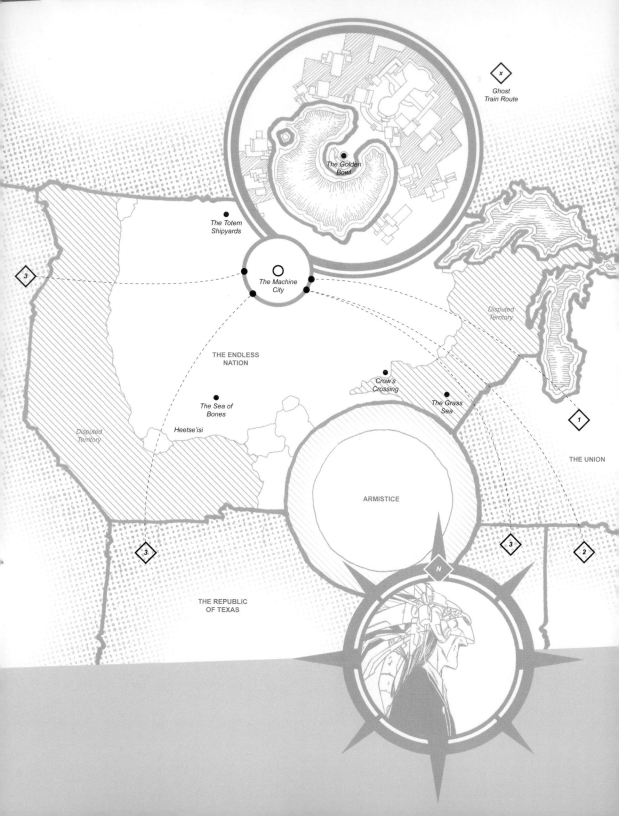

Ghost
Train Route

The Golden
Bowl

The Totem
Shipyards

The Machine
City

3

Disputed
Territory

THE ENDLESS
NATION

Crow's
Crossing

The Sea of
Bones

The Grass
Sea

1

Heetse'isi

Disputed
Territory

ARMISTICE

THE UNION

3

2

N

THE REPUBLIC
OF TEXAS

_HE NATION
OF THE AMERICAN ENDLESS

MOTTO:
"Verify"

Capital:	Unknown
Language:	Lakota
Government:	Communal Tribe
Current leadership:	Unknown
	Unknown
	Unknown
Independence:	1943
Area:	812,999 sq mi
Population:	Unknown
GDP:	Unknown
Currency:	Unknown
Military strength:	■■■■■■■■■■
Economic strength:	■■■■■■■■■■
Political stability:	■■■■□□□□□□
Long term viability:	■■■■■■■■■□
	(Estimated)

MACHINES
OF THE MACHINE STATE

Beyond the Sea of Bones, nestled deep within the Heetse'isi, is the Machine State of the Endless Nation. This godless state was born in the total rejection of the mythic beliefs that for generations had been the ideological bedrock of North America's indigenous people, and the embracing of the great idea 'progress.' There is no record of the internal revolution which resulted in the Machine State, only the oral history of cast-out believers who now reside in the dead country. One day there was no Machine State, and then the next there was.

Delivered to trading nations nonstop by Ghost Trains, the machines of the Endless Nation have become the technological backbone of the majority of the civilized world. From automated transportation systems, to advanced weaponry, to thinking machine companions, there is almost no part of daily citizens' lives that are not bettered by the Machine State.

Watch groups have long speculated the possibility of kill switches in all Endless Nation products, but rigorous investigations and thorough testing have proven these rumors to be just as unfounded as ones suggesting the existence of Endless Nation next generation technology being withheld from market.

[05] THE KINGDOM

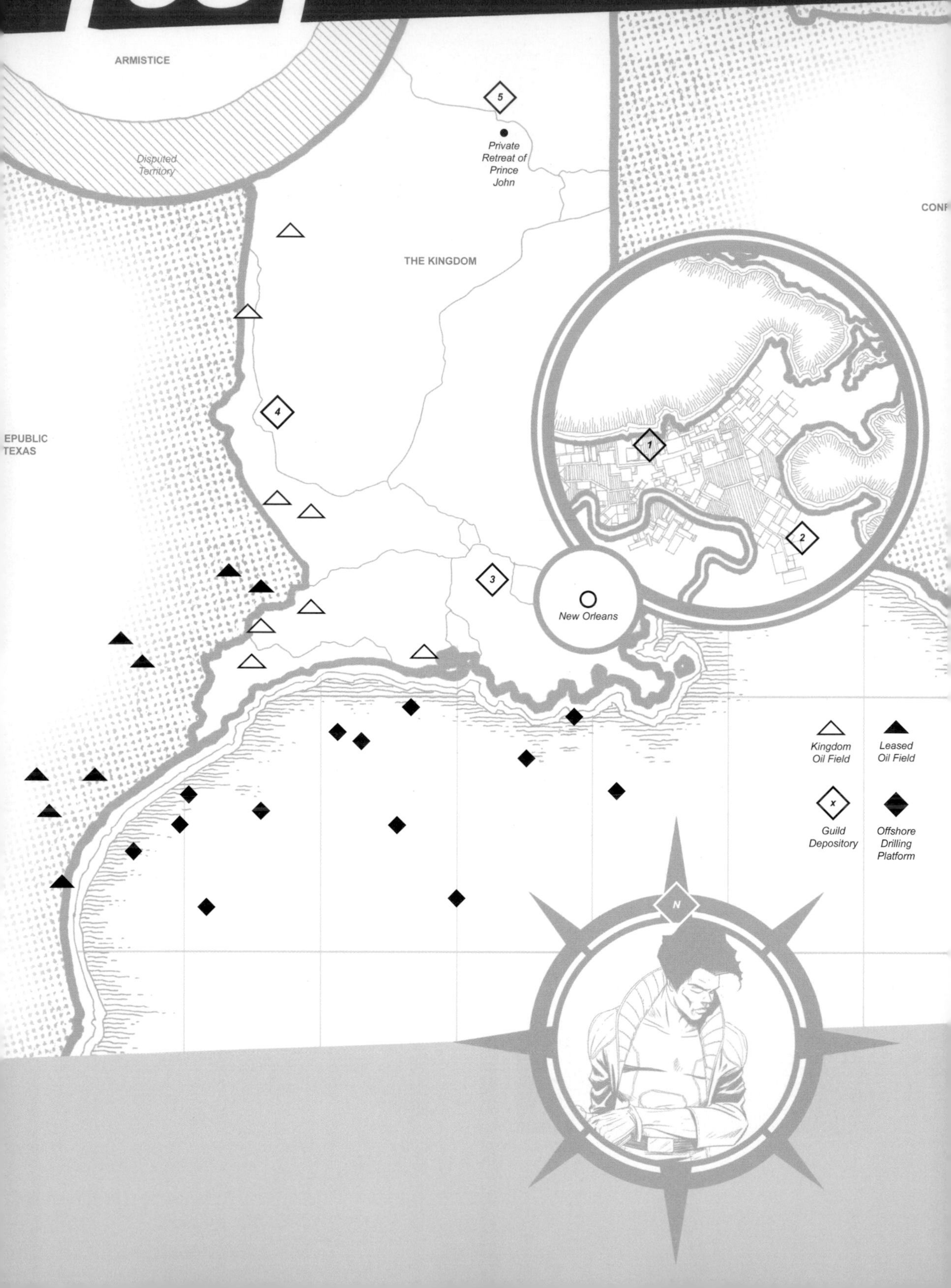

ARMISTICE
Disputed Territory
5
Private Retreat of Prince John
CONF
THE KINGDOM
4
EPUBLIC TEXAS
1
2
3
New Orleans
Kingdom Oil Field
Leased Oil Field
x
Guild Depository
Offshore Drilling Platform
N

KINGDOM
OF NEW ORLEANS

MOTTO:
"With these hands"

Capital:	The Freeport of New Orleans
Language:	English
Government:	Monarchy
Current leadership:	King Joseph Freeman III
	John Freeman [Crown Prince]
	Naomi Adams [Vizier]
Independence:	1941
Area:	323,024 sq mi
Population:	65,191,803
GDP:	$7.998 trillion
Currency:	tella
Military strength:	███░░░░░░░
Economic strength:	██████████
Political stability:	█████████░░
Long term viability:	████████░░

THE CROWN
INTERNAL MEMO

Secret Report to the King from his Vizier.
Re: The Banking Guild and Sibling Infighting.

The most current reports from the guild show reserves at fairly volatile levels. All five guild banks are floating Union loans that represent anywhere from five to seven percent of current reserves.

Extended out for more than twelve months, the guild is estimating that this number could grow to as high as fifty percent of all Kingdom holdings. It is the recommendation of this office that any extension beyond six months be strongly measured against potential future returns and potential default.

In accordance with these latest projections, this office also recommends the crown consider the potential upheaval that a failed Union state might have on the current line of succession within the heir dynamic.

The legitimacy of the Crown Prince John Freeman should be a concern.

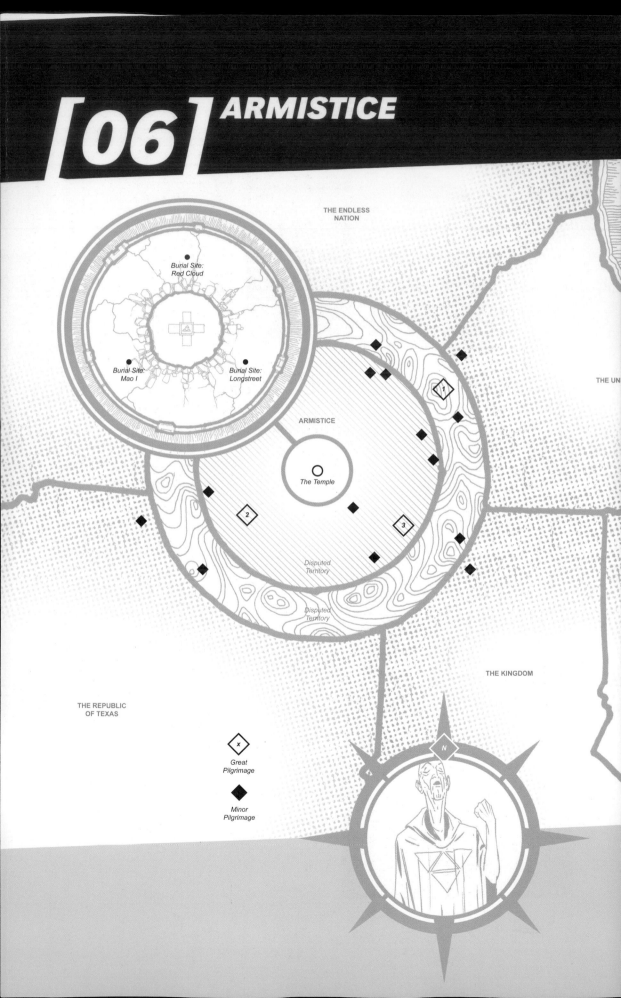

THE ENDLESS
NATION

*Burial Site:
Red Cloud*

*Burial Site:
Mao I*

*Burial Site:
Longstreet*

ARMISTICE

The Temple

THE UN

*Disputed
Territory*

*Disputed
Territory*

THE KINGDOM

THE REPUBLIC
OF TEXAS

*Great
Pilgrimage*

*Minor
Pilgrimage*

ARMISTICE

THE TEMPLE OF THE MESSAGE

MOTTO:
"I have heard the Message"

Capital:	None
Language:	Mandarin, English, Lakota
Government:	Theocracy
Current leadership:	The Prophet Ezra Orion
Independence:	1958
Area:	93,021 sq mi
Population:	1
GDP:	none
Currency:	none

Military strength:	■
Economic strength:	■
Political stability:	■■■
Long term viability:	■■■■■■

THE RETURN
OF THE PILGRIMS

At the close of the first year of the Apocalypse, when the Temple at Armistice fell, it was assumed by many that the Message -- the original works of Longstreet, Mao and Red Cloud -- were lost forever.

Then came the Prophet Orion.

Ezra Orion was orphaned, then raised, and finally abandoned, by the Horsemen of the Apocalypse. The son of murdered Pilgrims, he consumed the Message he believed in -- he devoured the word as the word's temple collapsed around him.

The days that followed were ones of transformation, he became the true voice of his generation, and the old ways were reborn. The burning temple was a signal fire -- a beacon for the soon returned. They came to hear him speak. They came to hear the Message. The Pilgrims began returning to Armistice.

[07] THE PRA

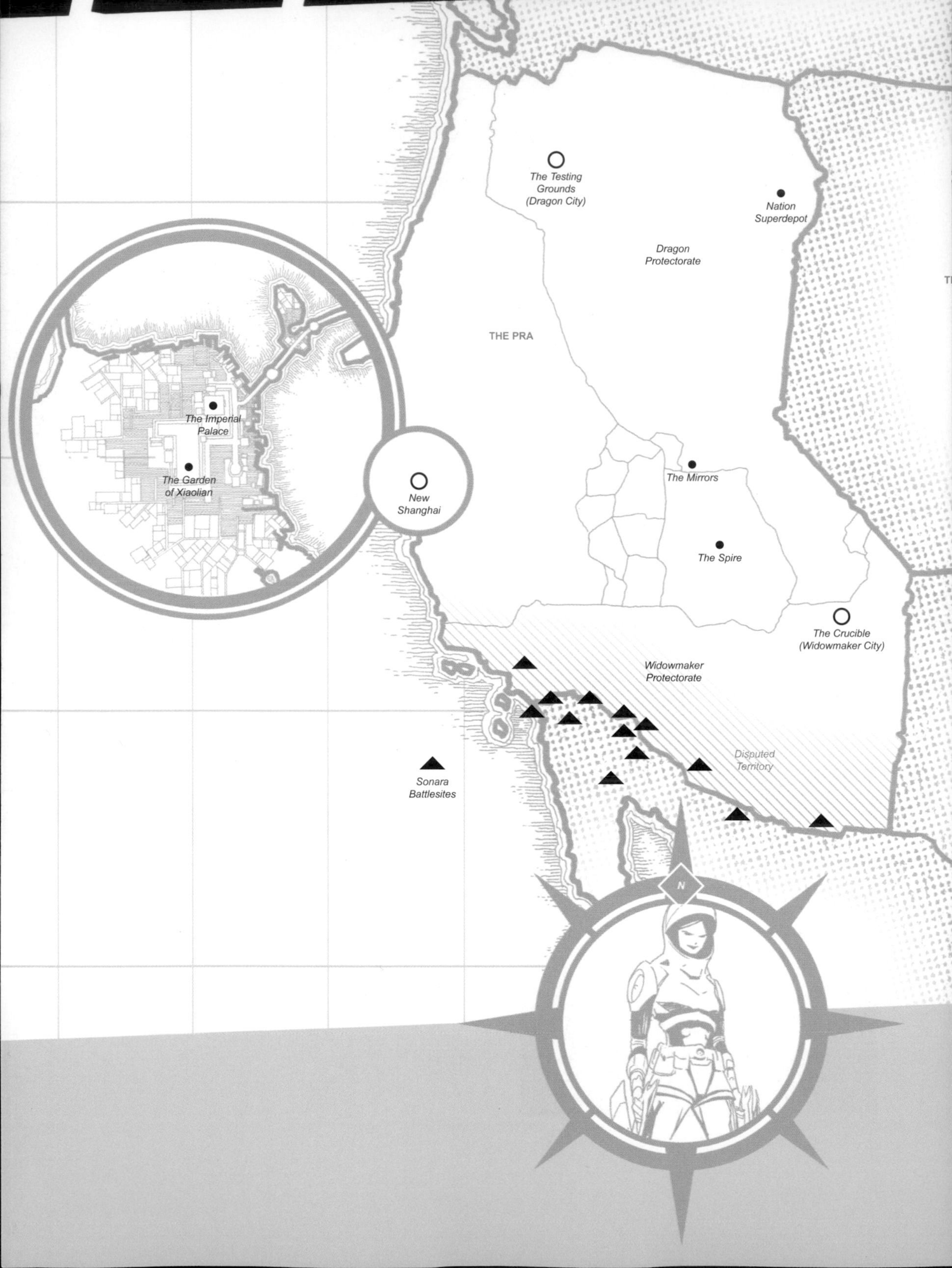

The Testing Grounds (Dragon City)
Nation Superdepot
Dragon Protectorate
THE PRA
The Imperial Palace
The Garden of Xiaolian
New Shanghai
The Mirrors
The Spire
The Crucible (Widowmaker City)
Widowmaker Protectorate
Disputed Territory
Sonara Battlesites
N

THE PRA

PEOPLE'S REPUBLIC OF AMERICA

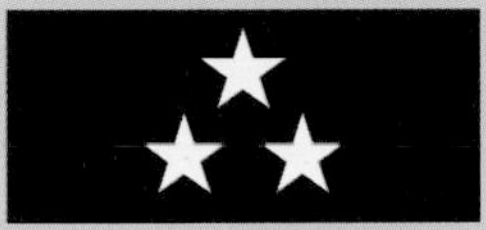

MOTTO:
"Tomorrow eternity"

Capital:	New Shanghai
Language:	Mandarin
Government:	Single-party socialist state
	Independent outlying protectorates
Current leadership:	Xiaolian Mao
	Guang Gao [Dragon]
	Li Pan [Widowmaker]
Independence:	1928
Area:	723,974 sq mi
Population:	126,788,811
GDP:	$6.568 trillion
Currency:	yuan
Military strength:	■■■■■■■■□□
Economic strength:	■■■■■■■□□□
Political stability:	■■■■■■■■■□
Long term viability:	■■■■■■■■□□

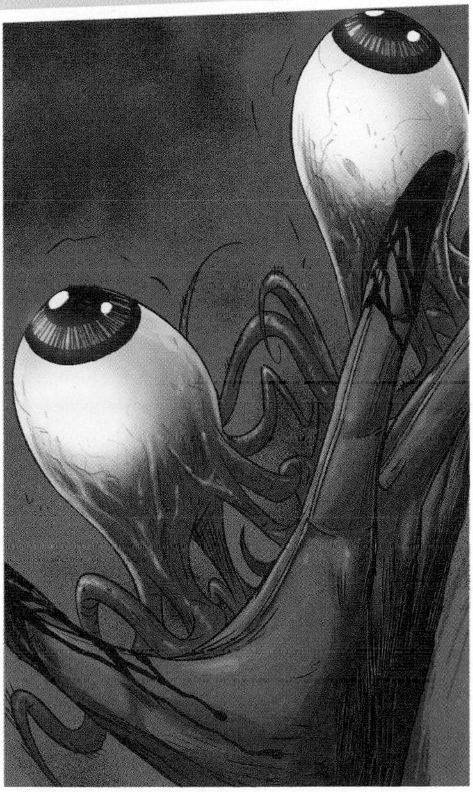

THE EYES

OF THE ORACLE

Now located in the Spire prison, the Oracle of Taconia is believed to have first appeared at the dawn of the day following the Fire in the Sky. Some believe this was the world's response to the apocalyptic Message -- a desire of the Great Mother to beat back the end times. Others believed the Oracle to be an environmental accelerant -- a binary catalyst increasing conflict for the coming age.

Either way, the power of the Oracle burned brightly, consuming a host every decade until, weary of her interference, the Four Horsemen captured her and separated the Oracle from her eyes. Imprisoned in the undying place of the Spire, the disconnected host and eyes were unable to regenerate and incapable of aging.

The Oracle remains imprisoned in the Spire, while the eyes are in the possession of the Pathfinder, Hunter and the President of the Confederacy, Archibald Chamberlain. One eye speaks the unvarnished truth, the other asks difficult questions no man can answer.

[08] TIMELINE
THE HISTORY OF AMERICA

THE UNION
OF THE UNITED STATES OF AMERICA

THE CONFEDERATE
STATES OF AMERICA

THE REPUBLIC
THE HISTORY OF AMERICA

THE NATION
OF THE AMERICAN ENDLESS/

THE KINGDOM
OF NEW ORLEANS

ARMISTICE
THE TEMPLE OF THE MESSAGE

THE PRA
THE PEOPLE'S REPUBLIC OF AMERICA

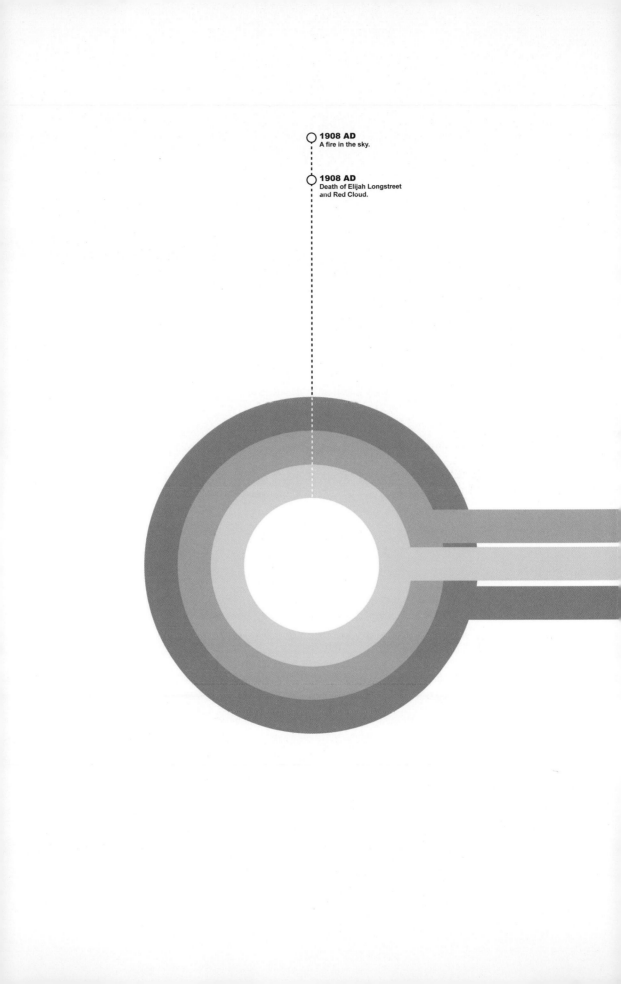

1908 AD
A fire in the sky.

1908 AD
Death of Elijah Longstreet
and Red Cloud.

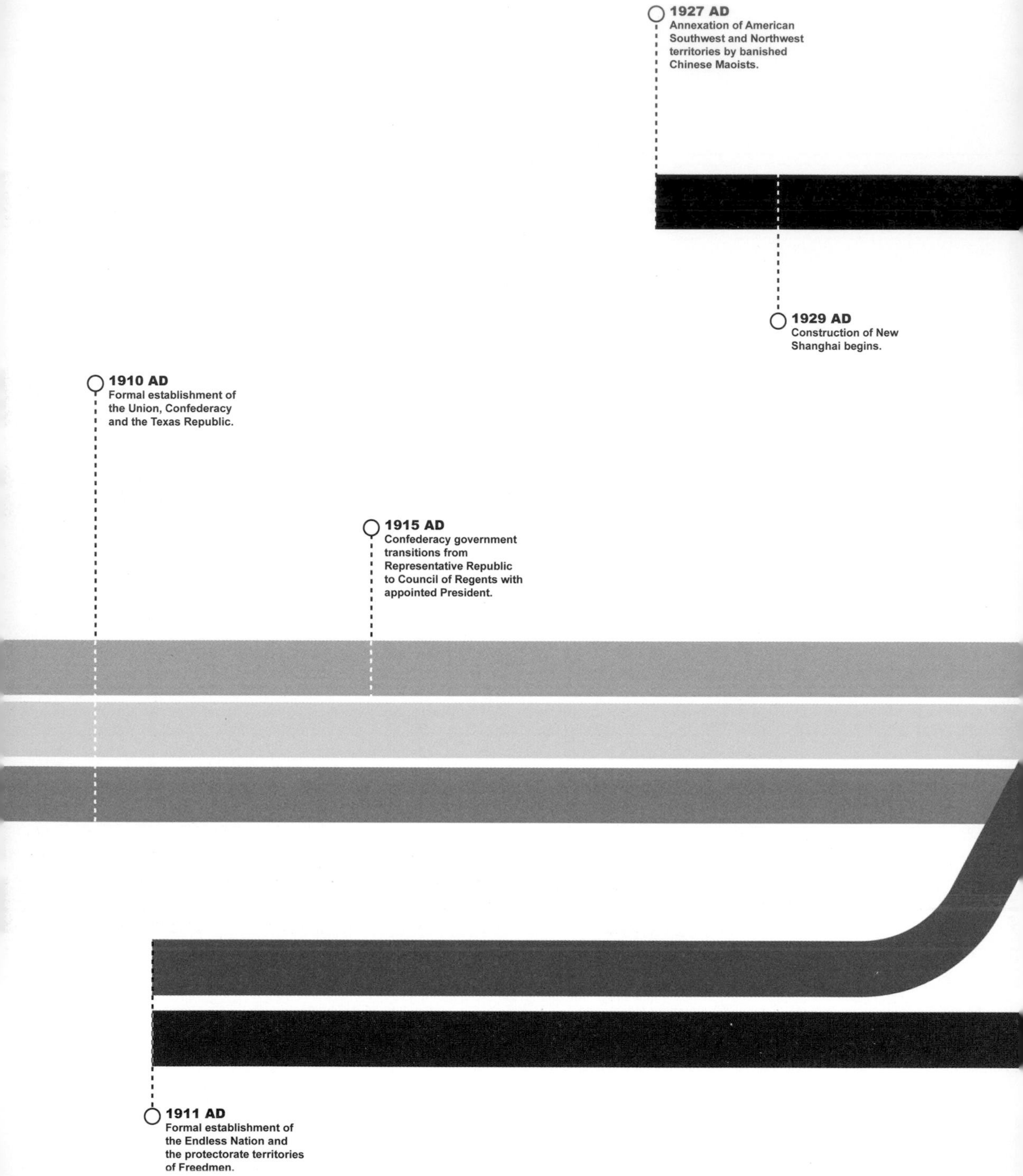
1927 AD
Annexation of American Southwest and Northwest territories by banished Chinese Maoists.
1929 AD
Construction of New Shanghai begins.
1910 AD
Formal establishment of the Union, Confederacy and the Texas Republic.
1915 AD
Confederacy government transitions from Representative Republic to Council of Regents with appointed President.
1911 AD
Formal establishment of the Endless Nation and the protectorate territories of Freedmen.

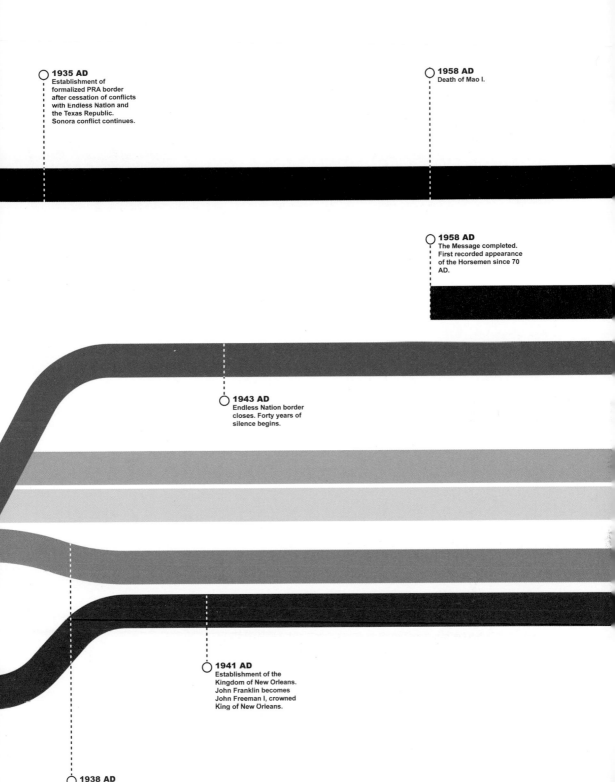

1935 AD
Establishment of
formalized PRA border
after cessation of conflicts
with Endless Nation and
the Texas Republic.
Sonora conflict continues.

1958 AD
Death of Mao I.

1958 AD
The Message completed.
First recorded appearance
of the Horsemen since 70
AD.

1943 AD
Endless Nation border
closes. Forty years of
silence begins.

1941 AD
Establishment of the
Kingdom of New Orleans.
John Franklin becomes
John Freeman I, crowned
King of New Orleans.

1938 AD
Negotiation of southern oil
rights with the Texas
Republic by freedman
John Franklin.

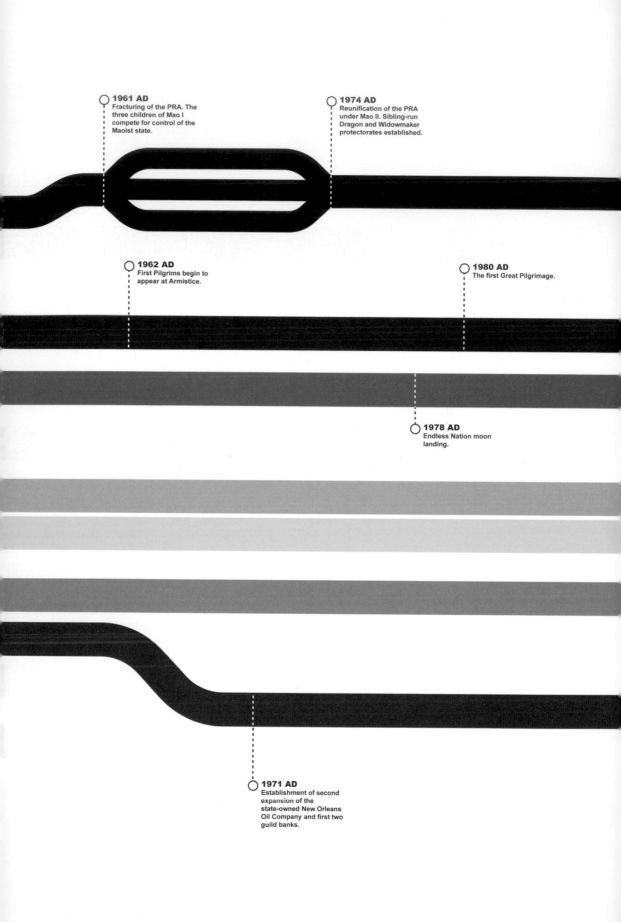

1961 AD
Fracturing of the PRA. The
three children of Mao I
compete for control of the
Maoist state.

1974 AD
Reunification of the PRA
under Mao II. Sibling-run
Dragon and Widowmaker
protectorates established.

1962 AD
First Pilgrims begin to
appear at Armistice.

1980 AD
The first Great Pilgrimage.

1978 AD
Endless Nation moon
landing.

1971 AD
Establishment of second
expansion of the
state-owned New Orleans
Oil Company and first two
guild banks.

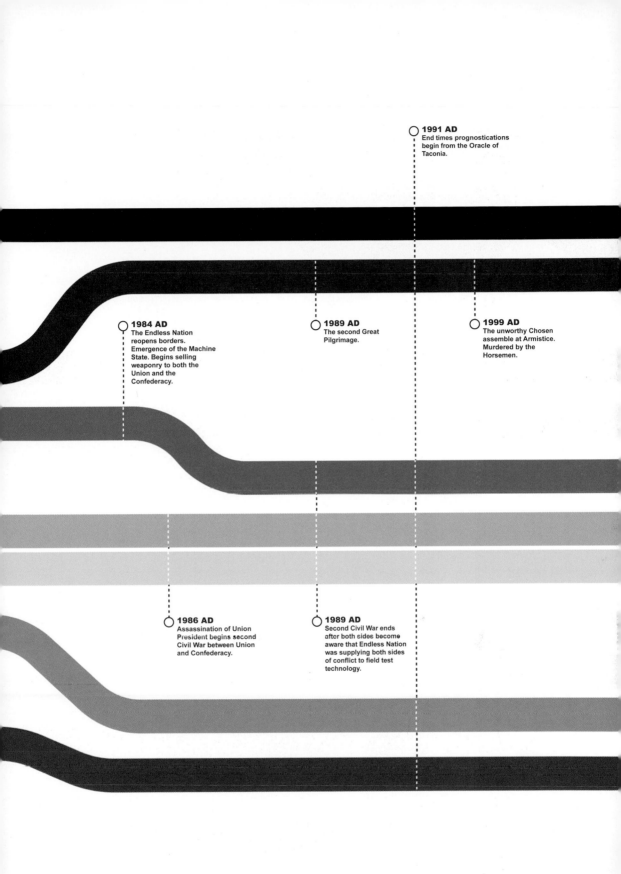

1991 AD
End times prognostications begin from the Oracle of Taconia.

1984 AD
The Endless Nation reopens borders. Emergence of the Machine State. Begins selling weaponry to both the Union and the Confederacy.

1989 AD
The second Great Pilgrimage.

1999 AD
The unworthy Chosen assemble at Armistice. Murdered by the Horsemen.

1986 AD
Assassination of Union President begins second Civil War between Union and Confederacy.

1989 AD
Second Civil War ends after both sides become aware that Endless Nation was supplying both sides of conflict to field test technology.

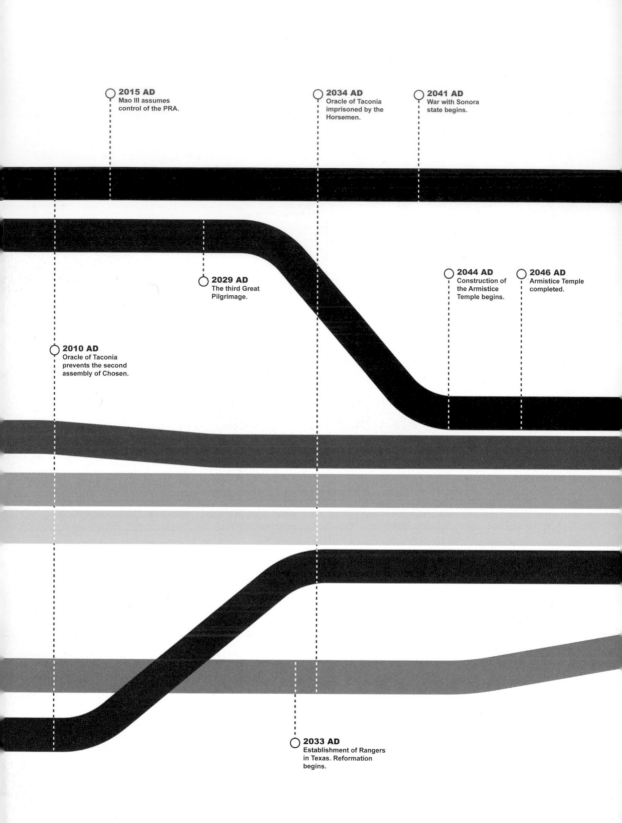

2015 AD
Mao III assumes
control of the PRA.

2034 AD
Oracle of Taconia
imprisoned by the
Horsemen.

2041 AD
War with Sonora
state begins.

2029 AD
The third Great
Pilgrimage.

2044 AD
Construction of
the Armistice
Temple begins.

2046 AD
Armistice Temple
completed.

2010 AD
Oracle of Taconia
prevents the second
assembly of Chosen.

2033 AD
Establishment of Rangers
in Texas. Reformation
begins.

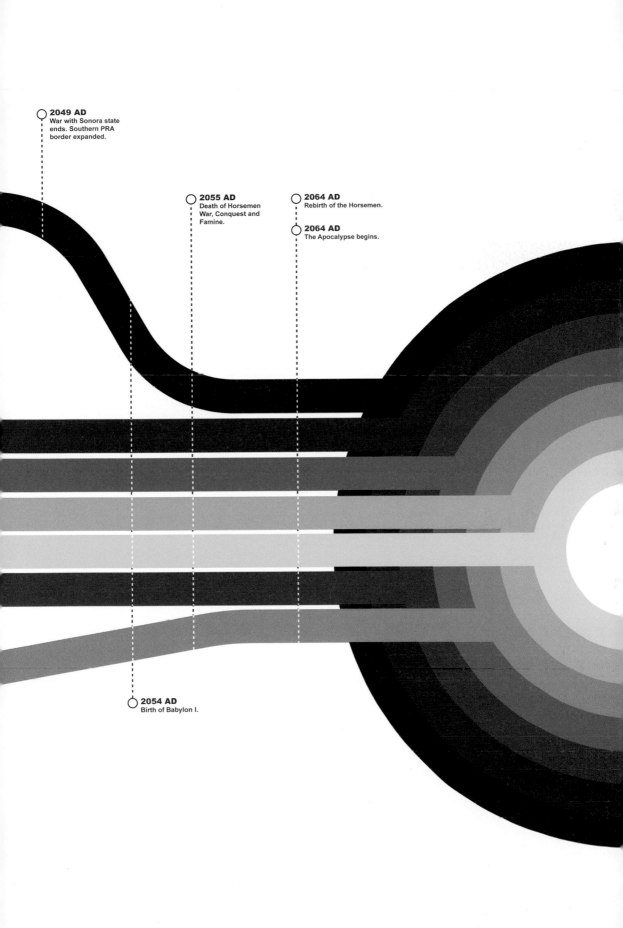

2049 AD
War with Sonora state
ends. Southern PRA
border expanded.

2055 AD
Death of Horsemen
War, Conquest and
Famine.

2064 AD
Rebirth of the Horsemen.

2064 AD
The Apocalypse begins.

2054 AD
Birth of Babylon I.

THE **FUTURE** HOLDS
DARKNESS AND **FIRE** AND
ASH.

SEE HOW IT **BURNS.** SEE
HOW IT **BREAKS.**

The Killing Fields of Texas.

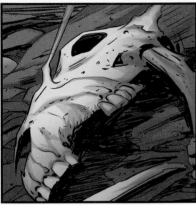

Would you look at this...

As far as the eye can see -- *scorched earth* and *those* consumed in its burning.

I know this place *well*. I have seen it in an endless number of other lands...

A people were *conquered* here...

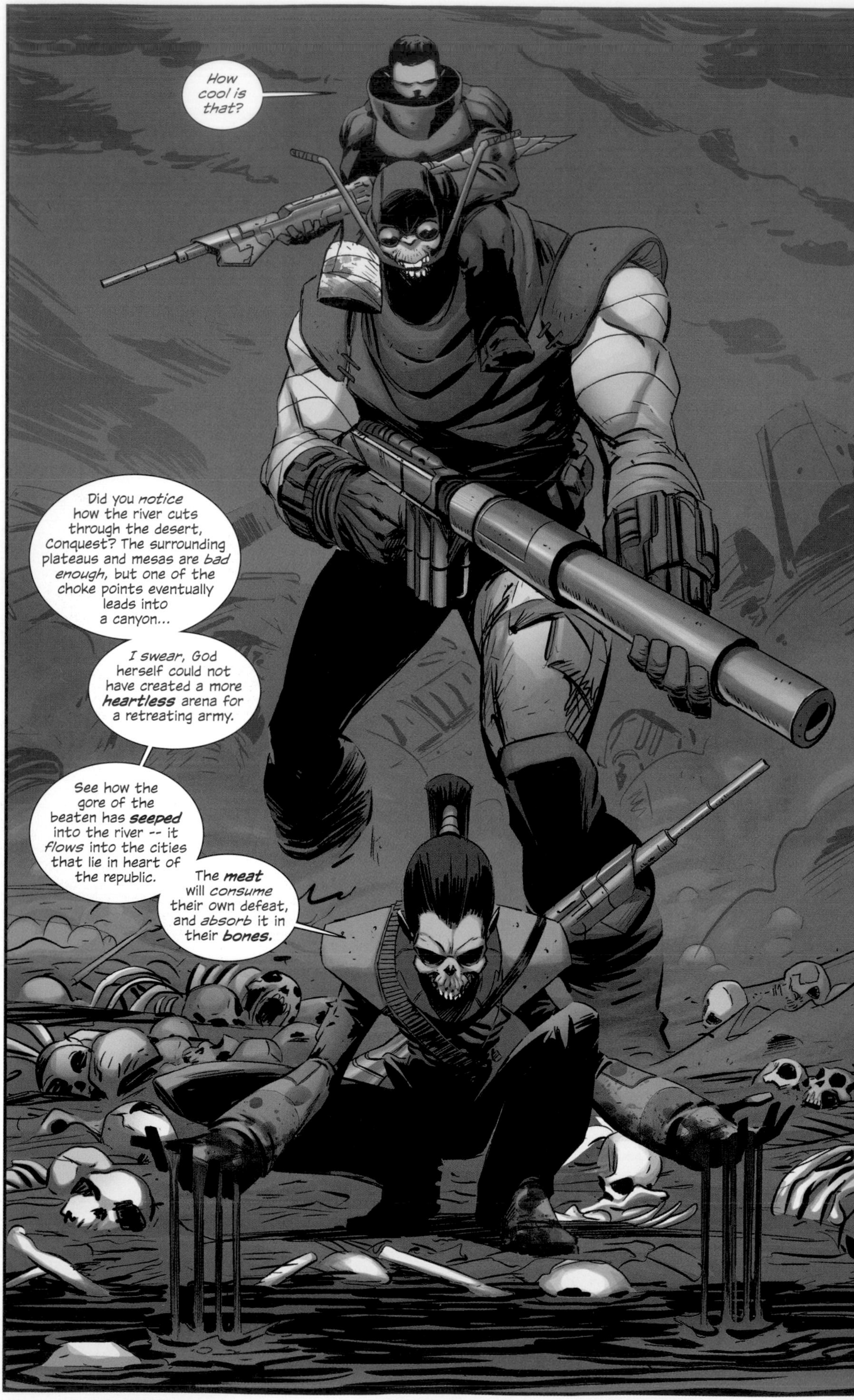
How cool is that?
Did you *notice* how the river cuts through the desert, Conquest? The surrounding plateaus and mesas are *bad enough*, but one of the choke points eventually leads into a canyon...
I swear, God herself could not have created a more ***heartless*** arena for a retreating army.
See how the gore of the beaten has ***seeped*** into the river -- it *flows* into the cities that lie in heart of the republic.
The ***meat*** will *consume* their own defeat, and *absorb* it in their ***bones.***

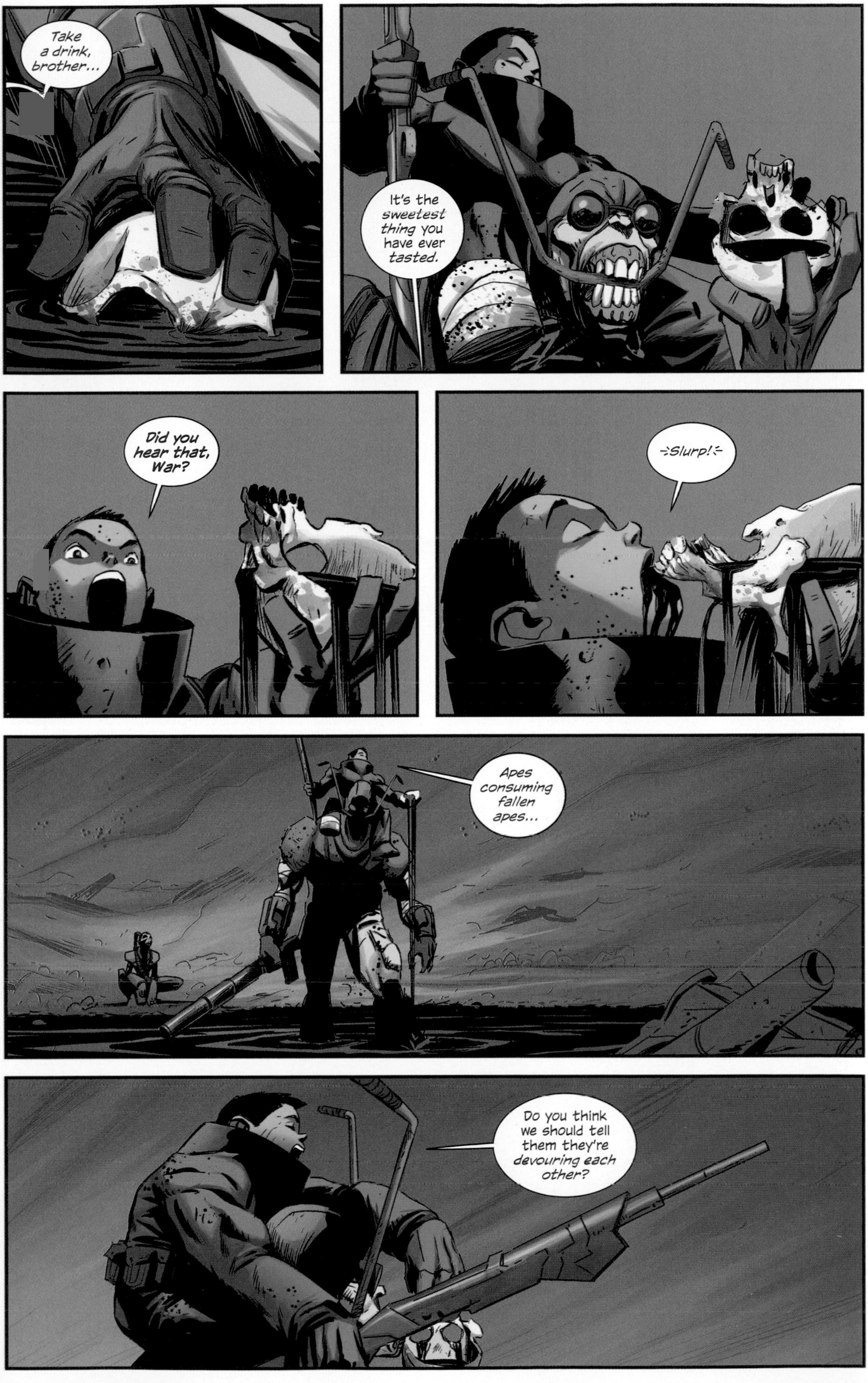

Take a drink, brother...
It's the *sweetest* thing you have ever tasted.
Did you hear that, War?
Slurp!
Apes consuming fallen apes...
Do you think we should tell them they're *devouring* each other?

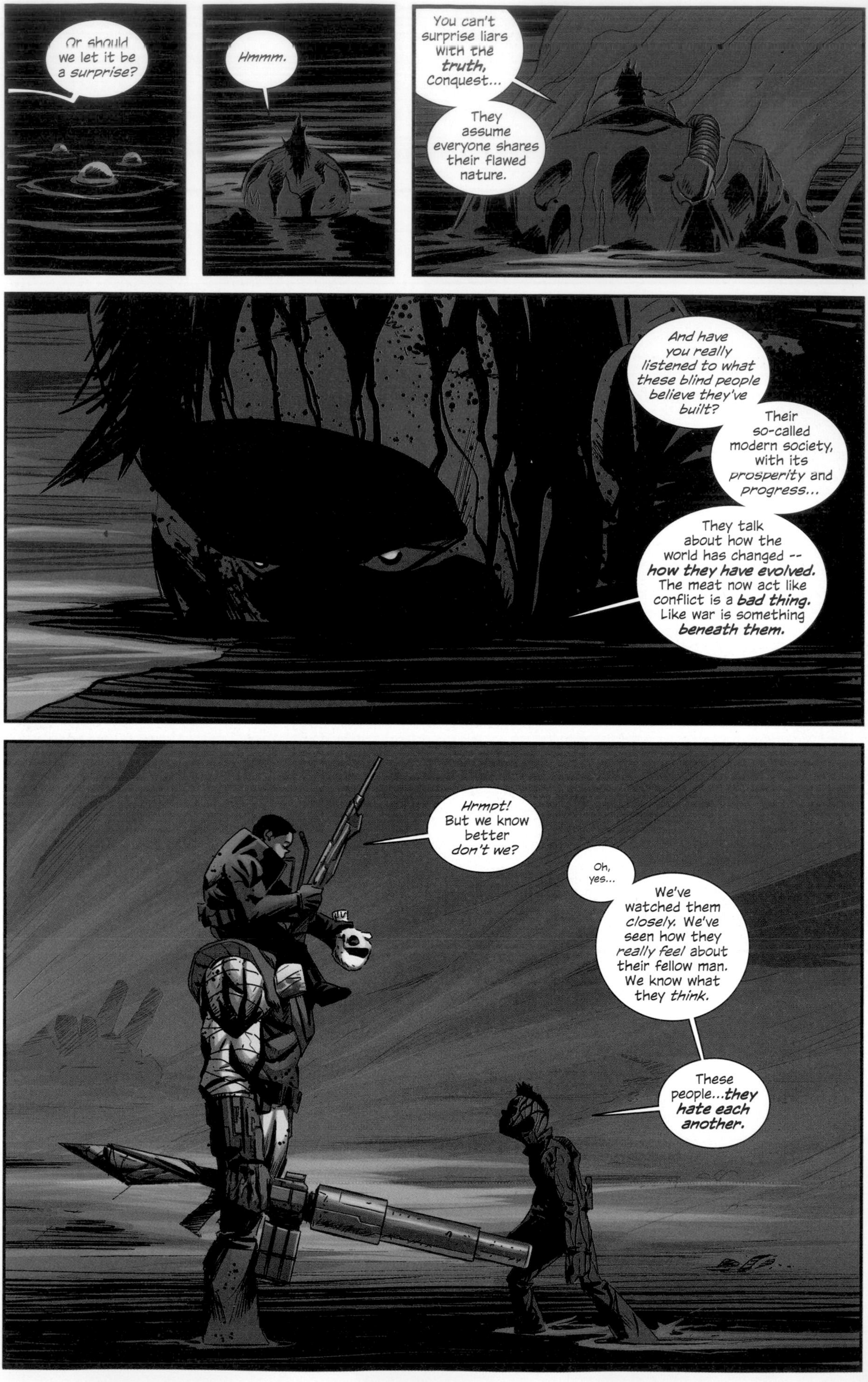
Or should we let it be a *surprise?*
Hmmm.
You can't surprise liars with the ***truth,*** Conquest...
They assume everyone shares their flawed nature.
And have you really listened to what these blind people believe they've built?
Their so-called modern society, with its *prosperity* and *progress...*
They talk about how the world has changed -- ***how they have evolved.*** The meat now act like conflict is a ***bad thing.*** Like war is something ***beneath them.***
Hrmpt! But we know better *don't we?*
Oh, yes...
We've watched them *closely.* We've seen how they *really feel* about their fellow man. We know what they *think.*
These people...***they hate each another.***

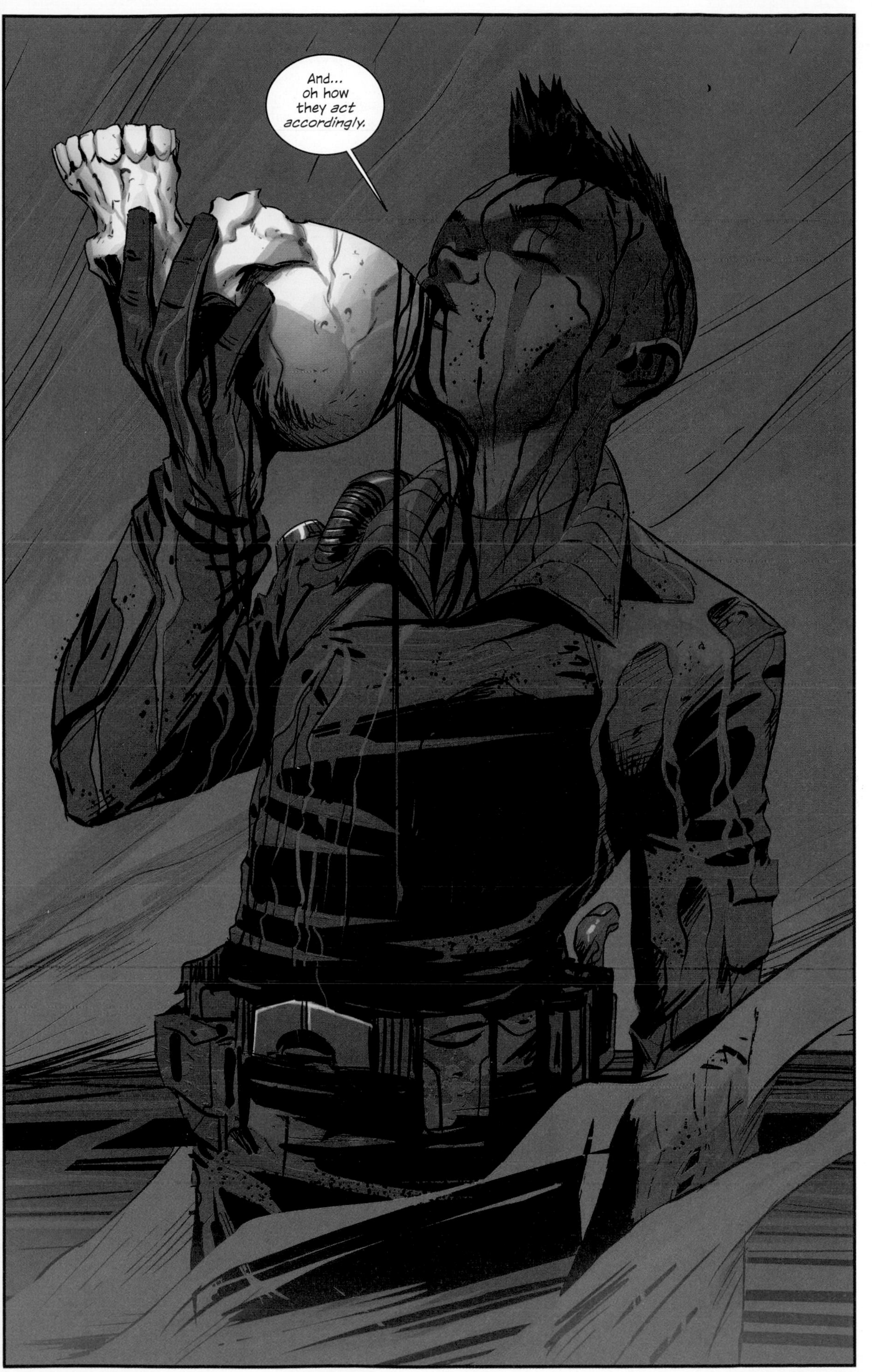
And... oh how they *act* accordingly.

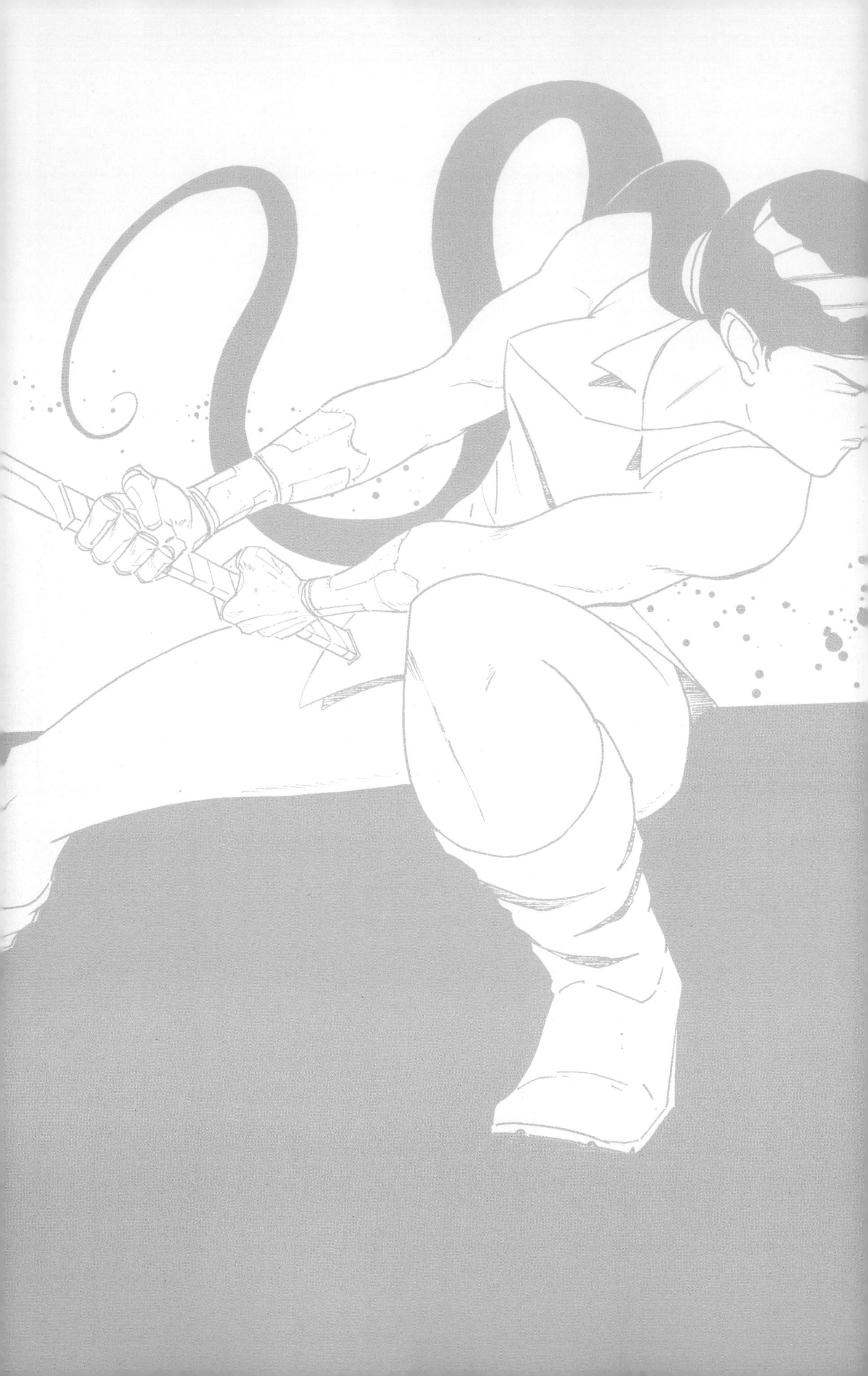

16

SIXTEEN: LET IT BURN

2065
THE APOCALYPSE: YEAR TWO

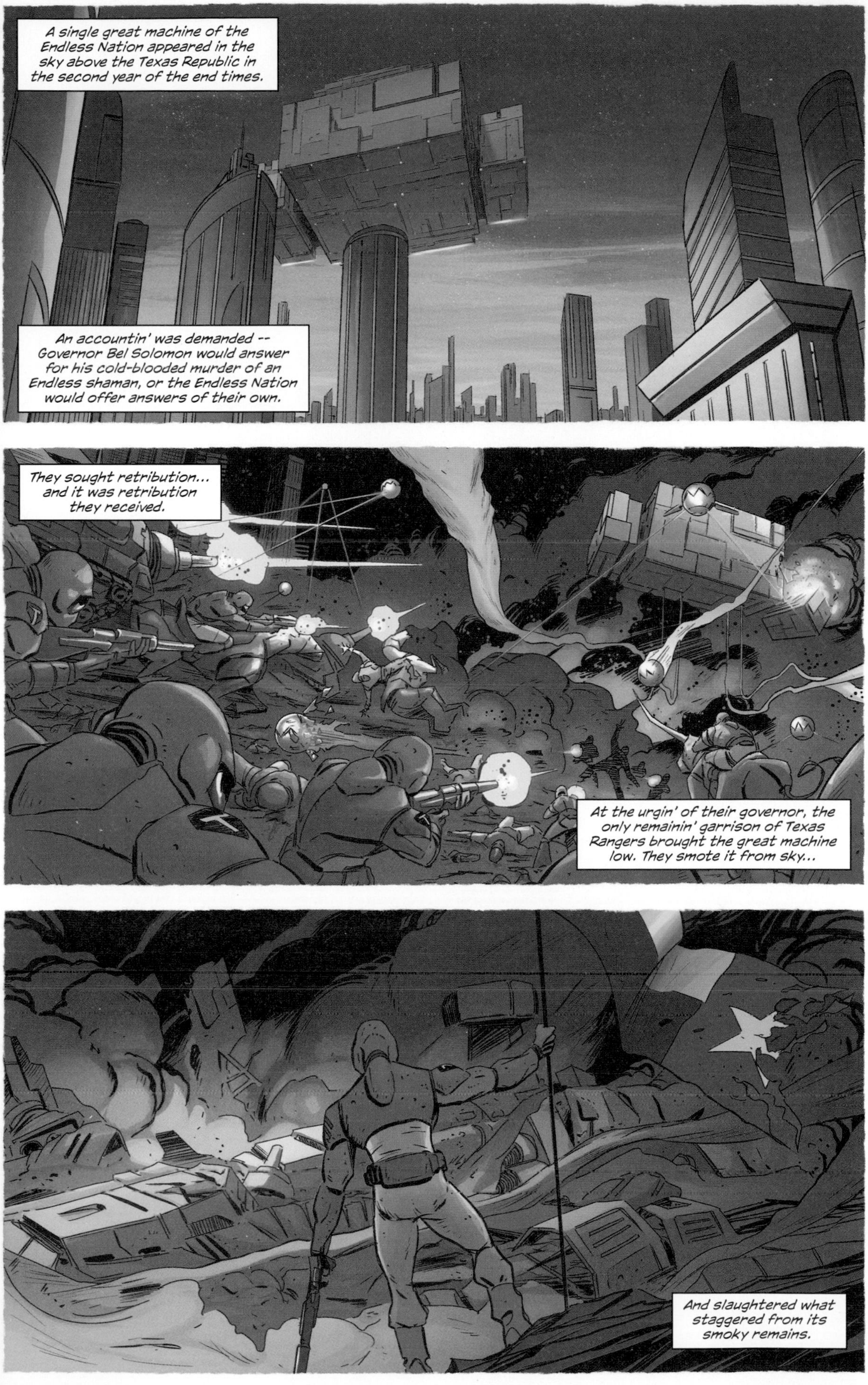
A single great machine of the Endless Nation appeared in the sky above the Texas Republic in the second year of the end times.
An accountin' was demanded -- Governor Bel Solomon would answer for his cold-blooded murder of an Endless shaman, or the Endless Nation would offer answers of their own.
They sought retribution... and it was retribution they received.
At the urgin' of their governor, the only remainin' garrison of Texas Rangers brought the great machine low. They smote it from sky...
And slaughtered what staggered from its smoky remains.

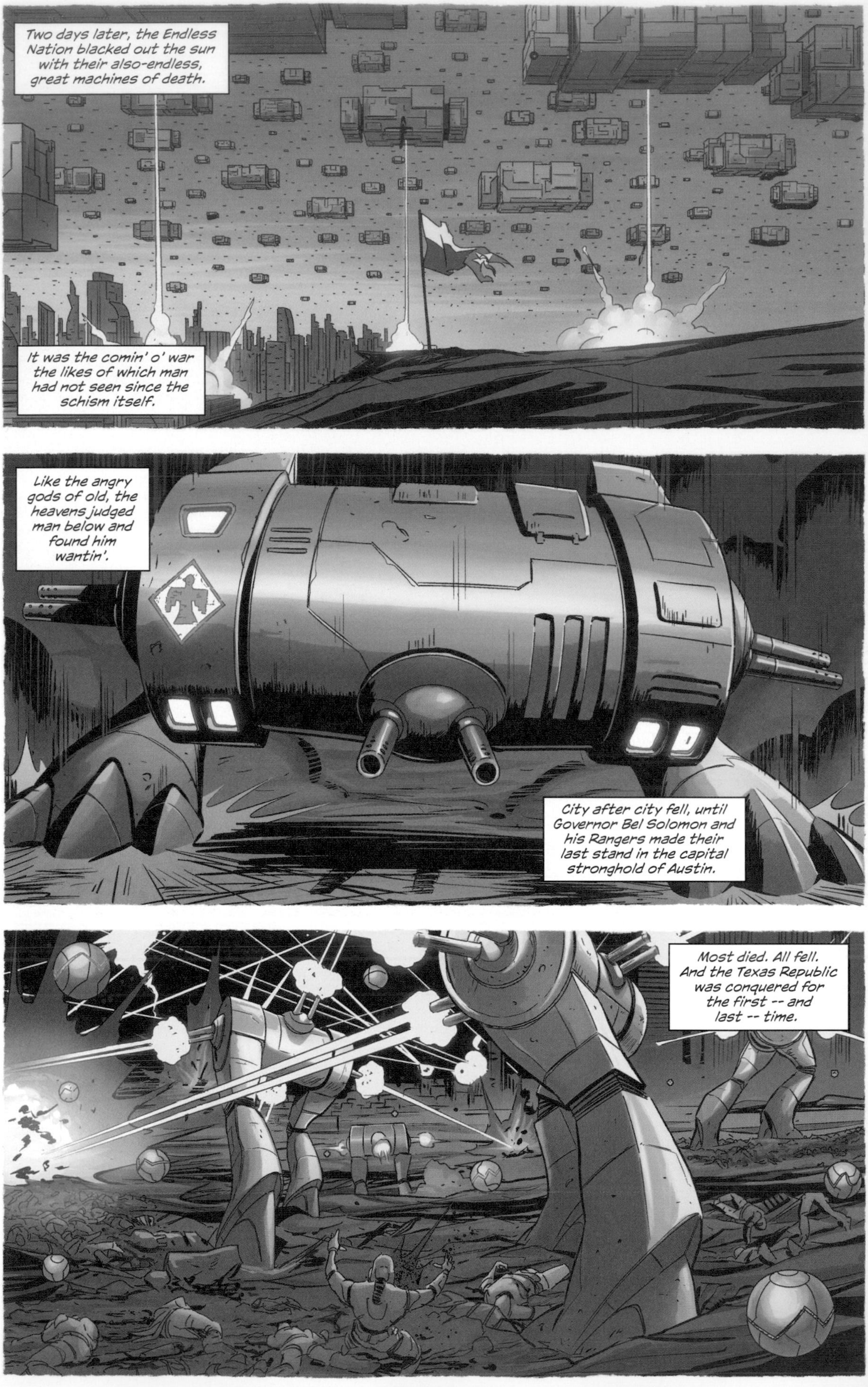
Two days later, the Endless Nation blacked out the sun with their also-endless, great machines of death.
It was the comin' o' war the likes of which man had not seen since the schism itself.
Like the angry gods of old, the heavens judged man below and found him wantin'.
City after city fell, until Governor Bel Solomon and his Rangers made their last stand in the capital stronghold of Austin.
Most died. All fell. And the Texas Republic was conquered for the first -- and last -- time.

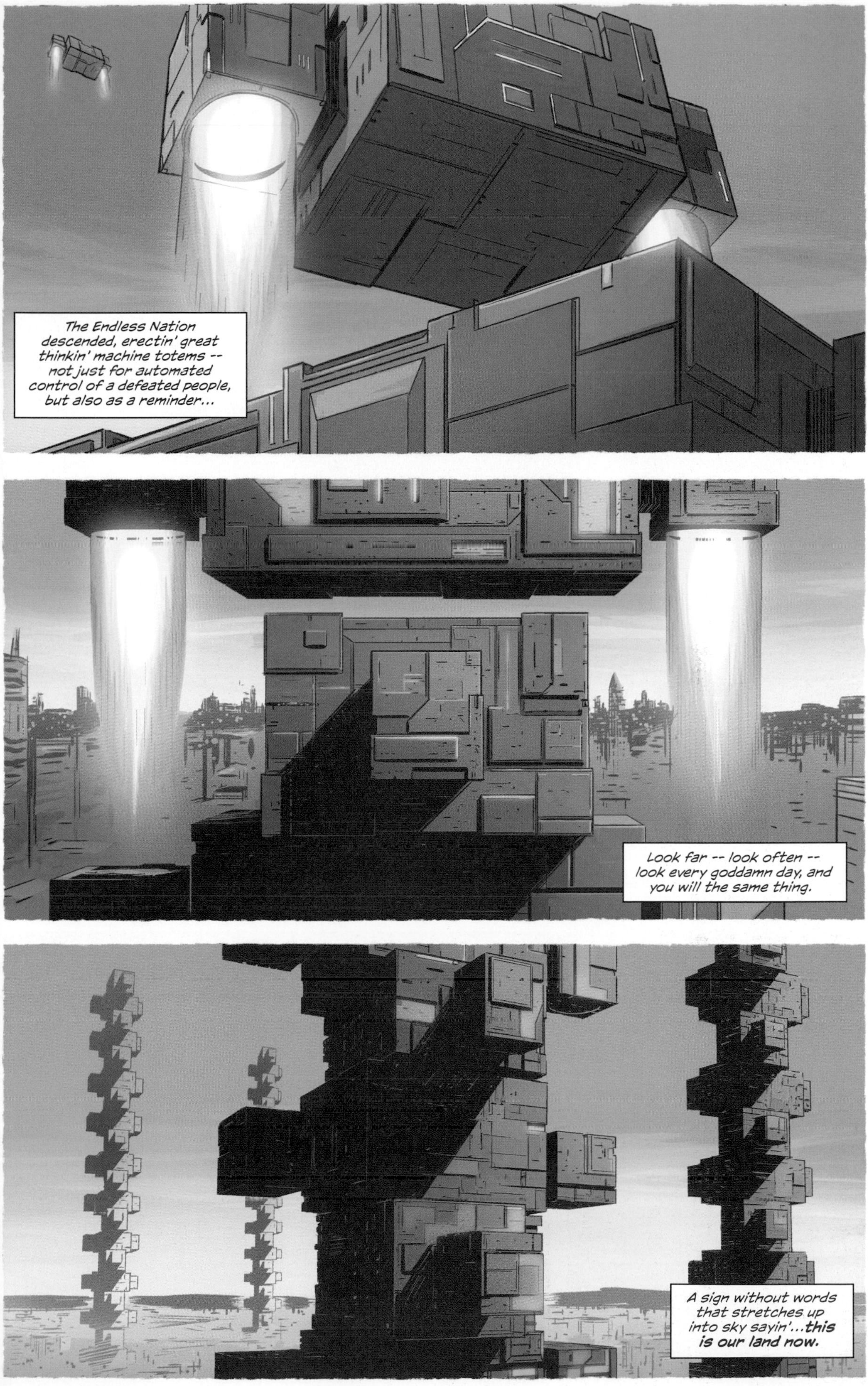
The Endless Nation descended, erectin' great thinkin' machine totems -- not just for automated control of a defeated people, but also as a reminder...
Look far -- look often -- look every goddamn day, and you will the same thing.
A sign without words that stretches up into sky sayin'...**this is our land now.**

This is justice.

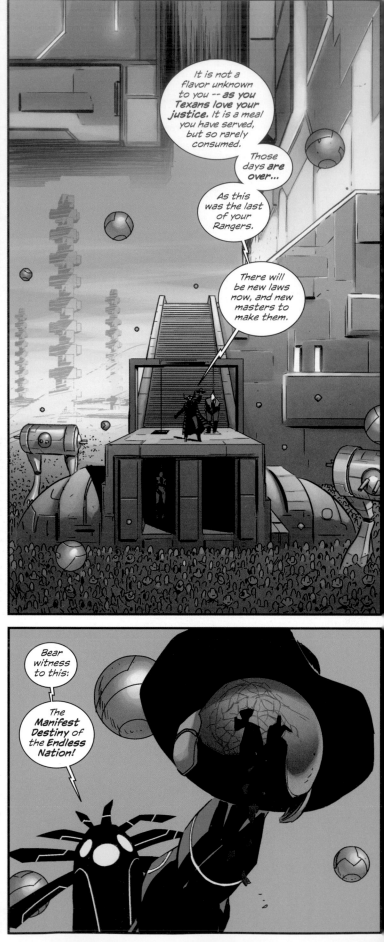

It is not a flavor unknown to you -- *as you Texans love your justice.* It is a meal you have served, but so rarely consumed.

Those days *are over...*

As this was the last of your Rangers.

There will be new laws now, and new masters to make them.

Bear witness to this:

The *Manifest Destiny* of the *Endless Nation!*

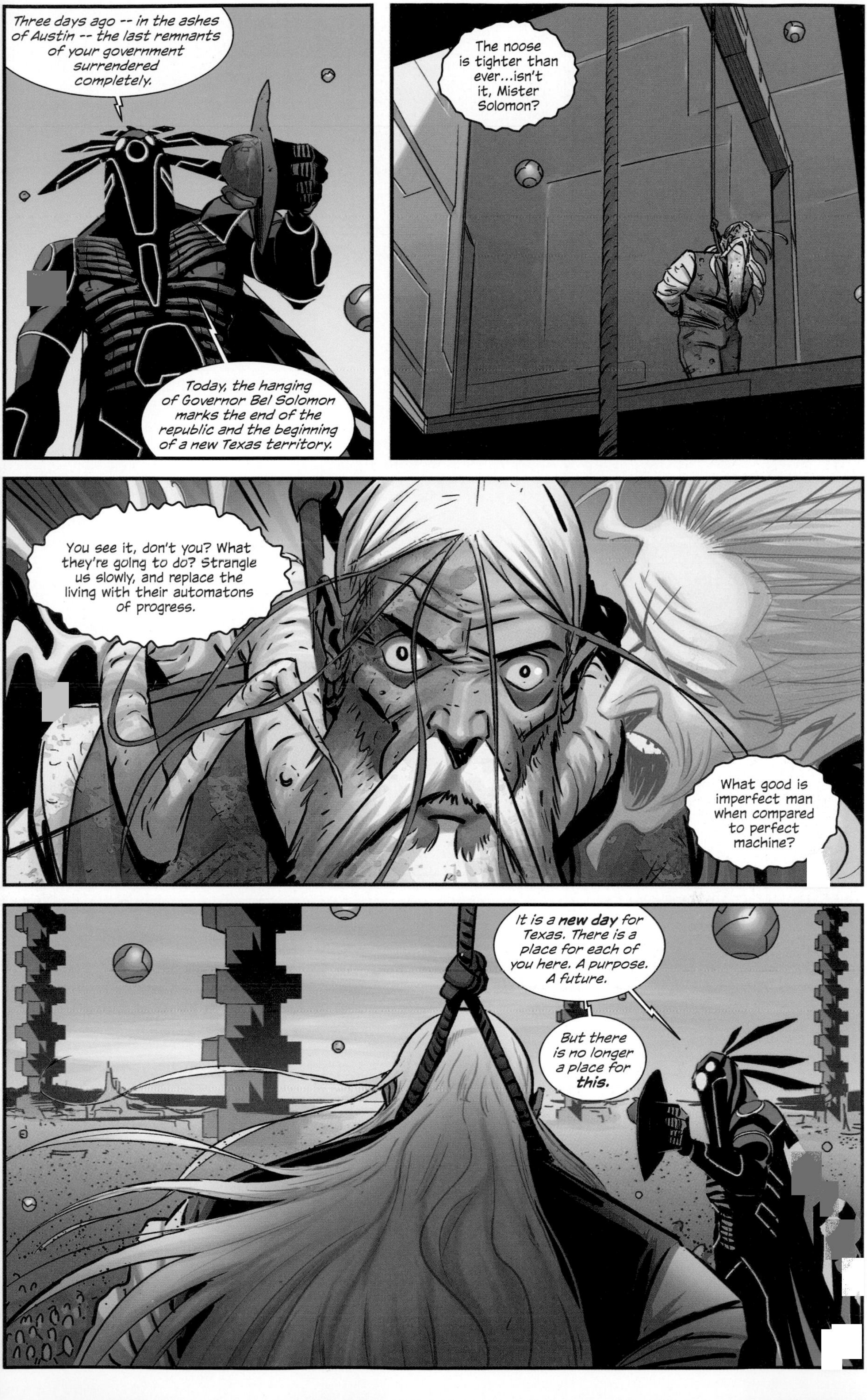
Three days ago -- in the ashes of Austin -- the last remnants of your government surrendered completely.
Today, the hanging of Governor Bel Solomon marks the end of the republic and the beginning of a new Texas territory.
The noose is tighter than ever...isn't it, Mister Solomon?
You see it, don't you? What they're going to do? Strangle us slowly, and replace the living with their automatons of progress.
What good is imperfect man when compared to perfect machine?
It is a **new day** for Texas. There is a place for each of you here. A purpose. A future.
But there is no longer a place for **this.**

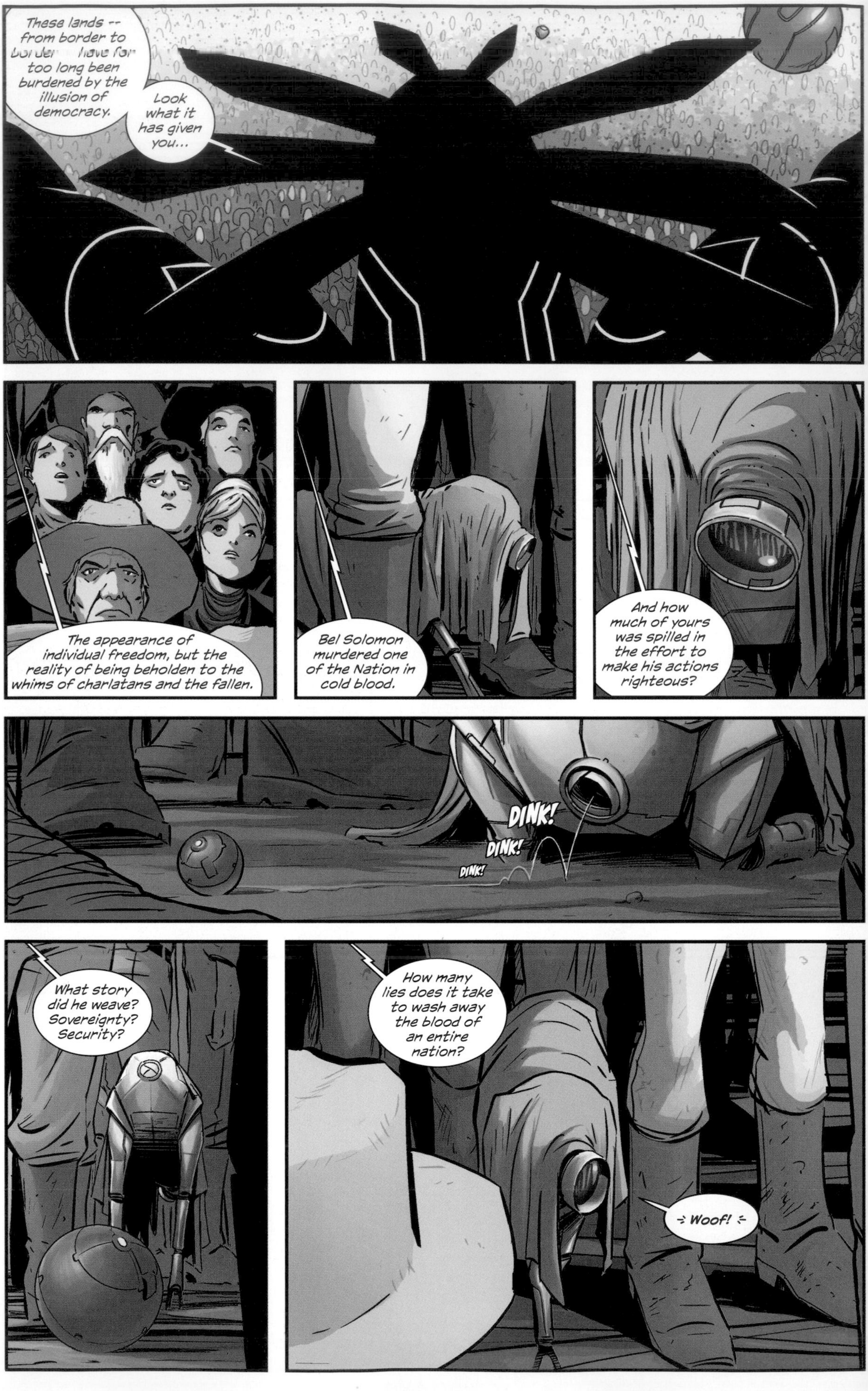
These lands -- from border to border -- have for too long been burdened by the illusion of democracy.
Look what it has given you...
The appearance of individual freedom, but the reality of being beholden to the whims of charlatans and the fallen.
Bel Solomon murdered one of the Nation in cold blood.
And how much of yours was spilled in the effort to make his actions righteous?
DINK!
DINK!
DINK!
What story did he weave? Sovereignty? Security?
How many lies does it take to wash away the blood of an entire nation?
Woof!

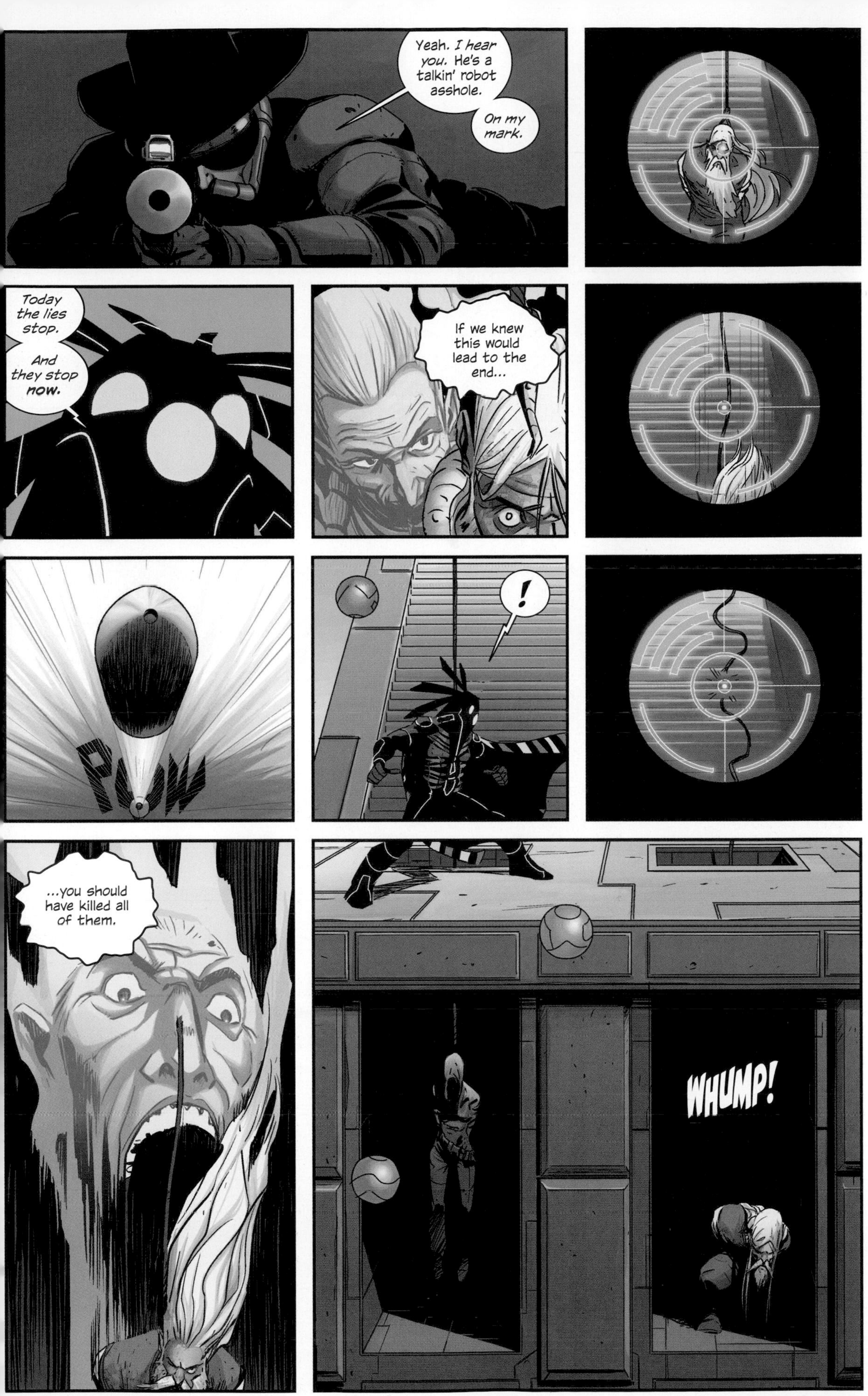

Yeah. I hear you. He's a talkin' robot asshole.
On my mark.
Today the lies stop.
And they stop now.
If we knew this would lead to the end...
POW
!
...you should have killed all of them.
WHUMP!

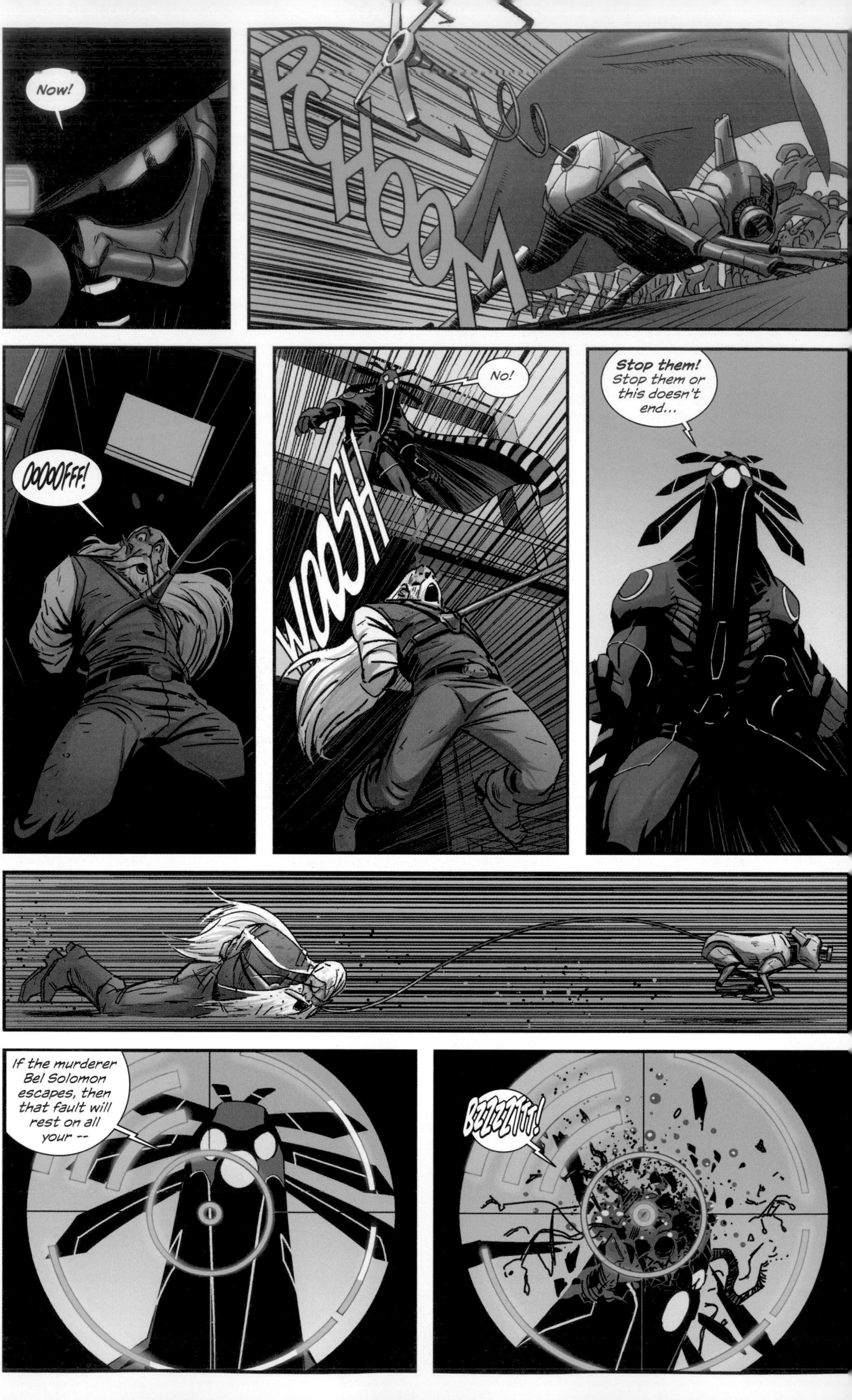
Now!
PCHOOM
OOOOOFFF!
No!
WOOSH
Stop them! Stop them or this doesn't end...
If the murderer Bel Solomon escapes, then that fault will rest on all your --
BZZZZTTT!

Nice fetch, dog...
Woof!
PSSSH
Now give yourself some cover and head this way.
I'm two clicks out.

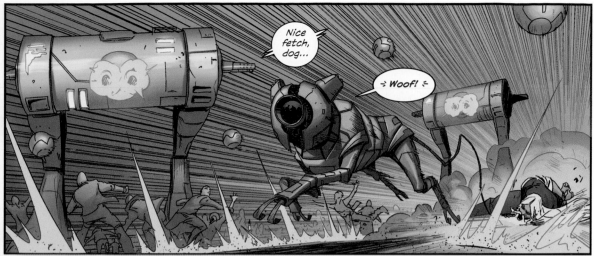

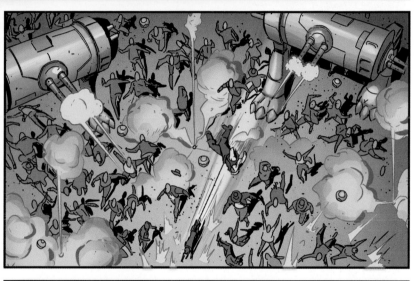

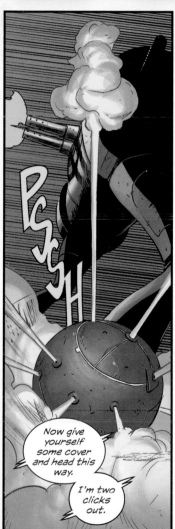

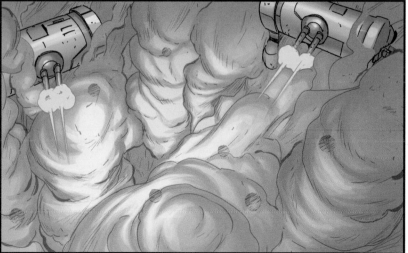

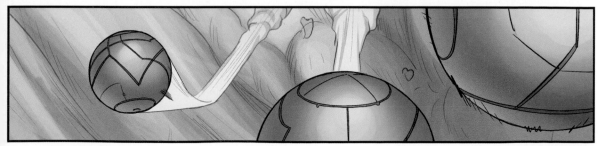

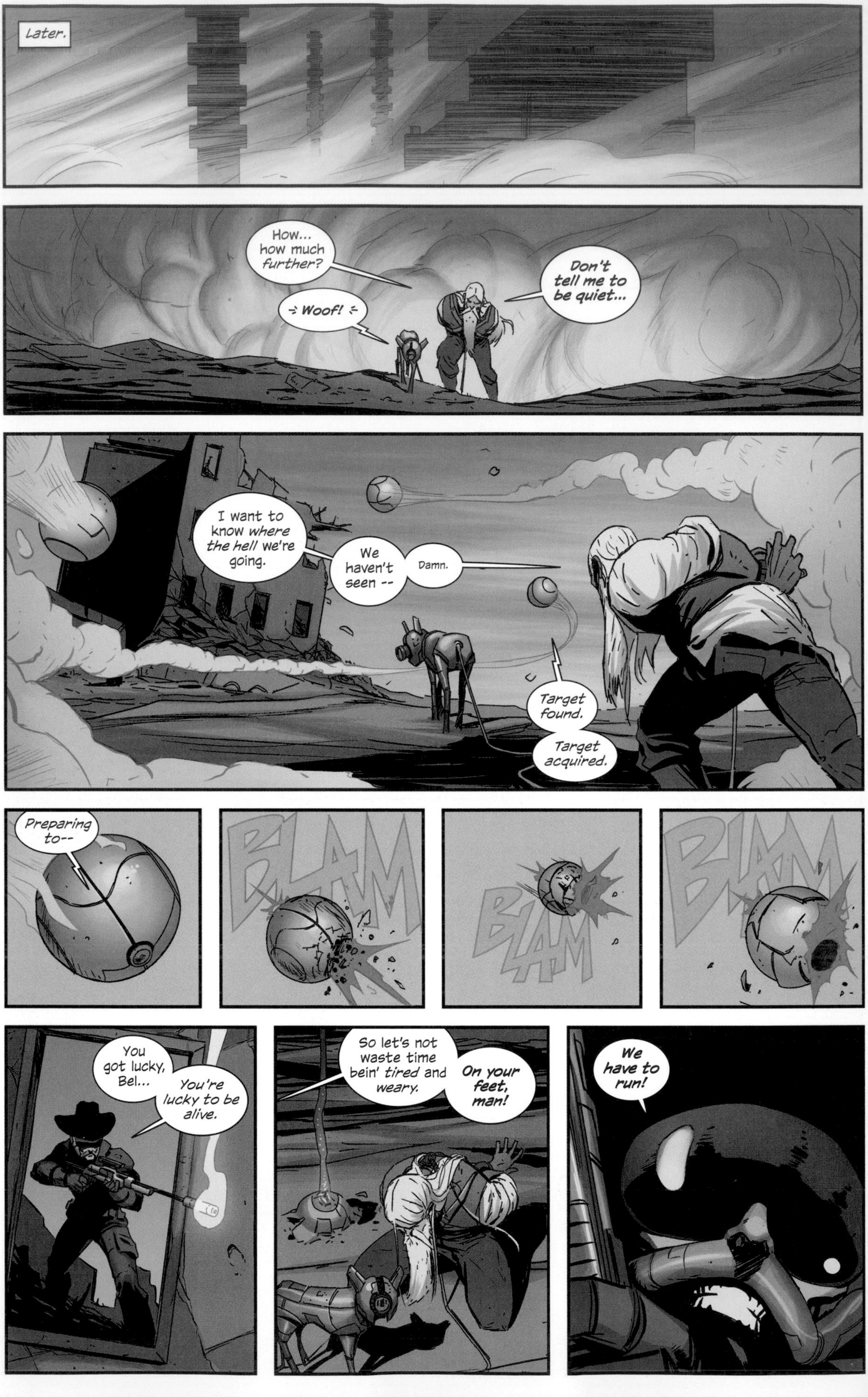
Later.
How... how much further?
Woof!
Don't tell me to be quiet...
I want to know where the hell we're going.
We haven't seen --
Damn.
Target found.
Target acquired.
Preparing to--
BLAM
BLAM
BLAM
You got lucky, Bel...
You're lucky to be alive.
So let's not waste time bein' tired and weary.
On your feet, man!
We have to run!

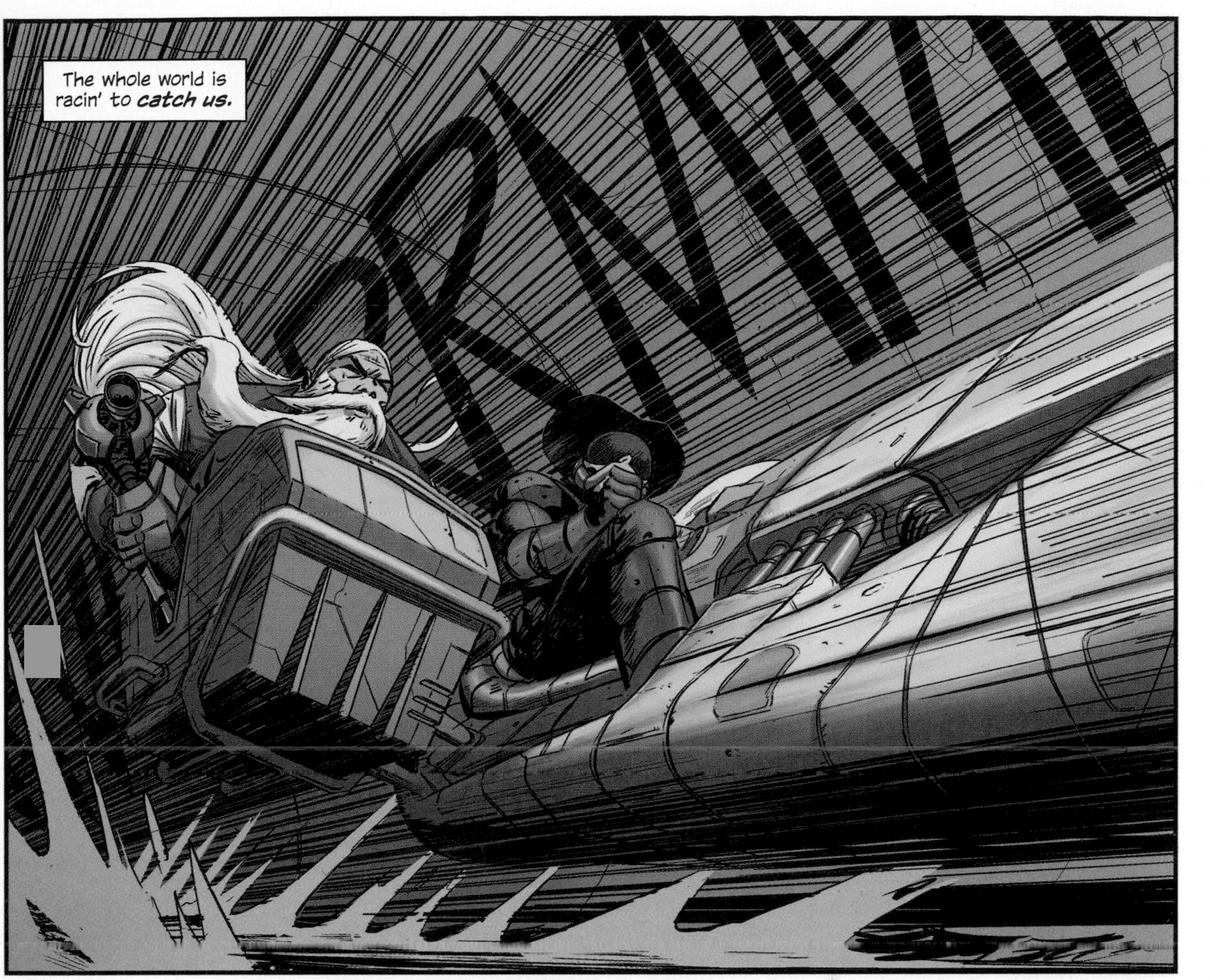
The whole world is racin' to **catch us.**

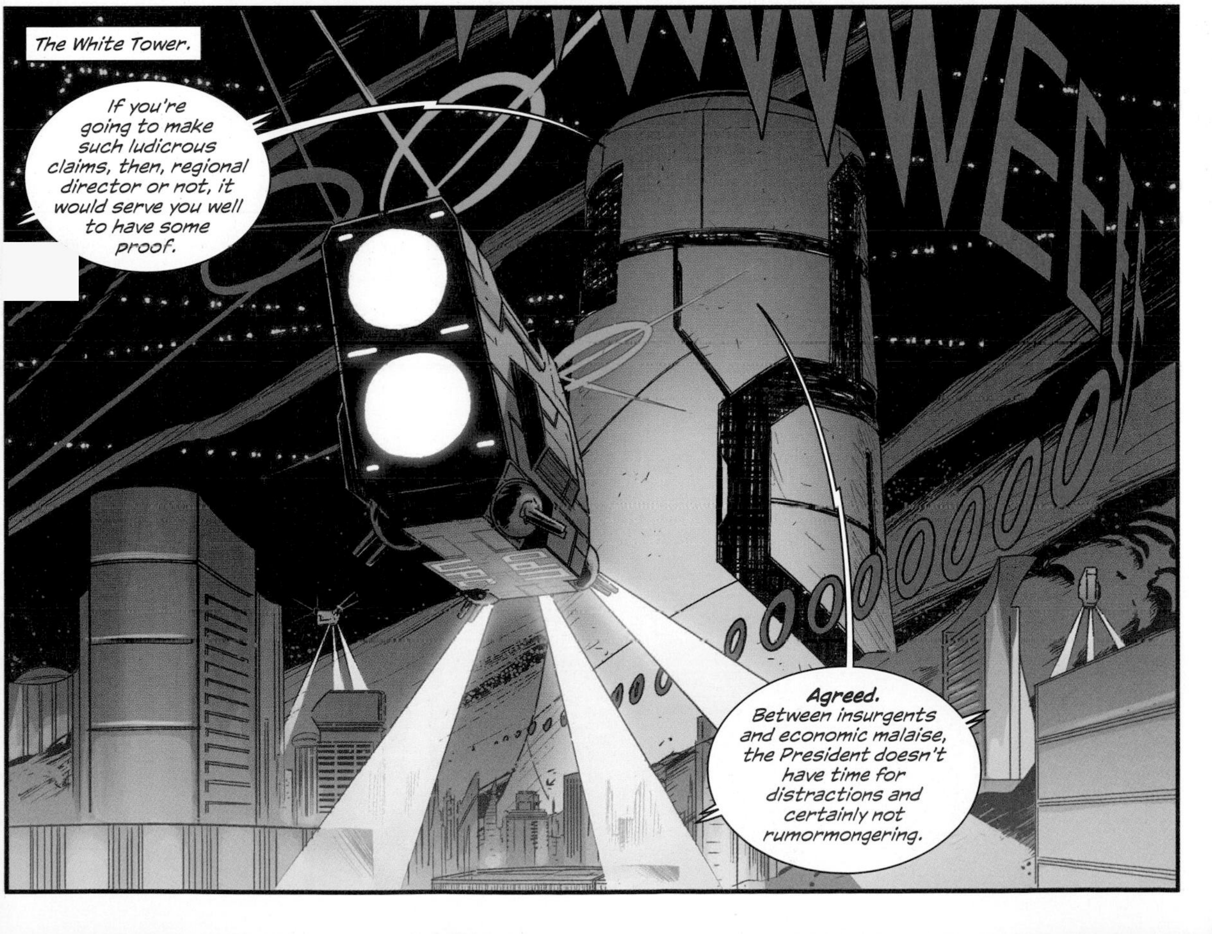
The White Tower.
If you're going to make such ludicrous claims, then, regional director or not, it would serve you well to have some proof.
Agreed. *Between insurgents and economic malaise, the President doesn't have time for distractions and certainly not rumormongering.*

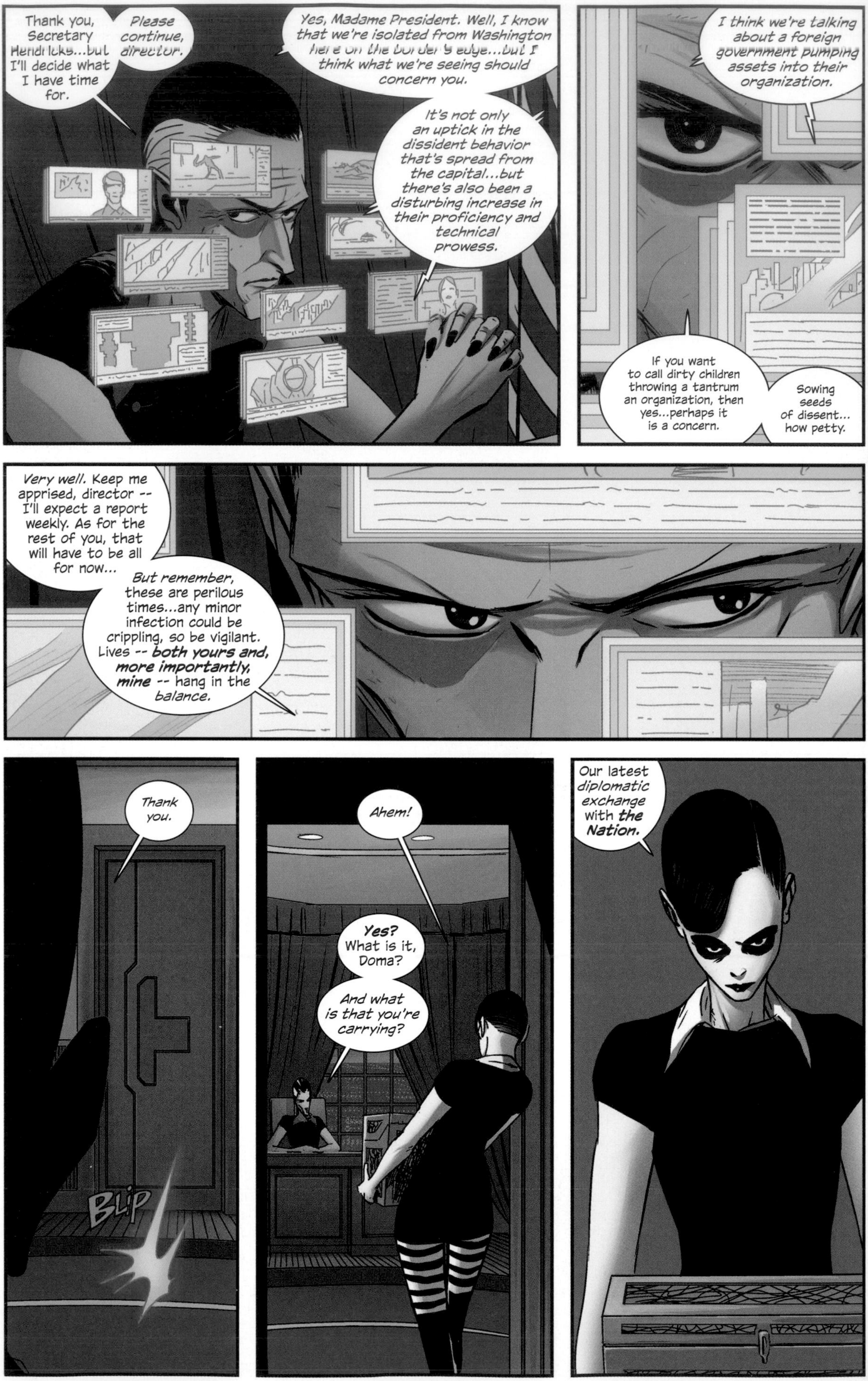
Thank you, Secretary Hendricks...but I'll decide what I have time for.
Please continue, director.
Yes, Madame President. Well, I know that we're isolated from Washington here on the border's edge...but I think what we're seeing should concern you.
It's not only an uptick in the dissident behavior that's spread from the capital...but there's also been a disturbing increase in their proficiency and technical prowess.
I think we're talking about a foreign government pumping assets into their organization.
If you want to call dirty children throwing a tantrum an organization, then yes...perhaps it is a concern.
Sowing seeds of dissent... how petty.
Very well. Keep me apprised, director -- I'll expect a report weekly. As for the rest of you, that will have to be all for now...
But remember, these are perilous times...any minor infection could be crippling, so be vigilant. Lives -- both yours and, more importantly, mine -- hang in the balance.
Thank you.
BLIP
Ahem!
Yes? What is it, Doma?
And what is that you're carrying?
Our latest diplomatic exchange with the Nation.

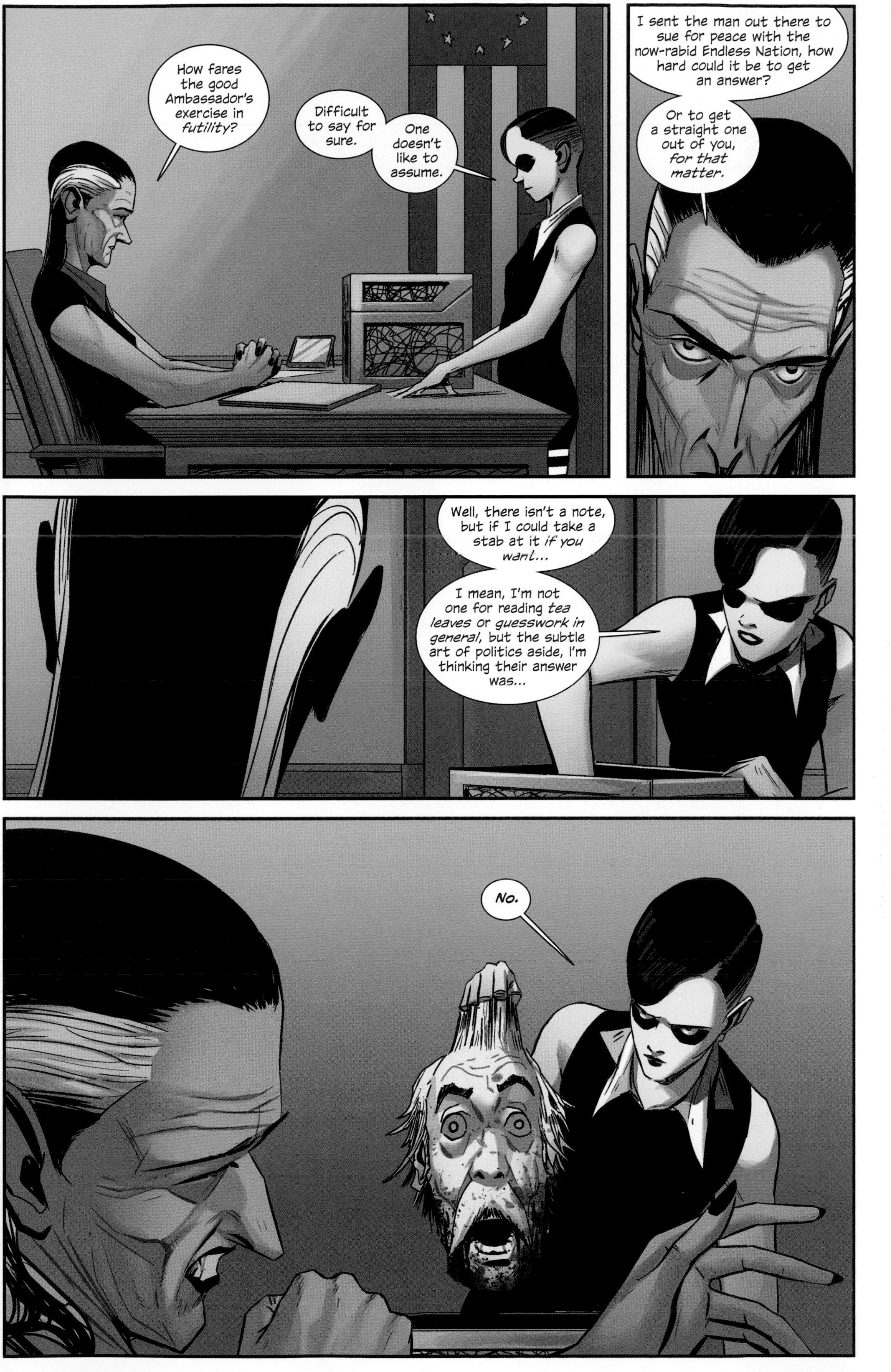
How fares the good Ambassador's exercise in *futility?*
Difficult to say for sure.
One doesn't like to assume.
I sent the man out there to sue for peace with the now-rabid Endless Nation, how hard could it be to get an answer?
Or to get a straight one out of you, *for that matter.*
Well, there isn't a note, but if I could take a stab at it *if you want...*
I mean, I'm not one for reading *tea leaves* or *guesswork in general*, but the subtle art of politics aside, I'm thinking their answer was...
No.

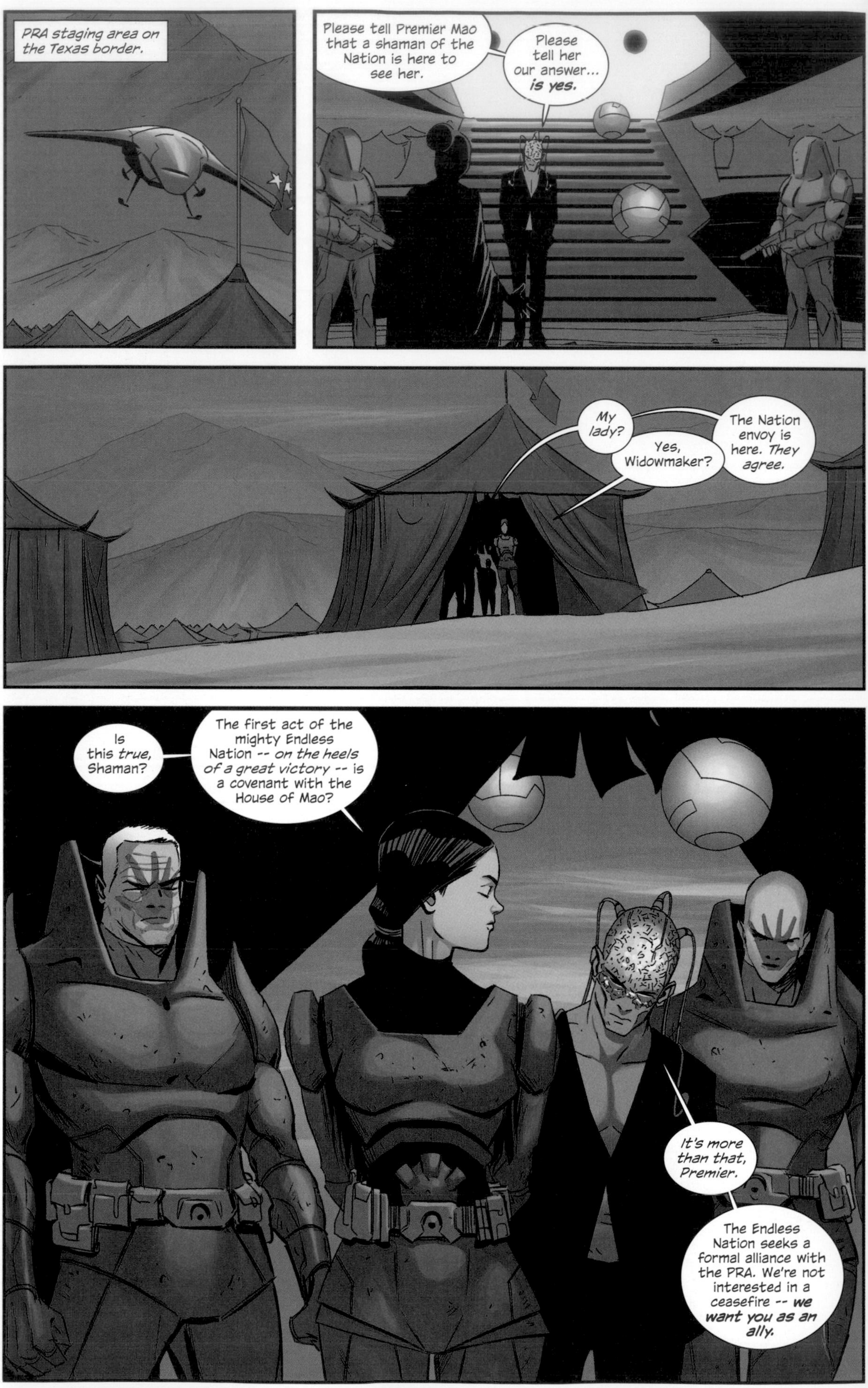
PRA staging area on the Texas border.
Please tell Premier Mao that a shaman of the Nation is here to see her.
Please tell her our answer... *is yes.*
My lady?
Yes, Widowmaker?
The Nation envoy is here. *They agree.*
Is this *true,* Shaman?
The first act of the mighty Endless Nation -- *on the heels of a great victory* -- is a covenant with the House of Mao?
It's more than that, Premier.
The Endless Nation seeks a formal alliance with the PRA. We're not interested in a ceasefire -- ***we want you as an ally.***

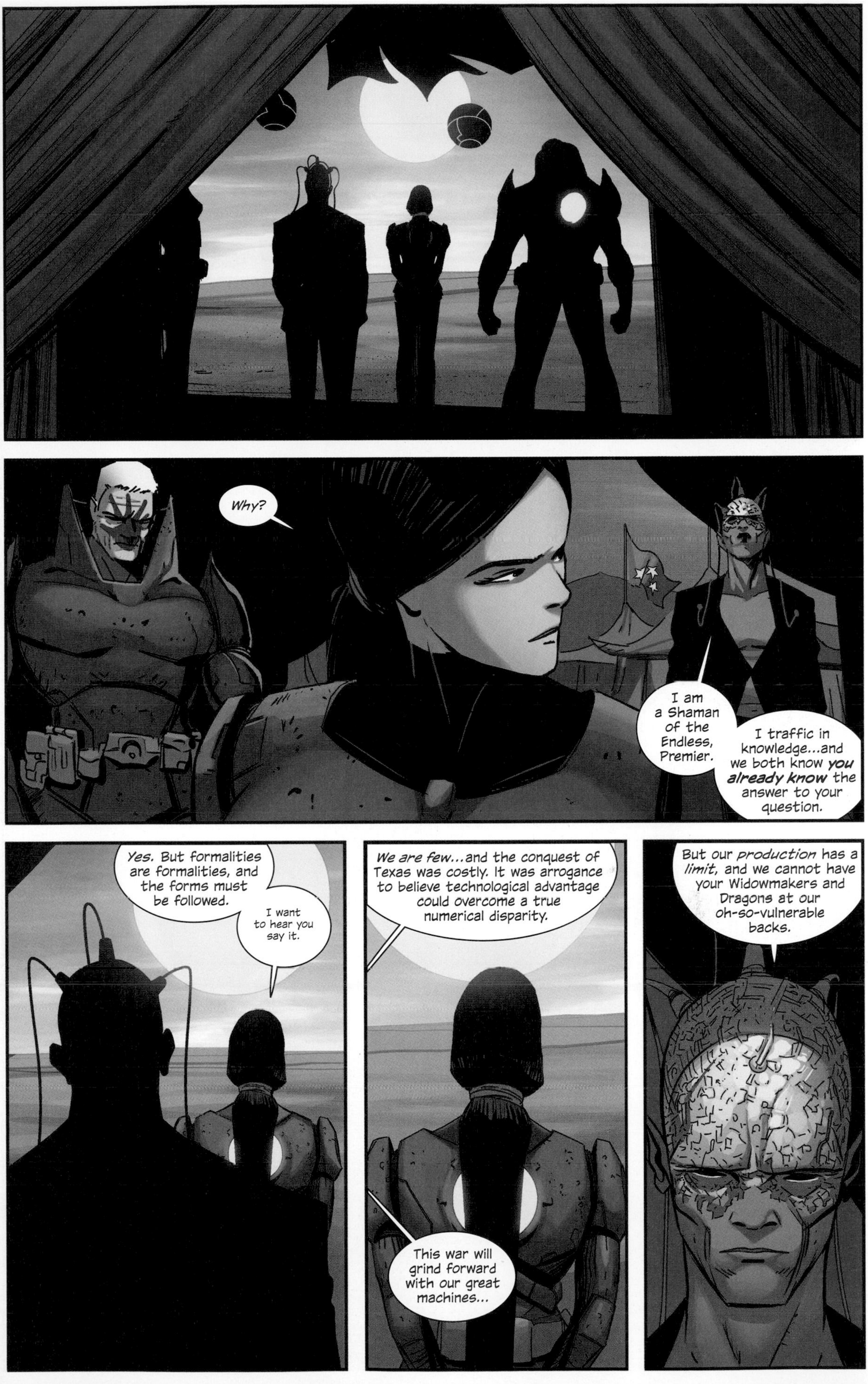

Why?
I am a Shaman of the Endless, Premier.
I traffic in knowledge...and we both know ***you already know*** the answer to your question.
Yes. But formalities are formalities, and the forms must be followed.
I want to hear you say it.
*We are few...*and the conquest of Texas was costly. It was arrogance to believe technological advantage could overcome a true numerical disparity.
This war will grind forward with our great machines...
But our *production* has a *limit,* and we cannot have your Widowmakers and Dragons at our oh-so-vulnerable backs.

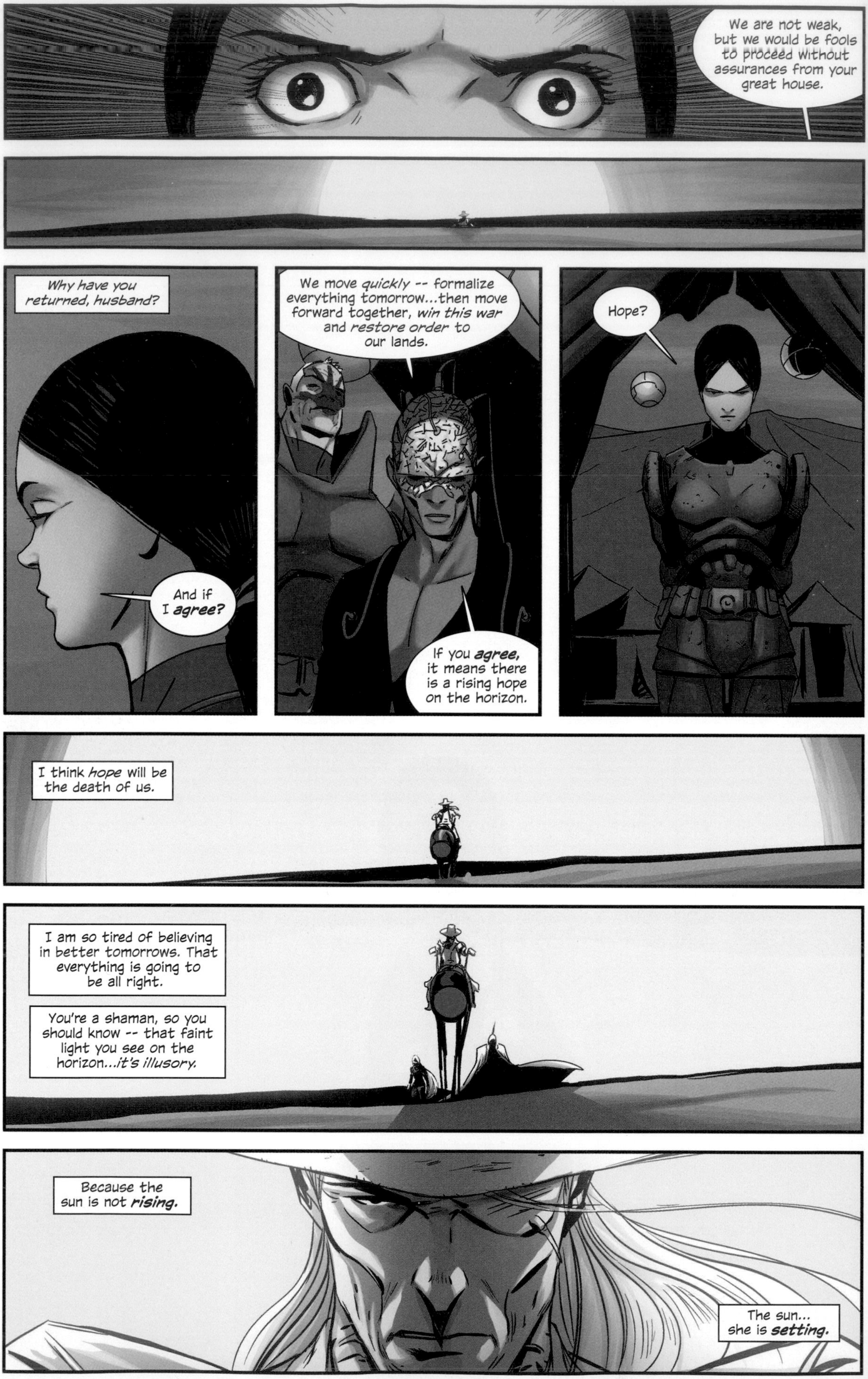
We are not weak, but we would be fools to proceed without assurances from your great house.
Why have you returned, husband?
And if I ***agree?***
We move *quickly* -- formalize everything tomorrow...then move forward together, *win this war* and *restore order* to our lands.
If you ***agree,*** it means there is a rising hope on the horizon.
Hope?
I think *hope* will be the death of us.
I am so tired of believing in better tomorrows. That everything is going to be all right.
You're a shaman, so you should know -- that faint light you see on the horizon...*it's illusory.*
Because the sun is not ***rising.***
The sun... she is ***setting.***

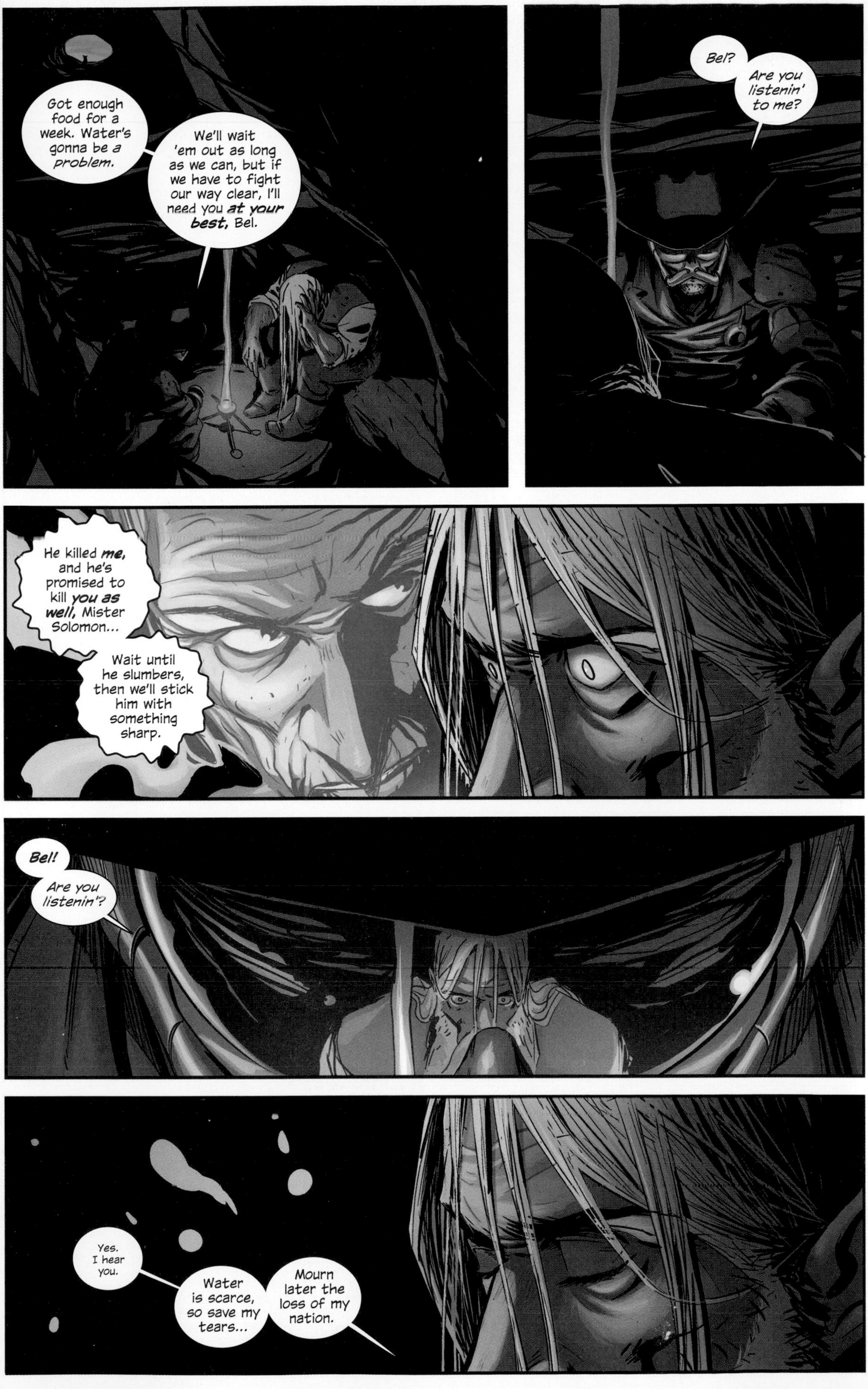

Got enough food for a week. Water's gonna be a *problem.*
We'll wait 'em out as long as we can, but if we have to fight our way clear, I'll need you ***at your best,*** Bel.
Bel?
Are you listenin' to me?
He killed ***me,*** and he's promised to kill ***you as well,*** Mister Solomon...
Wait until he slumbers, then we'll stick him with something sharp.
Bel!
Are you listenin'?
Yes. I hear you.
Water is scarce, so save my tears...
Mourn later the loss of my nation.

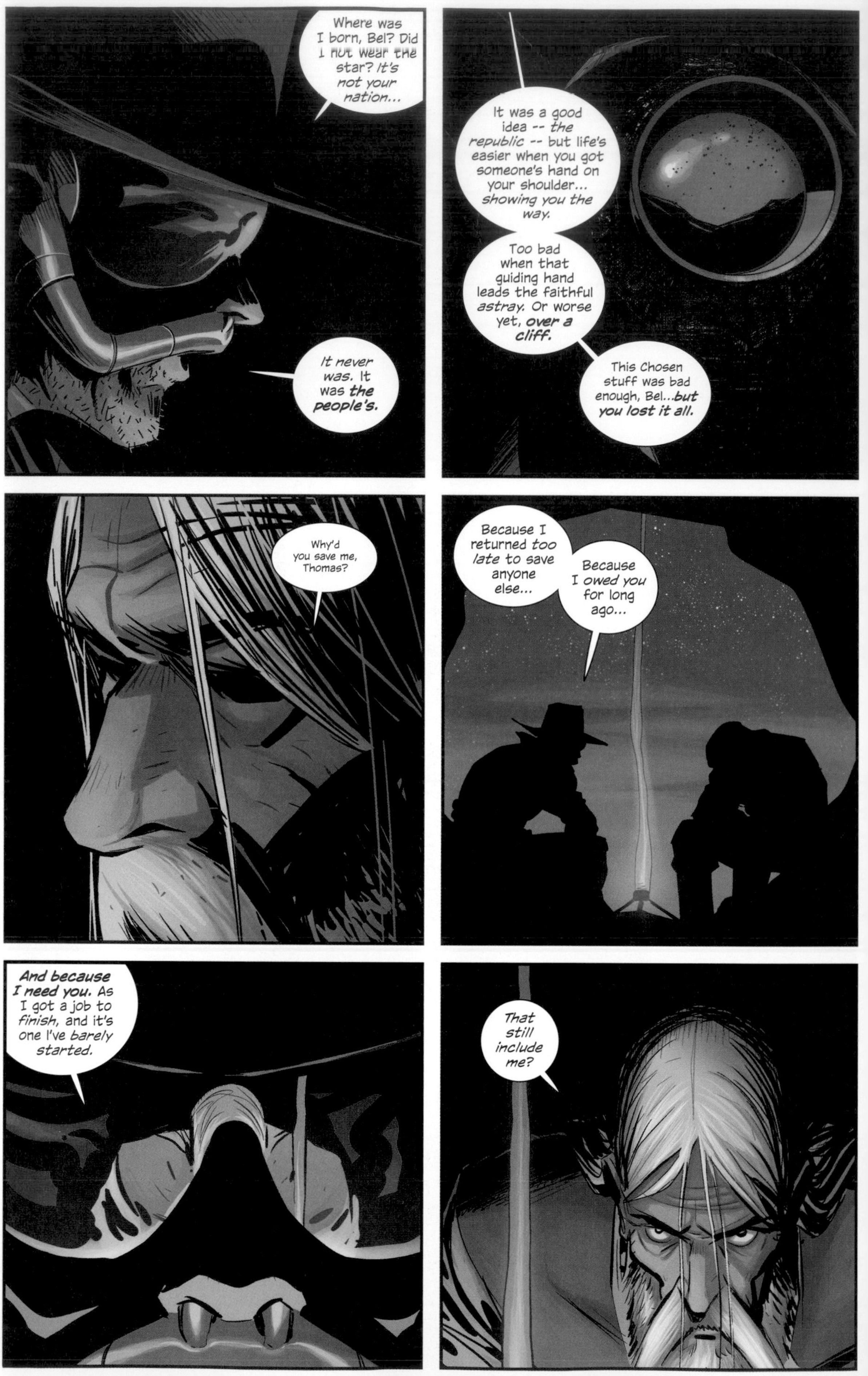
Where was I born, Bel? Did I not wear the star? It's not your nation...
It never was. It was the people's.
It was a good idea -- the republic -- but life's easier when you got someone's hand on your shoulder... showing you the way.
Too bad when that guiding hand leads the faithful astray. Or worse yet, over a cliff.
This Chosen stuff was bad enough, Bel...but you lost it all.
Why'd you save me, Thomas?
Because I returned too late to save anyone else...
Because I owed you for long ago...
And because I need you. As I got a job to finish, and it's one I've barely started.
That still include me?

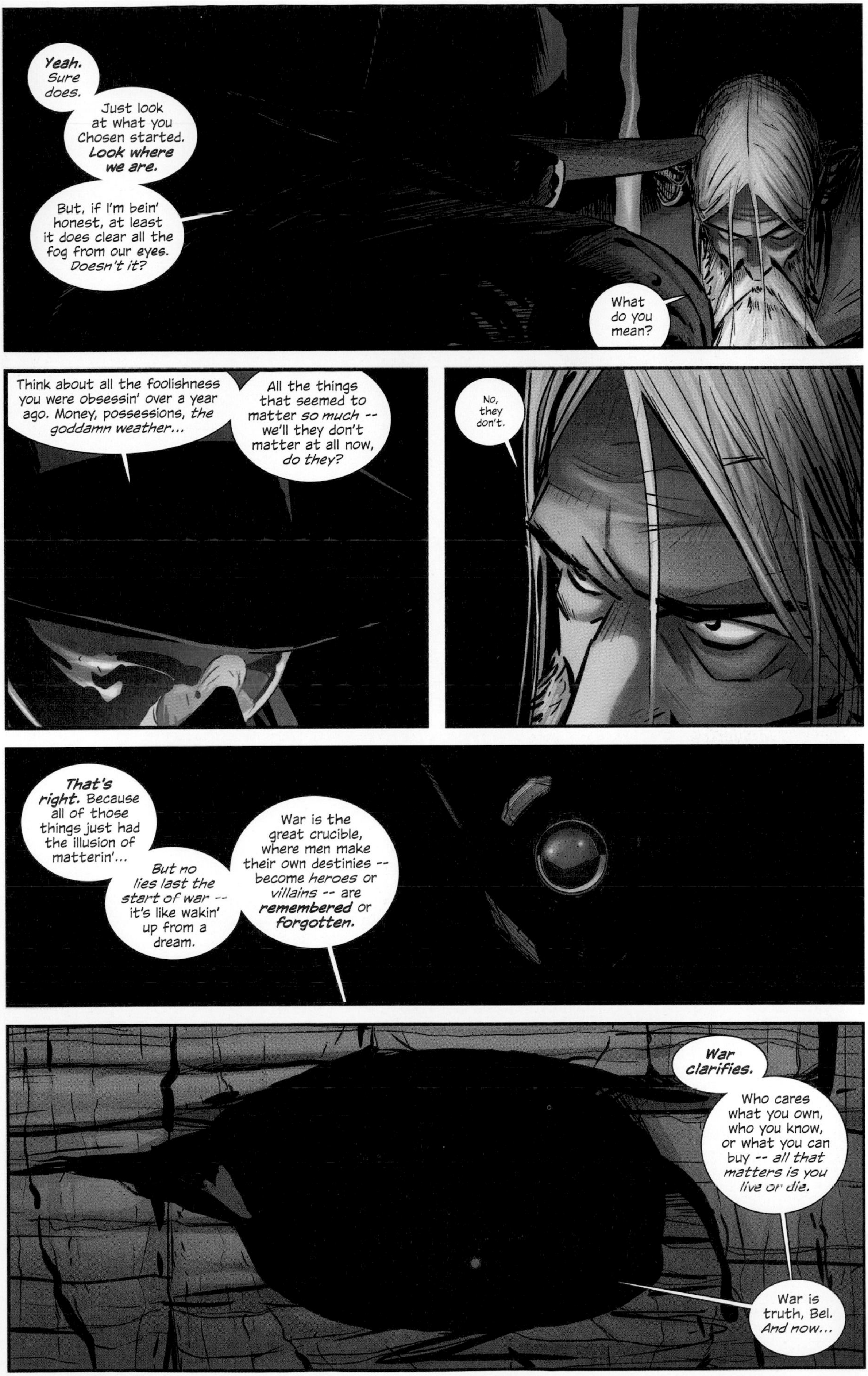

Yeah. Sure does.
Just look at what you Chosen started. Look where we are.
But, if I'm bein' honest, at least it does clear all the fog from our eyes. Doesn't it?
What do you mean?
Think about all the foolishness you were obsessin' over a year ago. Money, possessions, the goddamn weather...
All the things that seemed to matter so much -- we'll they don't matter at all now, do they?
No, they don't.
That's right. Because all of those things just had the illusion of matterin'...
But no lies last the start of war -- it's like wakin' up from a dream.
War is the great crucible, where men make their own destinies -- become heroes or villains -- are remembered or forgotten.
War clarifies.
Who cares what you own, who you know, or what you can buy -- all that matters is you live or die.
War is truth, Bel. And now...

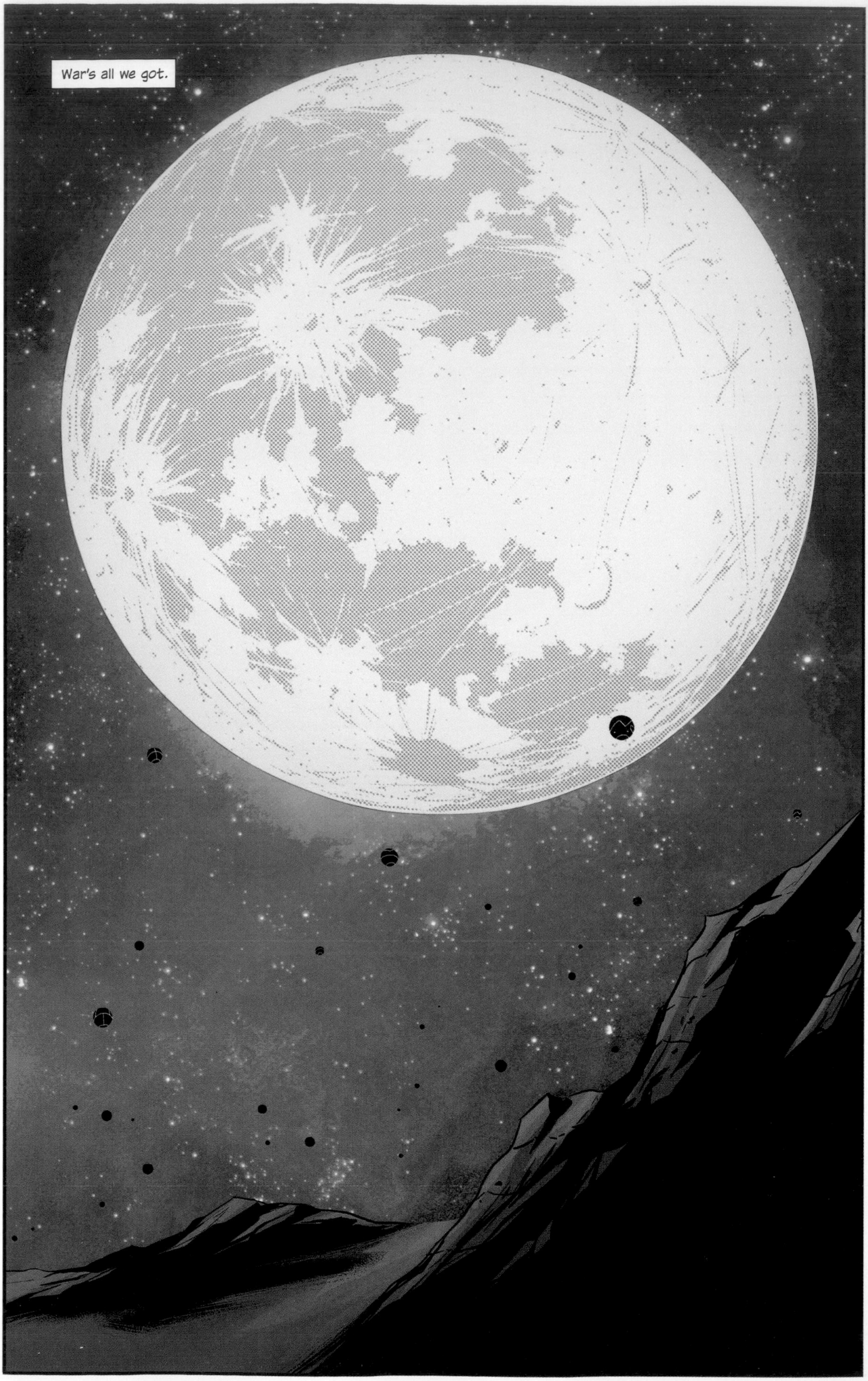
War's all we got.

LOOK WHAT THEY **GIVE YOU.**

JUST SO THEY CAN **TAKE IT AWAY.**

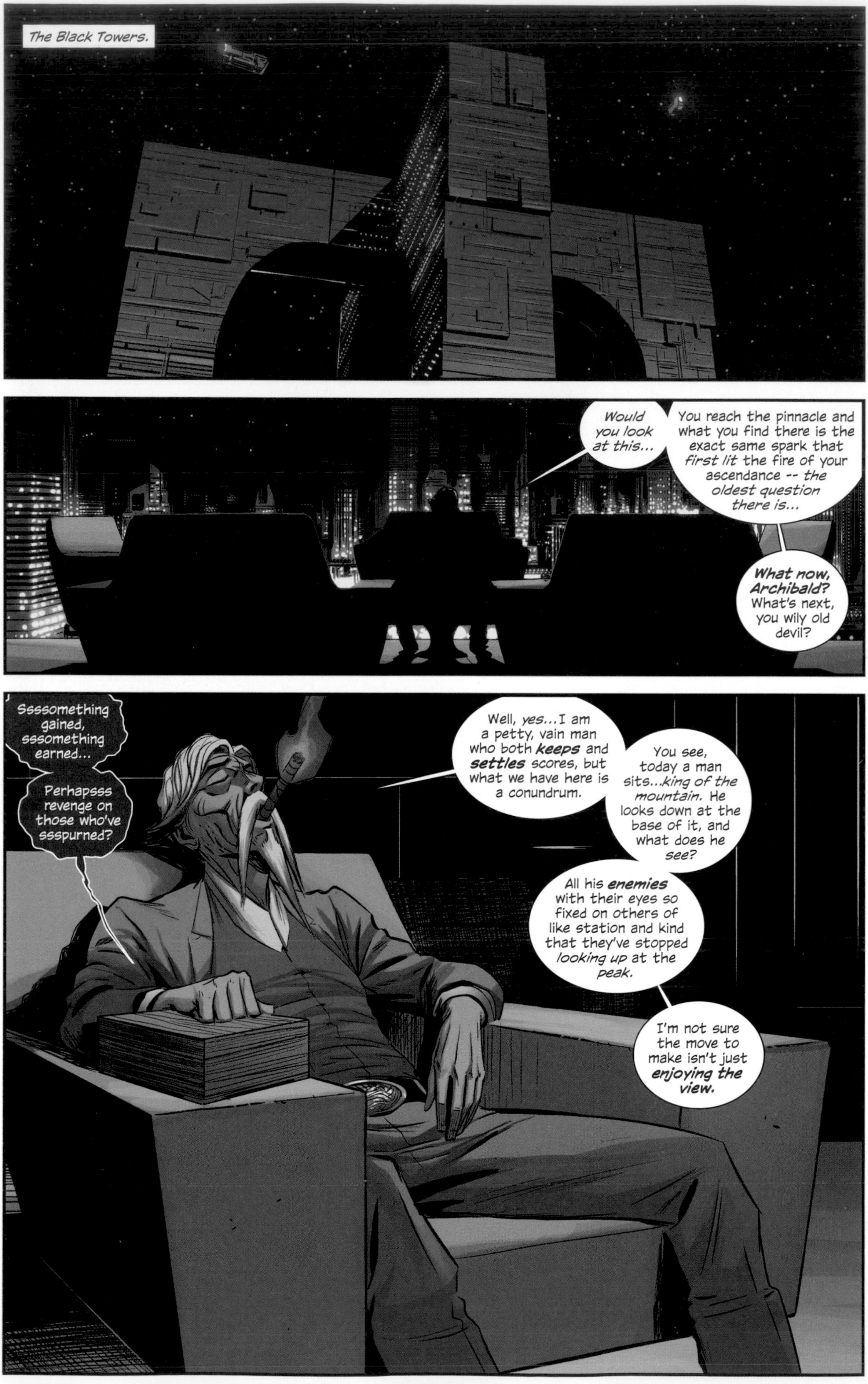

The Black Towers.
Would you look at this...
You reach the pinnacle and what you find there is the exact same spark that first lit the fire of your ascendance -- the oldest question there is...
What now, Archibald? What's next, you wily old devil?
Ssssomething gained, sssomething earned...
Perhapsss revenge on those who've ssspurned?
Well, yes...I am a petty, vain man who both keeps and settles scores, but what we have here is a conundrum.
You see, today a man sits...king of the mountain. He looks down at the base of it, and what does he see?
All his enemies with their eyes so fixed on others of like station and kind that they've stopped looking up at the peak.
I'm not sure the move to make isn't just enjoying the view.

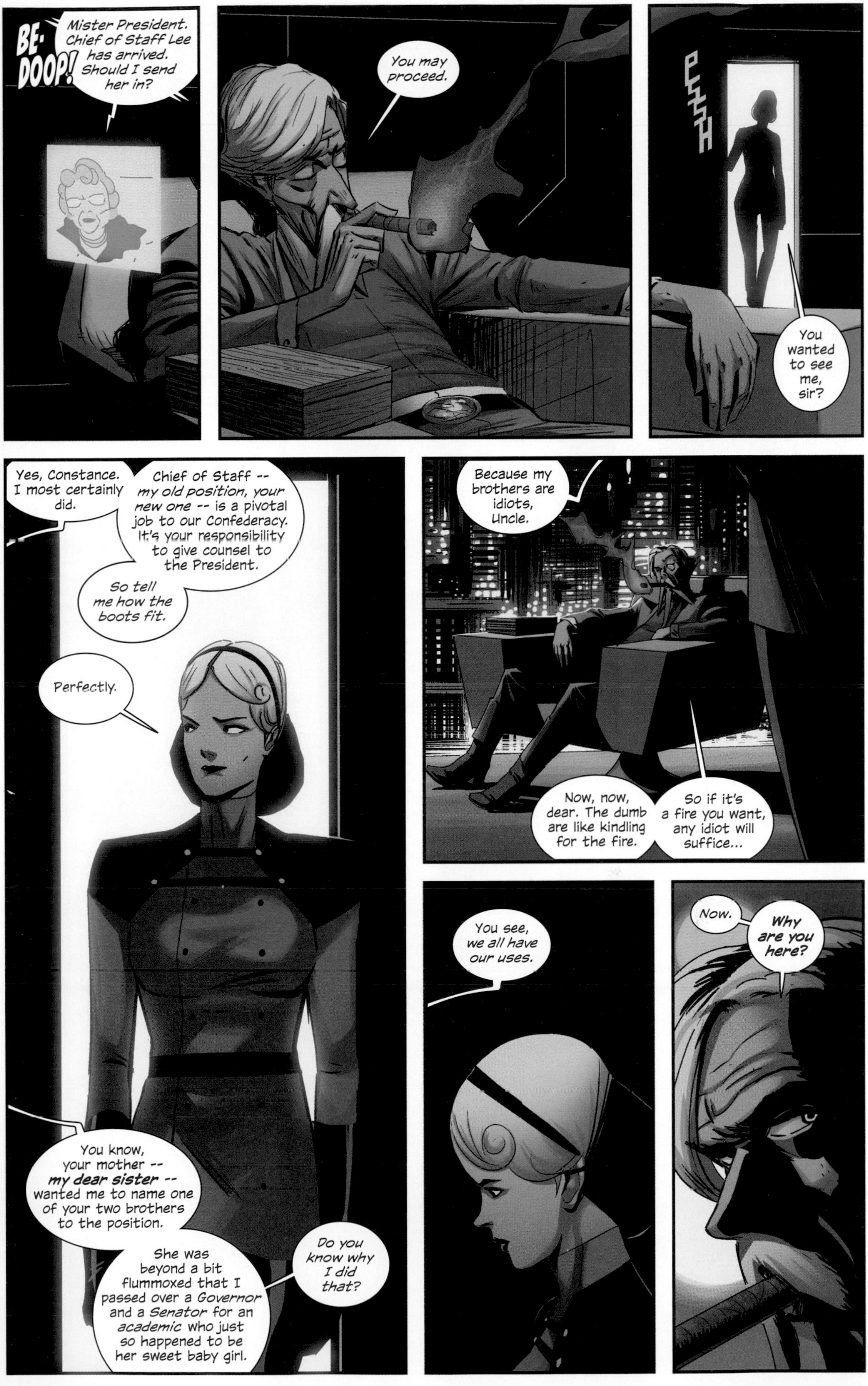
BE-DOOP!
Mister President. Chief of Staff Lee has arrived. Should I send her in?
You may proceed.
PSSH
You wanted to see me, sir?
Yes, Constance. I most certainly did.
Chief of Staff -- *my old position, your new one* -- is a pivotal job to our Confederacy. It's your responsibility to give counsel to the President.
So tell me how the boots fit.
Perfectly.
You know, your mother -- ***my dear sister*** -- wanted me to name one of your two brothers to the position.
She was beyond a bit flummoxed that I passed over a *Governor* and a *Senator* for an *academic* who just so happened to be her sweet baby girl.
Do you know why I did that?
Because my brothers are idiots, Uncle.
Now, now, dear. The dumb are like kindling for the fire.
So if it's a fire you want, any idiot will suffice...
You see, we all have our uses.
Now.
Why are you here?

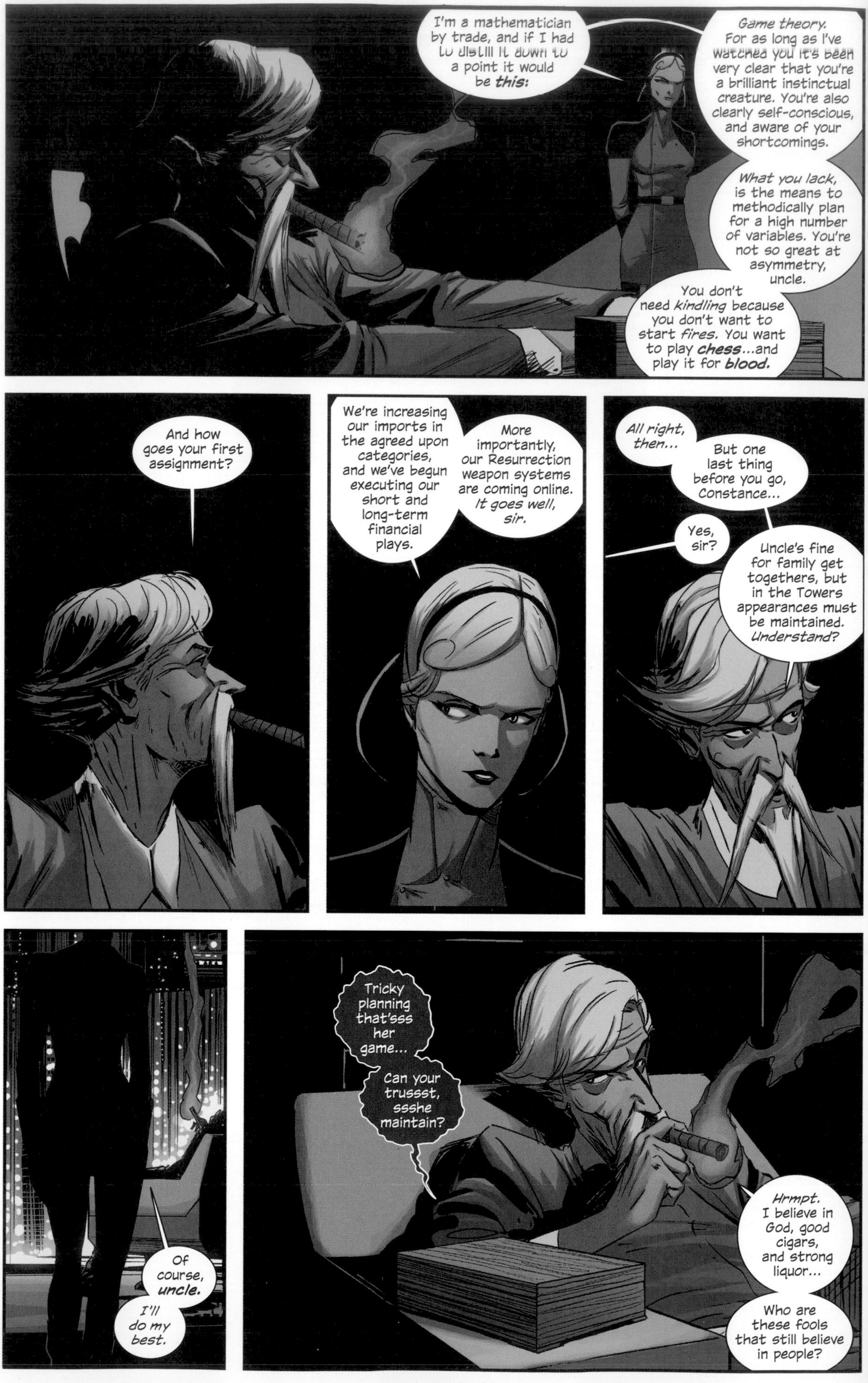
I'm a mathematician by trade, and if I had to distill it down to a point it would be *this:*
Game theory. For as long as I've watched you it's been very clear that you're a brilliant instinctual creature. You're also clearly self-conscious, and aware of your shortcomings.
What you lack, is the means to methodically plan for a high number of variables. You're not so great at asymmetry, uncle.
You don't need *kindling* because you don't want to start *fires.* You want to play ***chess***...and play it for ***blood.***
And how goes your first assignment?
We're increasing our imports in the agreed upon categories, and we've begun executing our short and long-term financial plays.
More importantly, our Resurrection weapon systems are coming online. *It goes well, sir.*
All right, then...
But one last thing before you go, Constance...
Yes, sir?
Uncle's fine for family get togethers, but in the Towers appearances must be maintained. *Understand?*
Of course, ***uncle.***
I'll do my best.
Tricky planning that'sss her game...
Can your trussst, ssshe maintain?
Hrmpt. I believe in God, good cigars, and strong liquor...
Who are these fools that still believe in people?

FOREVER IS A LONG TIME
TO **FEEL.**

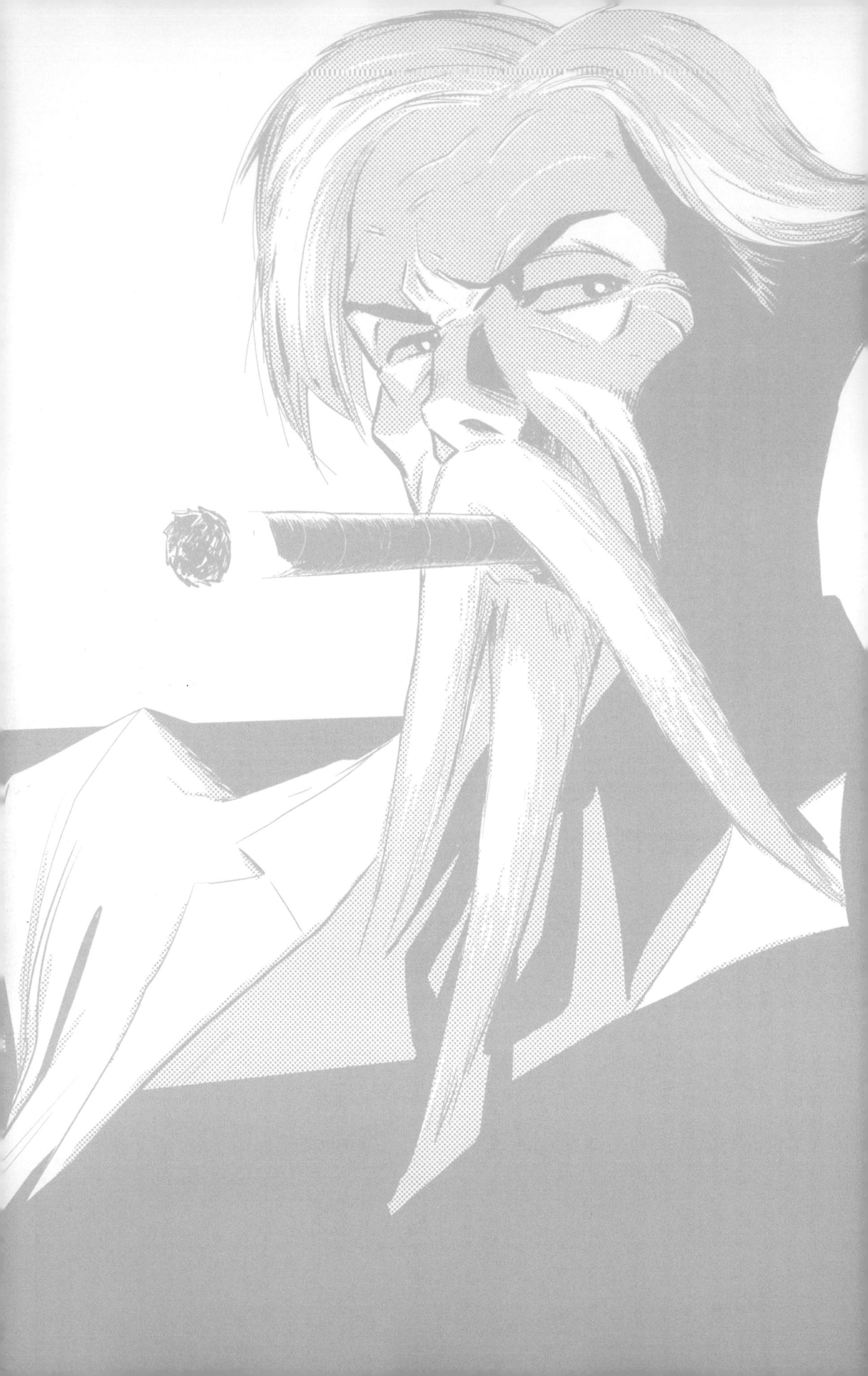

17

SEVENTEEN: THIS SACRED MEAL

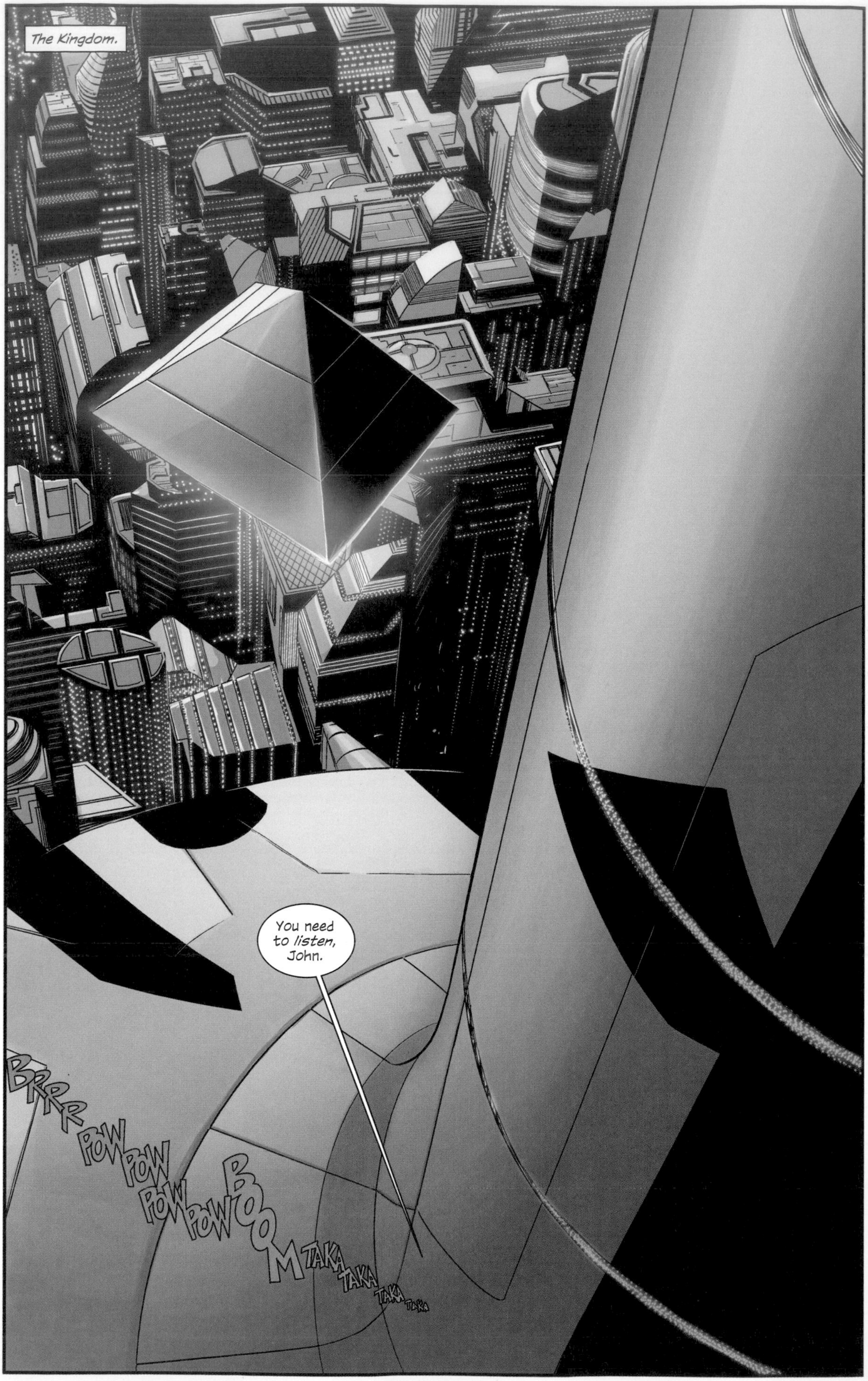
The Kingdom.
You need to listen, John.
BRRR
POW POW POW POW
BOOOM
TAKA TAKA TAKA TAKA

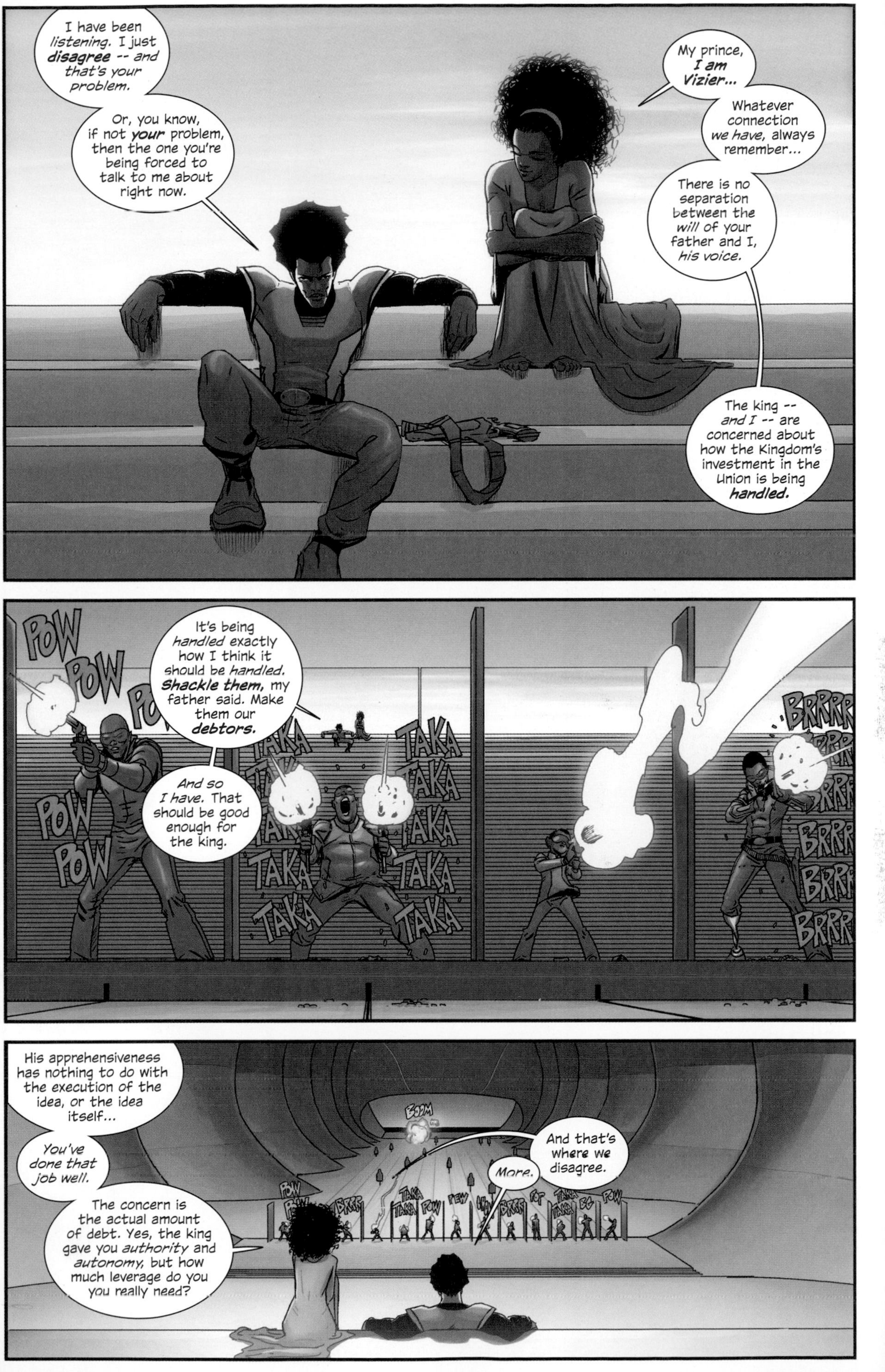

I have been listening. I just disagree -- and that's your problem.
Or, you know, if not your problem, then the one you're being forced to talk to me about right now.
My prince, I am Vizier...
Whatever connection we have, always remember...
There is no separation between the will of your father and I, his voice.
The king -- and I -- are concerned about how the Kingdom's investment in the Union is being handled.
POW POW POW
POW POW
It's being handled exactly how I think it should be handled. Shackle them, my father said. Make them our debtors.
And so I have. That should be good enough for the king.
TAKA TAKA TAKA TAKA TAKA TAKA
TAKA TAKA TAKA TAKA TAKA TAKA
BRRRR BRRRR BRRRR BRRRR BRRRR BRRRR
His apprehensiveness has nothing to do with the execution of the idea, or the idea itself...
You've done that job well.
The concern is the actual amount of debt. Yes, the king gave you authority and autonomy, but how much leverage do you you really need?
More.
And that's where we disagree.

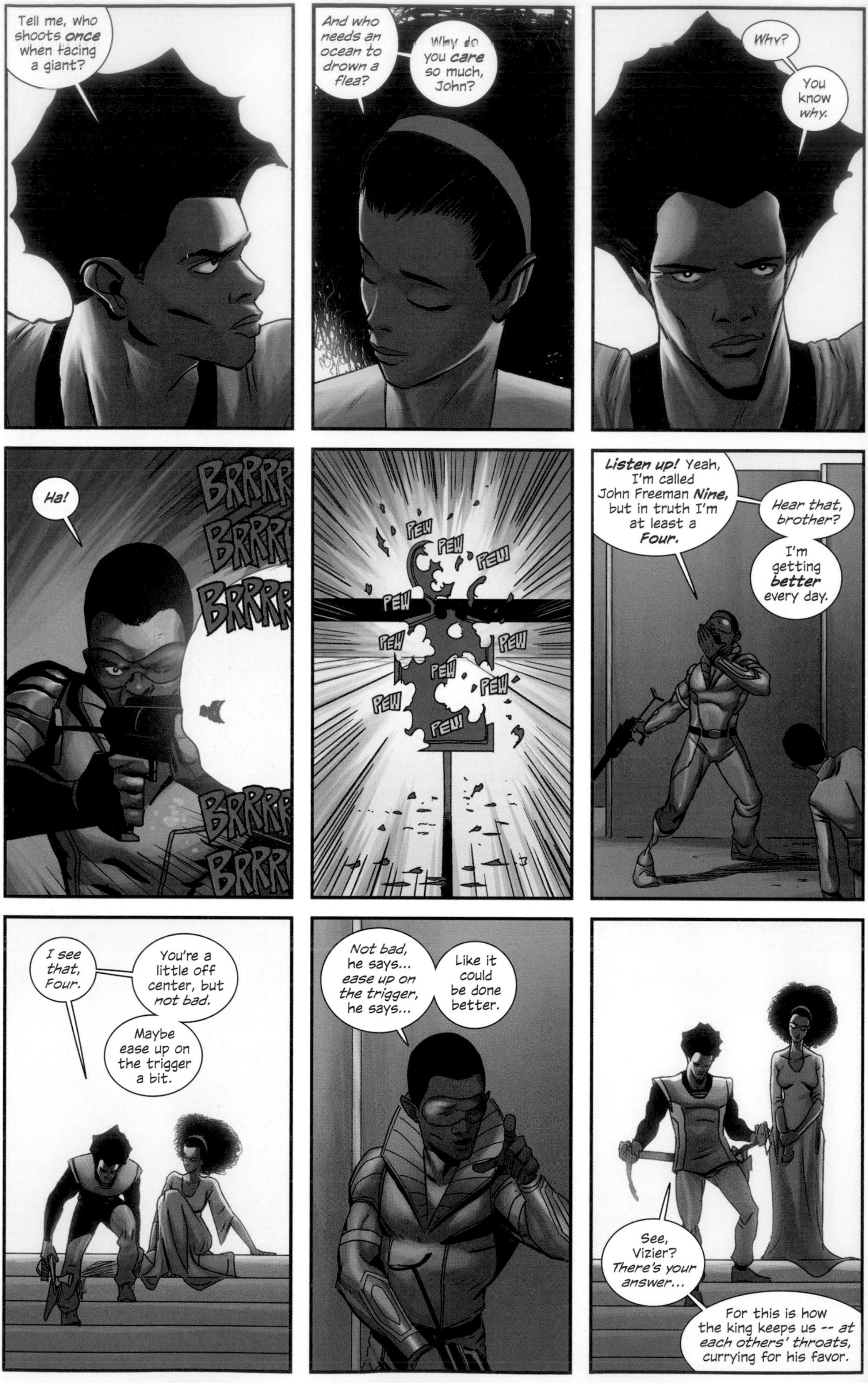

Tell me, who shoots **once** when facing a giant?
And who needs an ocean to drown a flea?
Why do you **care** so much, John?
Why?
You know why.
Ha!
BRRRR
BRRRR
BRRRR
BRRRR
BRRRR
PEW PEW PEW PEW PEW PEW PEW PEW PEW PEW
Listen up! Yeah, I'm called John Freeman ***Nine,*** but in truth I'm at least a ***Four.***
Hear that, brother?
I'm getting ***better*** every day.
I see that, Four.
You're a little off center, but *not bad.*
Maybe ease up on the trigger a bit.
Not bad, he says... ease up on the trigger, he says...
Like it could be done better.
See, Vizier? *There's your answer...*
For this is how the king keeps us -- *at each others' throats,* currying for his favor.

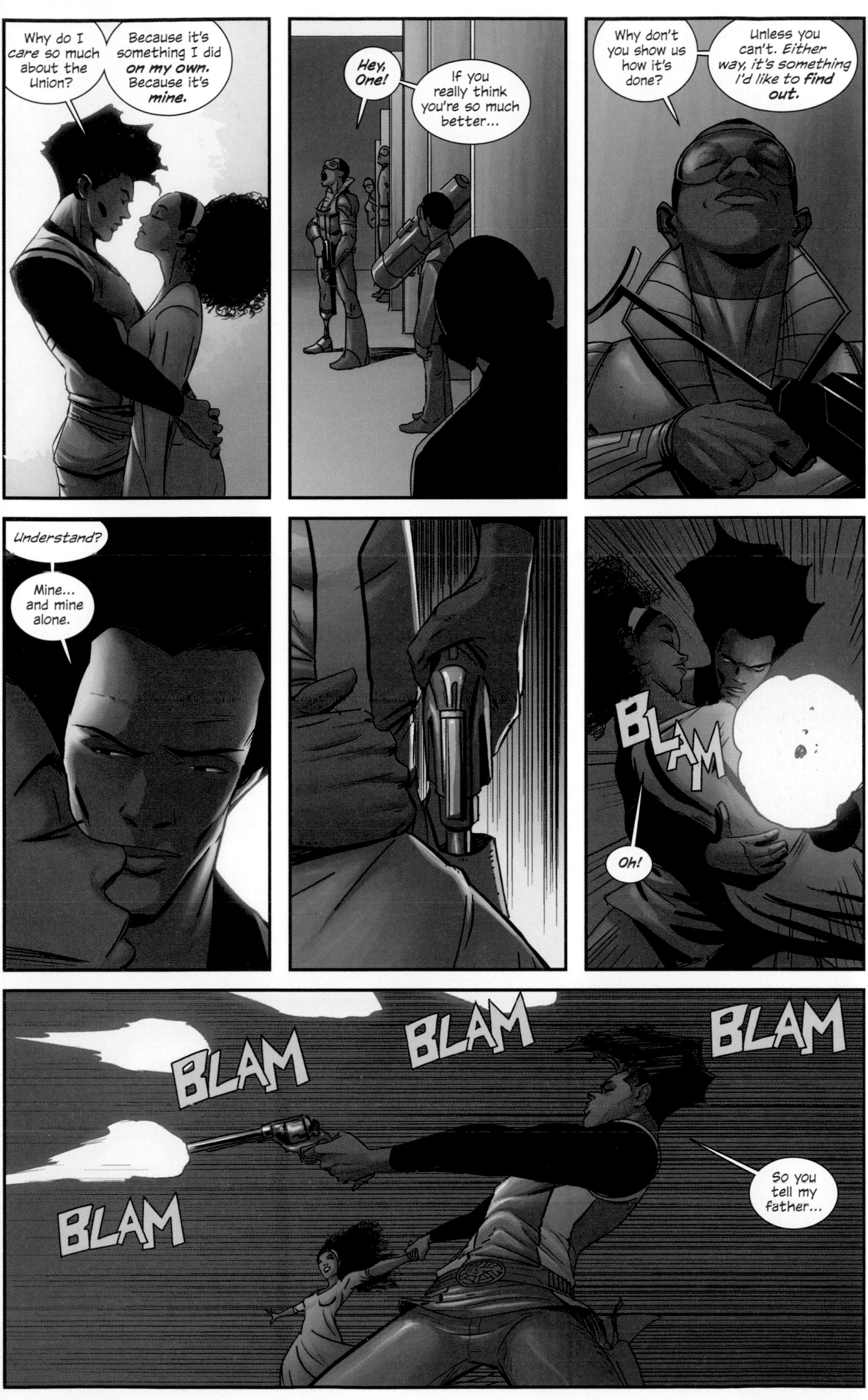

Why do I *care* so much about the Union?
Because it's something I did **on my own.** Because it's **mine.**
Hey, One!
If you really think you're so much better...
Why don't you show us how it's done?
Unless you can't. *Either way, it's something I'd like to* **find out.**
Understand?
Mine... and mine alone.
BLAM
Oh!
BLAM
BLAM
BLAM
BLAM
So you tell my father...

That you have delivered his message...

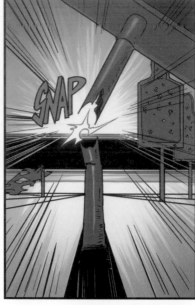

SNAP

BLAM

That I understood it...

But I disagree...

BLAM

AH!

And as long as the discretion remains mine...

BLAM

I have *made* my decision.

BLAM

AARGHH!!

SNAP

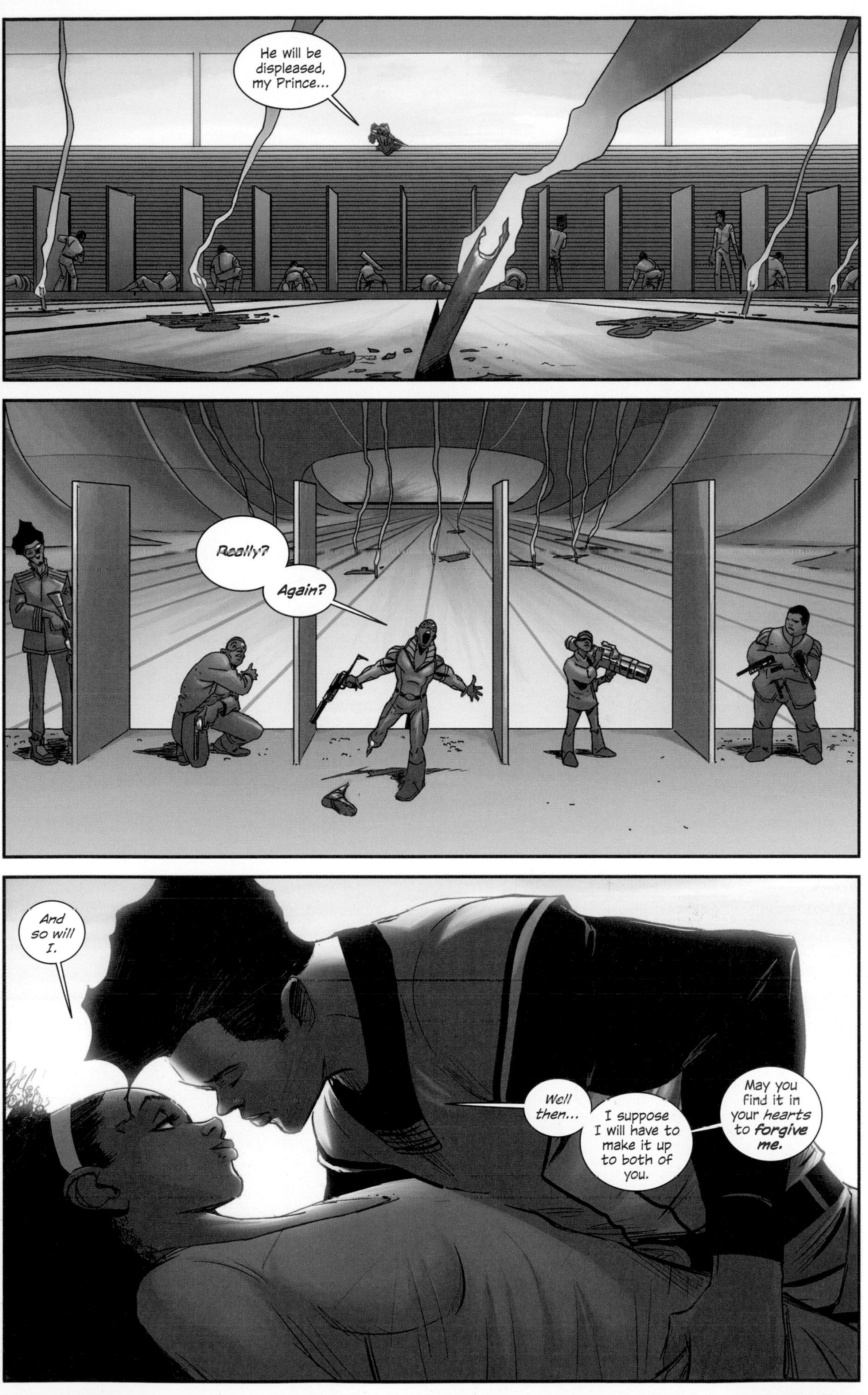
He will be displeased, my Prince...
Really?
Again?
And so will I.
Well then...
I suppose I will have to make it up to both of you.
May you find it in your *hearts* to ***forgive me.***

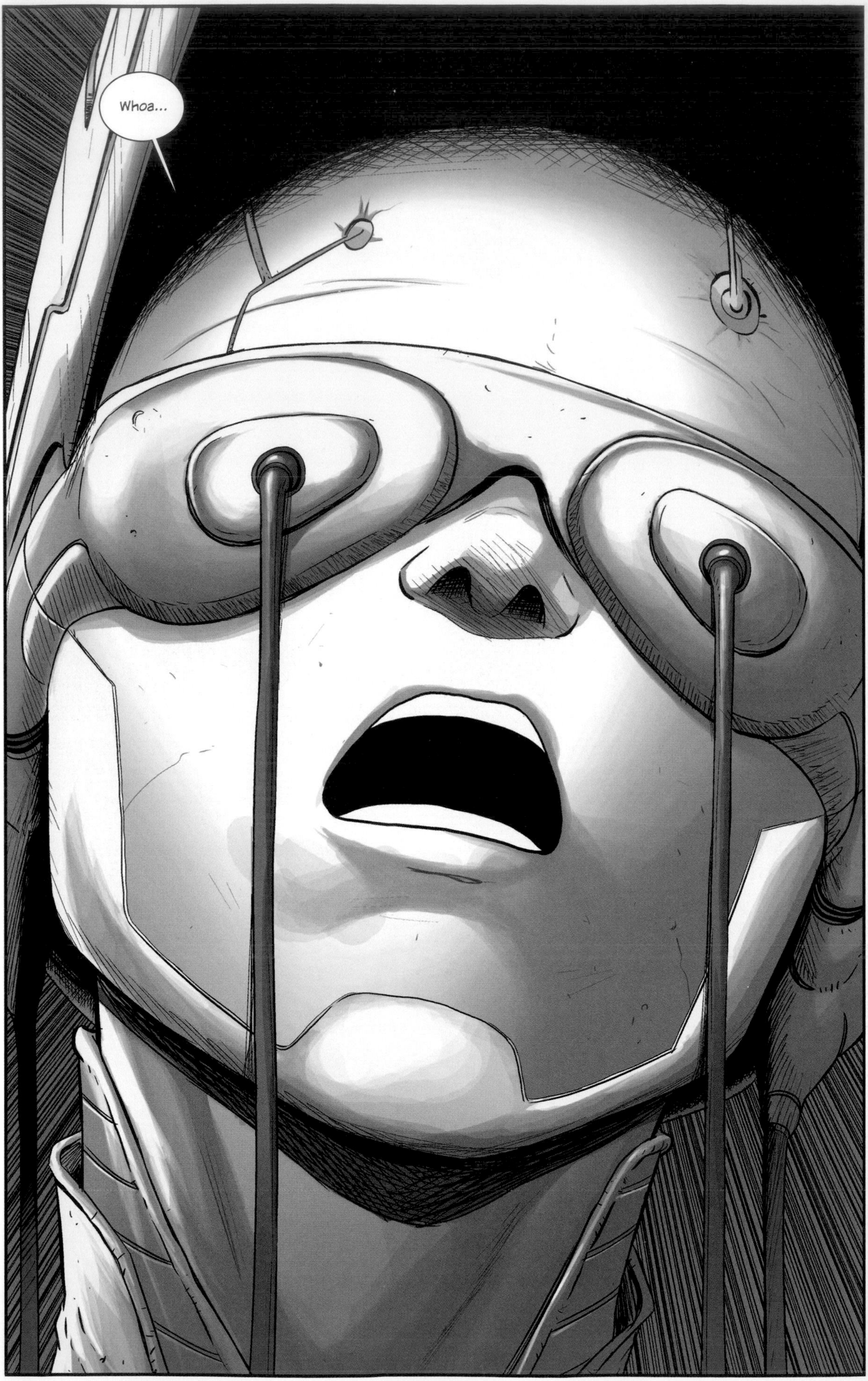
Whoa...

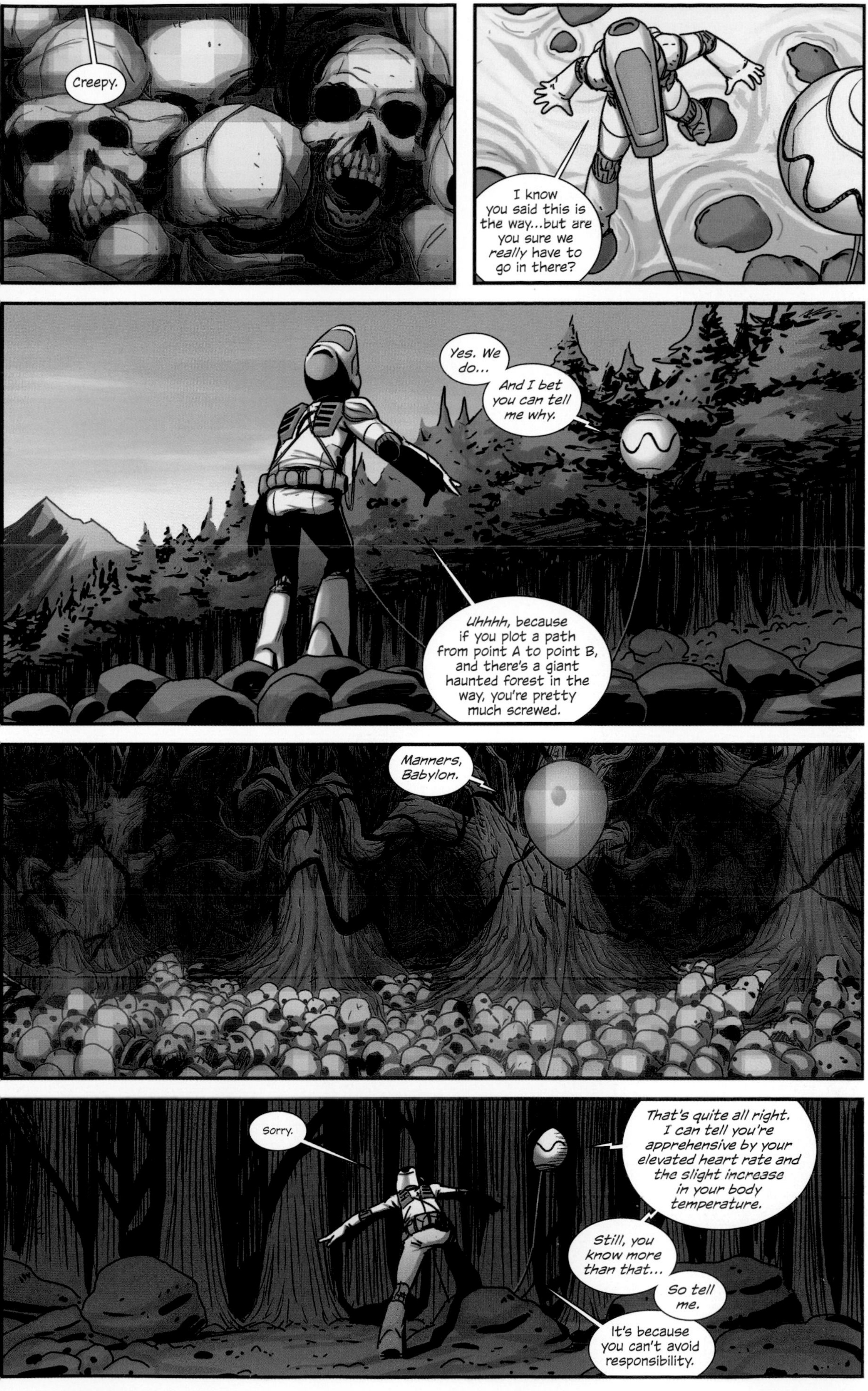
Creepy.
I know you said this is the way...but are you sure we *really* have to go in there?
Yes. We do...
And I bet you can tell me why.
Uhhhh, because if you plot a path from point A to point B, and there's a giant haunted forest in the way, you're pretty much screwed.
Manners, Babylon.
Sorry.
That's quite all right. I can tell you're apprehensive by your elevated heart rate and the slight increase in your body temperature.
Still, you know more than that...
So tell me.
It's because you can't avoid responsibility.

If you plot a path from age one to age whatever, along the way you'll meet the person you're eventually going to become.

And since growth can only be achieved through experiences...

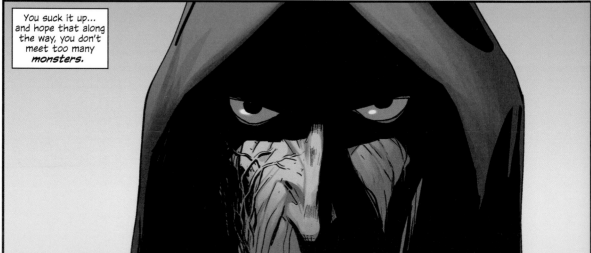

You suck it up... and hope that along the way, you don't meet too many *monsters*.

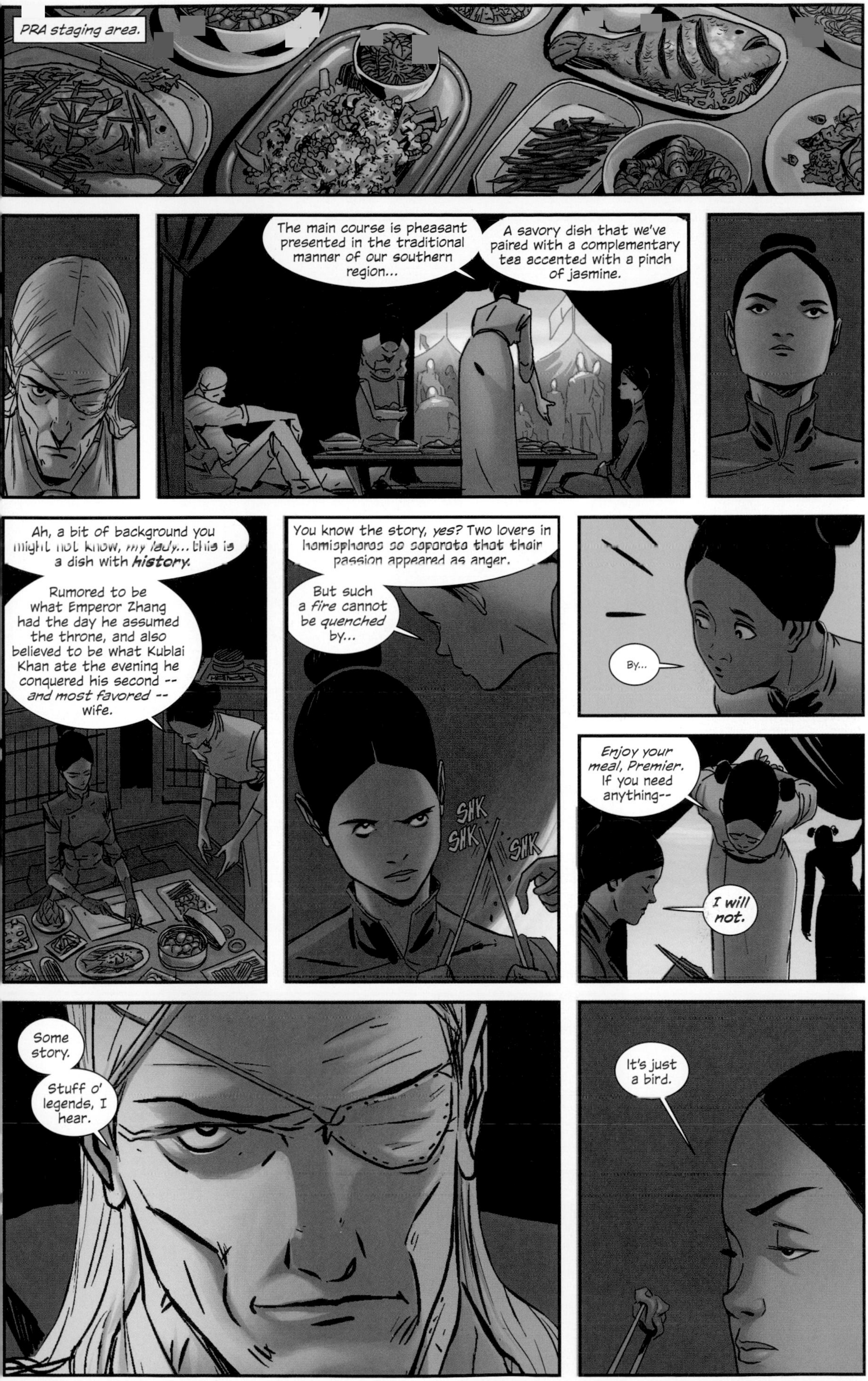
PRA staging area.
The main course is pheasant presented in the traditional manner of our southern region...
A savory dish that we've paired with a complementary tea accented with a pinch of jasmine.
Ah, a bit of background you might not know, *my lady*... this is a dish with ***history***.
Rumored to be what Emperor Zhang had the day he assumed the throne, and also believed to be what Kublai Khan ate the evening he conquered his second -- *and most favored* -- wife.
You know the story, *yes?* Two lovers in hemispheres so separate that their passion appeared as anger.
But such a *fire* cannot be *quenched* by...
SHK
SHK
SHK
By...
Enjoy your meal, Premier. If you need anything--
I will not.
Some story.
Stuff o' legends, I hear.
It's just a bird.

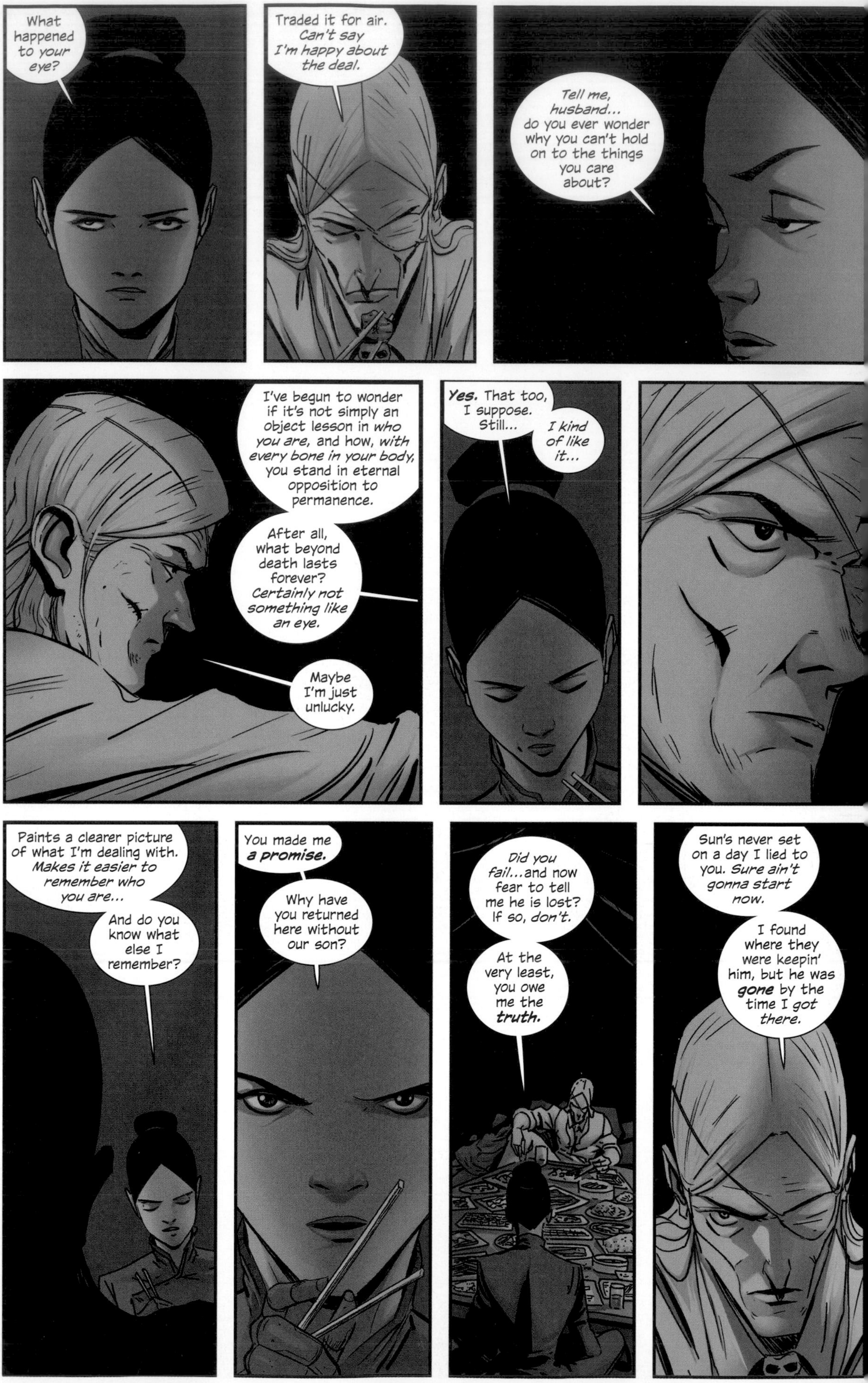
What happened to your eye?
Traded it for air. *Can't say I'm happy about the deal.*
Tell me, husband... do you ever wonder why you can't hold on to the things you care about?
I've begun to wonder if it's not simply an object lesson in *who you are,* and how, *with every bone in your body,* you stand in eternal opposition to permanence.
After all, what beyond death lasts forever? *Certainly not something like an eye.*
Maybe I'm just unlucky.
Yes. That too, I suppose. Still...
I kind of like it...
Paints a clearer picture of what I'm dealing with. *Makes it easier to remember who you are...*
And do you know what else I remember?
You made me ***a promise.***
Why have you returned here without our son?
*Did you fail...*and now fear to tell me he is lost? If so, *don't.*
At the very least, you owe me the ***truth.***
Sun's never set on a day I lied to you. *Sure ain't gonna start now.*
I found where they were keepin' him, but he was ***gone*** by the time I *got there.*

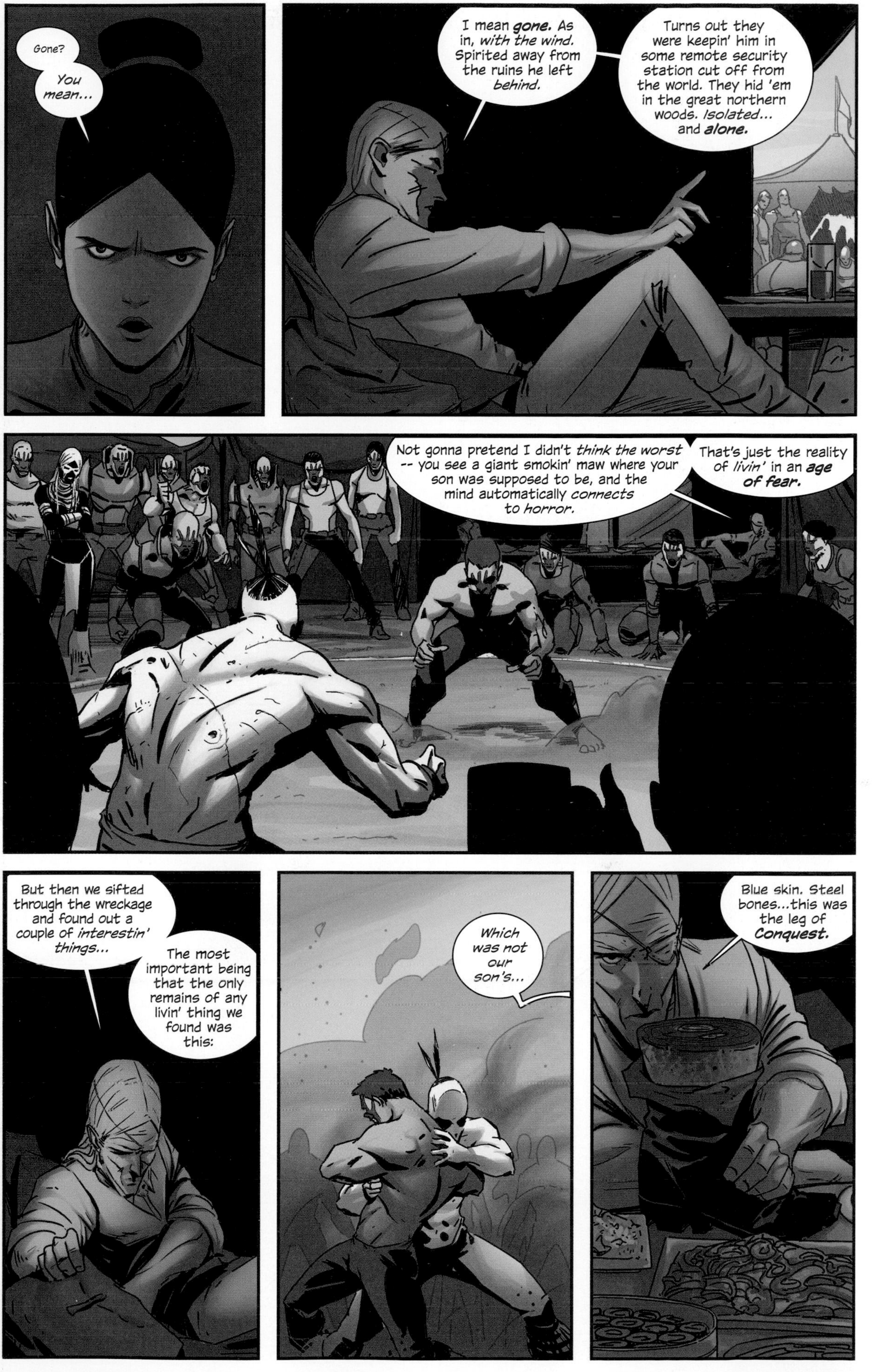
Gone?
You mean...
I mean gone. As in, with the wind. Spirited away from the ruins he left behind.
Turns out they were keepin' him in some remote security station cut off from the world. They hid 'em in the great northern woods. Isolated... and alone.
Not gonna pretend I didn't think the worst -- you see a giant smokin' maw where your son was supposed to be, and the mind automatically connects to horror.
That's just the reality of livin' in an age of fear.
But then we sifted through the wreckage and found out a couple of interestin' things...
The most important being that the only remains of any livin' thing we found was this:
Which was not our son's...
Blue skin. Steel bones...this was the leg of Conquest.

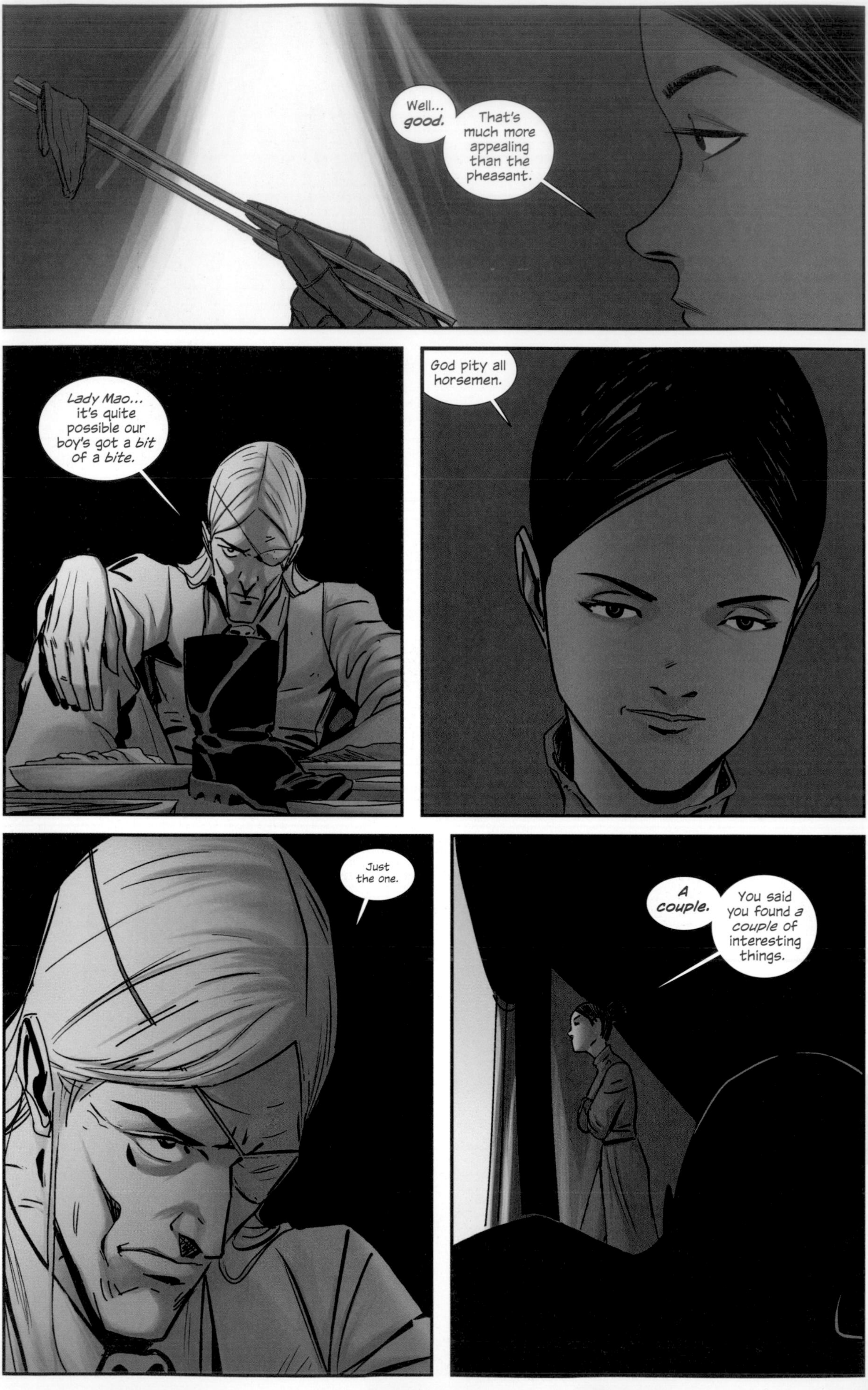
Well... *good.*
That's much more appealing than the pheasant.
Lady Mao... it's quite possible our boy's got a *bit* of a *bite.*
God pity all horsemen.
Just the one.
A couple.
You said you found a *couple* of interesting things.

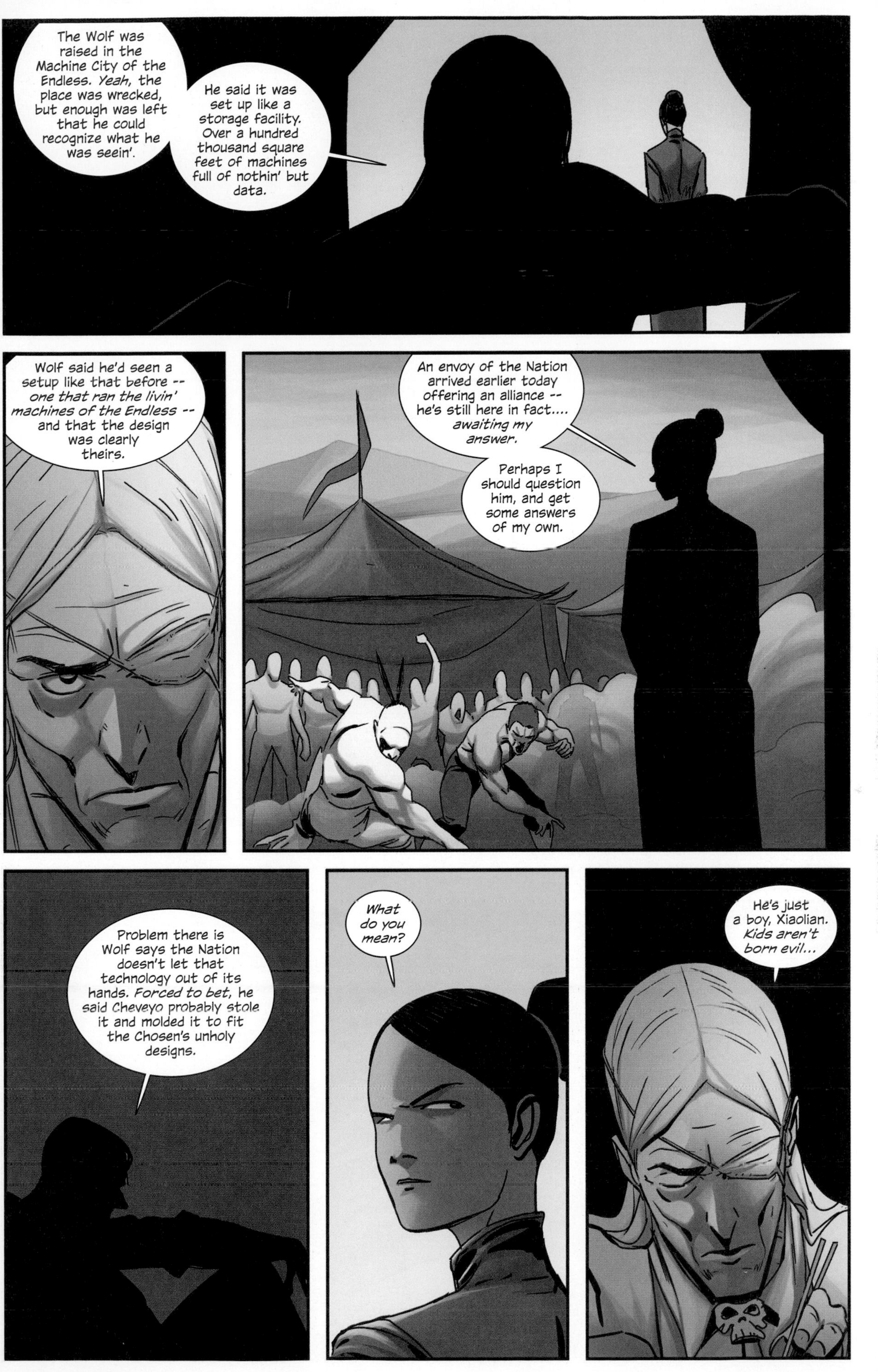
The Wolf was raised in the Machine City of the Endless. Yeah, the place was wrecked, but enough was left that he could recognize what he was seein'.
He said it was set up like a storage facility. Over a hundred thousand square feet of machines full of nothin' but data.
Wolf said he'd seen a setup like that before -- one that ran the livin' machines of the Endless -- and that the design was clearly theirs.
An envoy of the Nation arrived earlier today offering an alliance -- he's still here in fact.... awaiting my answer.
Perhaps I should question him, and get some answers of my own.
Problem there is Wolf says the Nation doesn't let that technology out of its hands. Forced to bet, he said Cheveyo probably stole it and molded it to fit the Chosen's unholy designs.
What do you mean?
He's just a boy, Xiaolian. Kids aren't born evil...

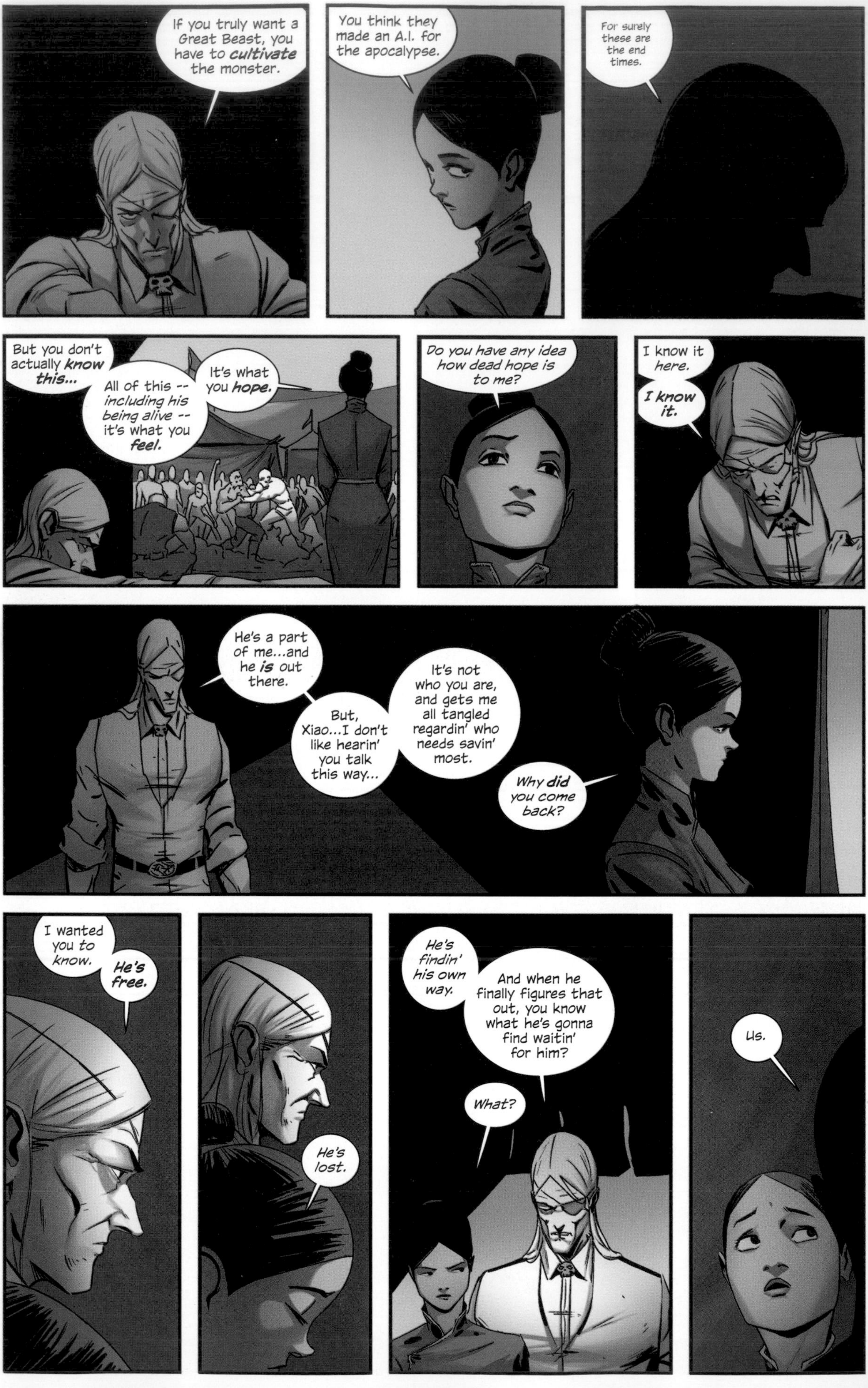

If you truly want a Great Beast, you have to cultivate the monster.
You think they made an A.I. for the apocalypse.
For surely these are the end times.
But you don't actually know this...
All of this -- including his being alive -- it's what you feel.
It's what you hope.
Do you have any idea how dead hope is to me?
I know it here.
I know it.
He's a part of me...and he is out there.
But, Xiao...I don't like hearin' you talk this way...
It's not who you are, and gets me all tangled regardin' who needs savin' most.
Why did you come back?
I wanted you to know.
He's free.
He's lost.
He's findin' his own way.
And when he finally figures that out, you know what he's gonna find waitin' for him?
What?
Us.

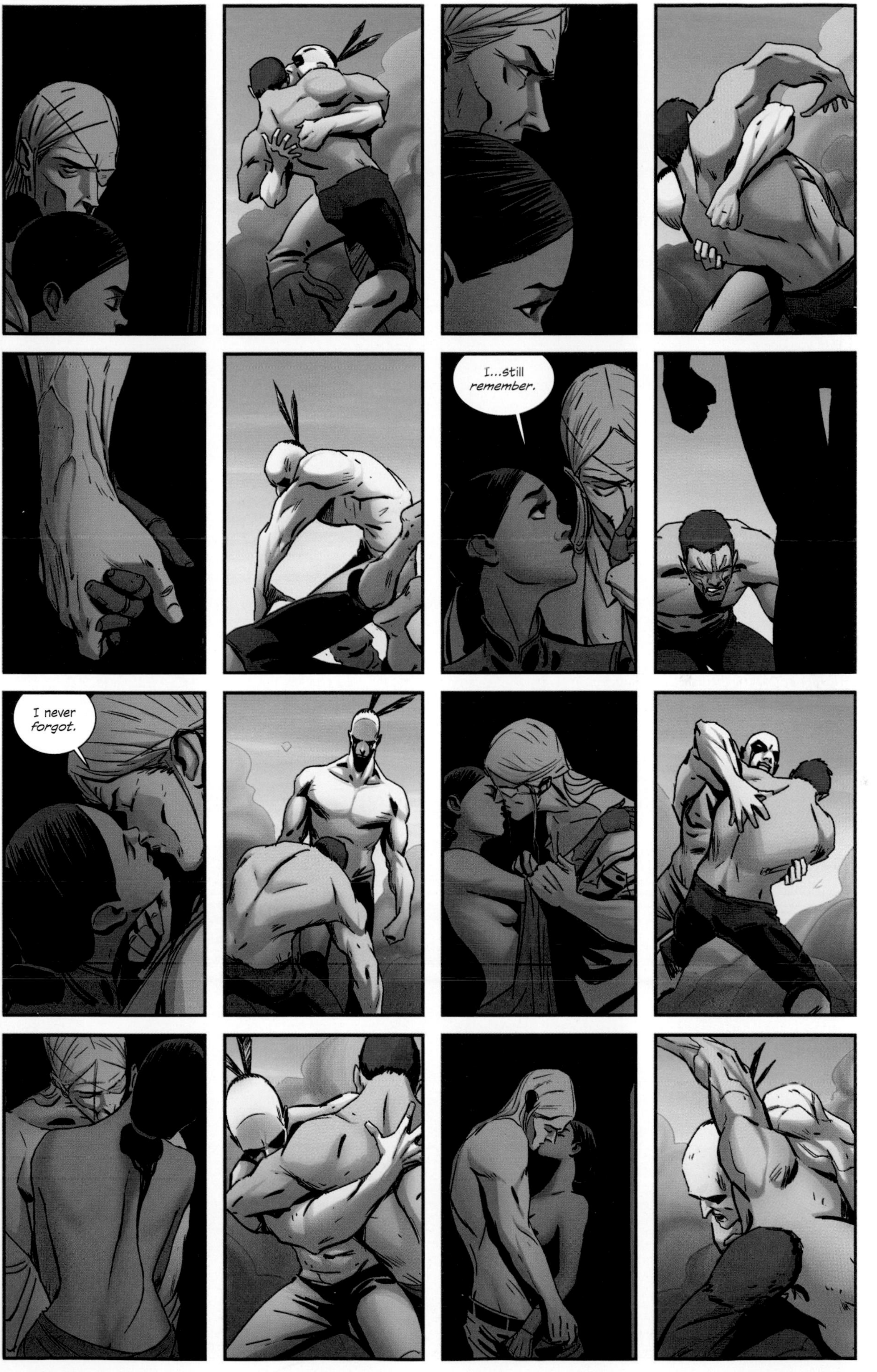
I...still remember.
I never forgot.

What followed was...*of the times.*

It was *The Message.*

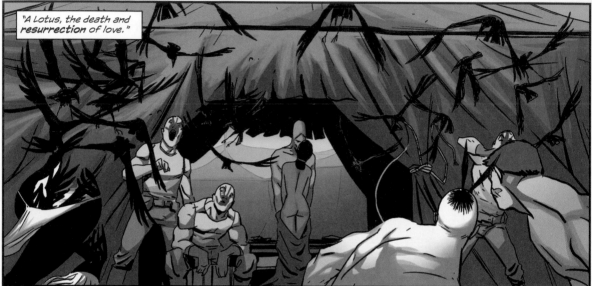

"A Lotus, the death and resurrection of love."

A fire that burned and could have lasted forever...*but did not.*

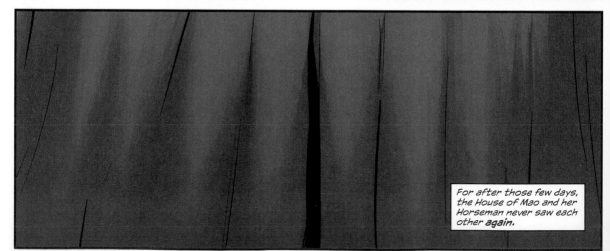

For after those few days, the House of Mao and her Horseman never saw each other *again.*

SPIN AGAINST THE **AXIS.**

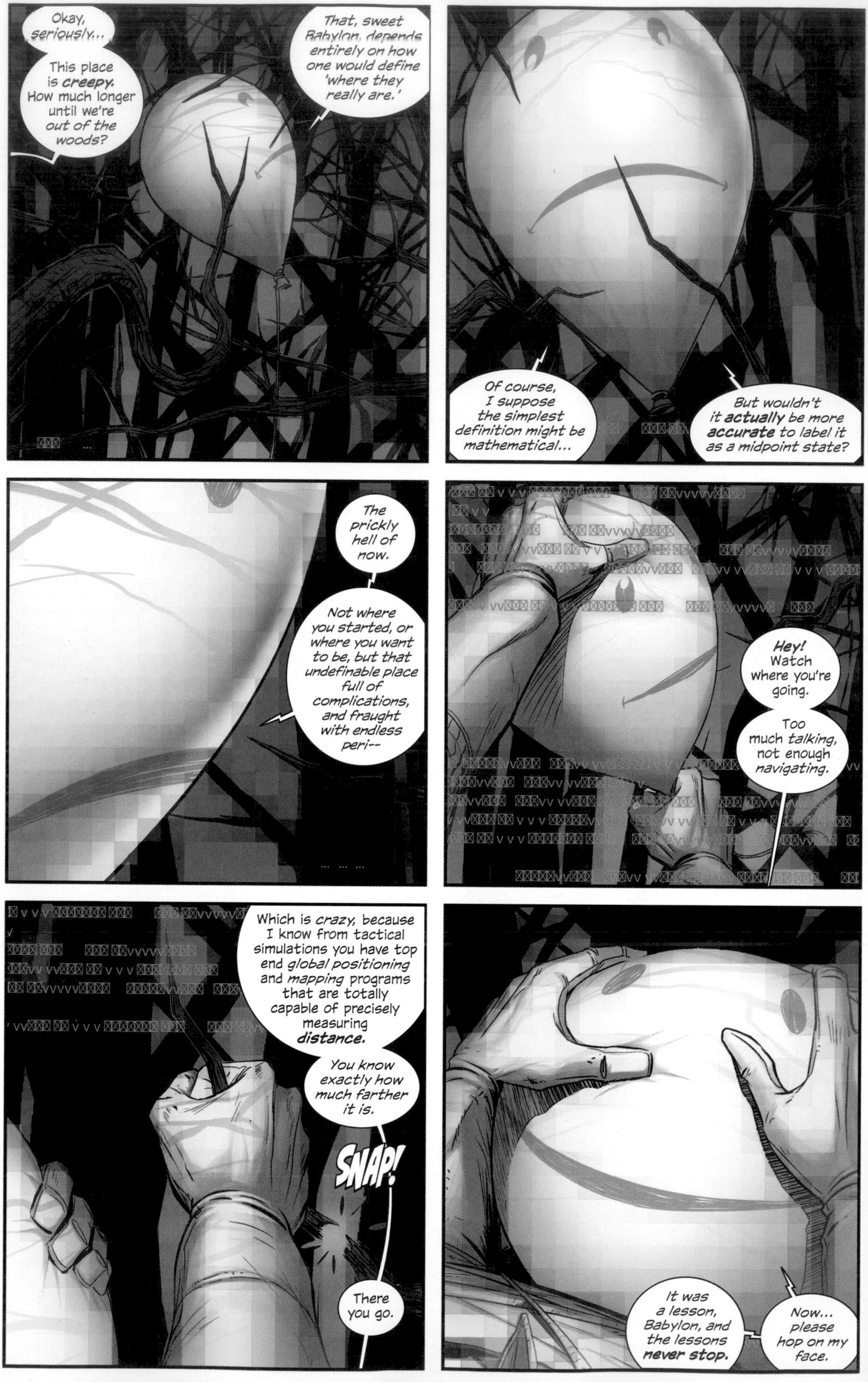

Okay, seriously...
This place is *creepy.* How much longer until we're out of the woods?
That, sweet Babylon, depends entirely on how one would define 'where they really are.'
Of course, I suppose the simplest definition might be mathematical...
But wouldn't it **actually** be more **accurate** to label it as a midpoint state?
The prickly hell of now.
Not where you started, or where you want to be, but that undefinable place full of complications, and fraught with endless peri--
Hey! Watch where you're going.
Too much *talking,* not enough *navigating.*
Which is *crazy,* because I know from tactical simulations you have top end *global positioning* and *mapping* programs that are totally capable of precisely measuring **distance.**
You know exactly how much farther it is.
SNAP!
There you go.
It was a lesson, Babylon, and the lessons **never stop.**
Now... please hop on my face.

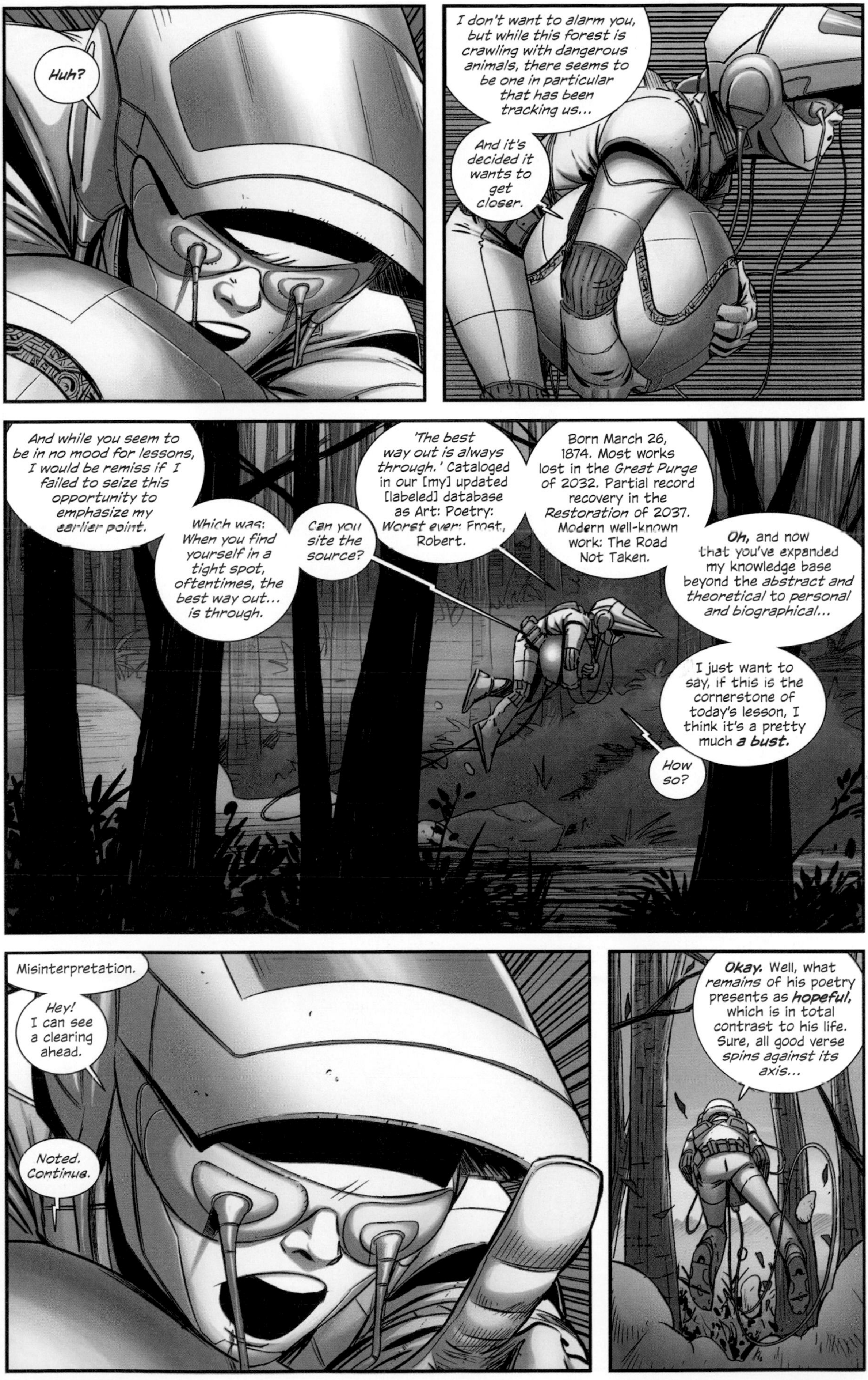

Huh?
I don't want to alarm you, but while this forest is crawling with dangerous animals, there seems to be one in particular that has been tracking us...
And it's decided it wants to get closer.
And while you seem to be in no mood for lessons, I would be remiss if I failed to seize this opportunity to emphasize my earlier point.
Which was: When you find yourself in a tight spot, oftentimes, the best way out... is through.
Can you site the source?
'The best way out is always through.' Cataloged in our [my] updated [labeled] database as Art: Poetry: Worst ever: Frost, Robert.
Born March 26, 1874. Most works lost in the Great Purge of 2032. Partial record recovery in the Restoration of 2037. Modern well-known work: The Road Not Taken.
Oh, and now that you've expanded my knowledge base beyond the abstract and theoretical to personal and biographical...
I just want to say, if this is the cornerstone of today's lesson, I think it's a pretty much a bust.
How so?
Misinterpretation.
Hey! I can see a clearing ahead.
Noted. Continue.
Okay. Well, what remains of his poetry presents as hopeful, which is in total contrast to his life. Sure, all good verse spins against its axis...

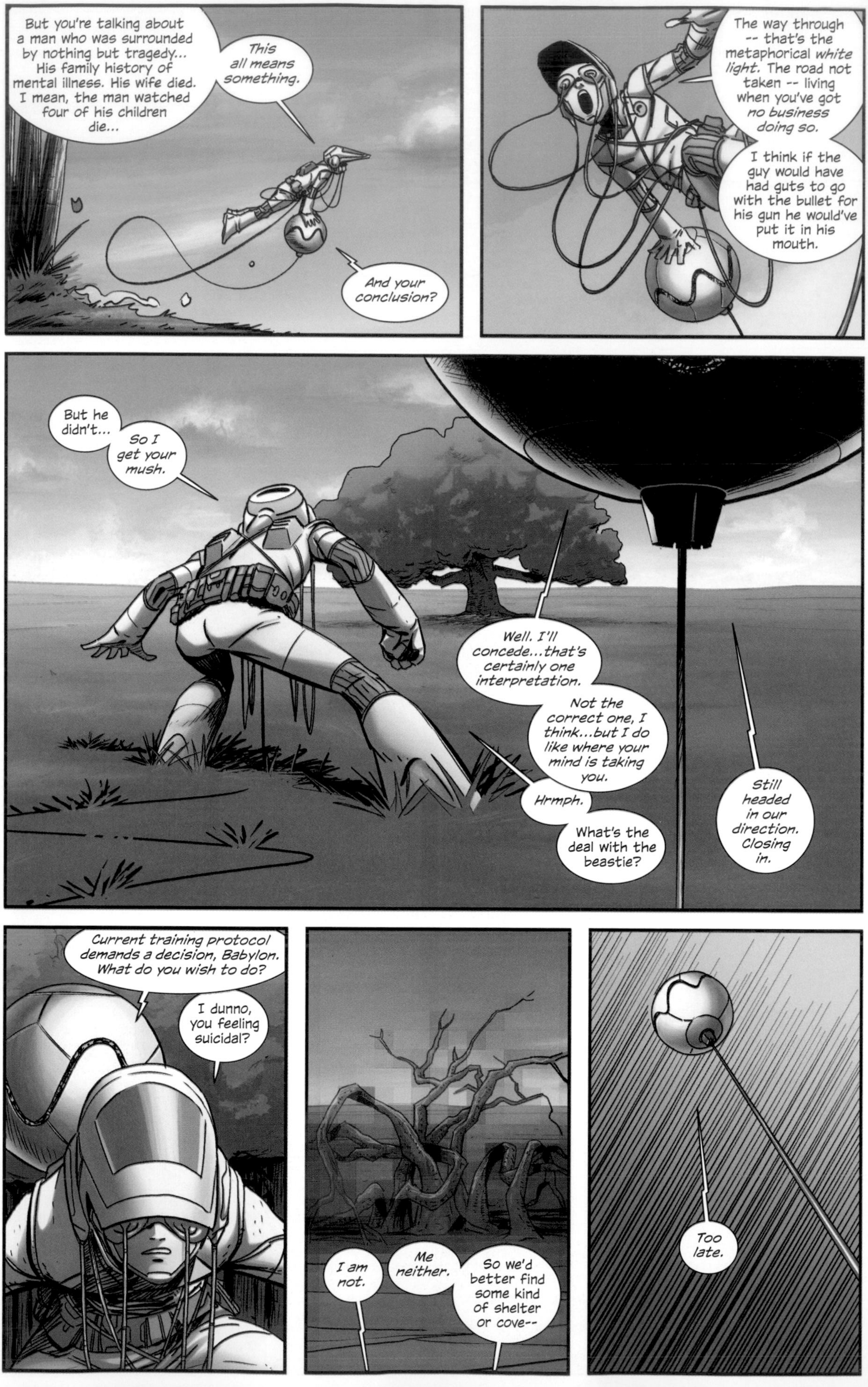
But you're talking about a man who was surrounded by nothing but tragedy... His family history of mental illness. His wife died. I mean, the man watched four of his children die...
This all means something.
And your conclusion?
The way through -- that's the metaphorical *white light*. The road not taken -- living when you've got *no business* doing so.
I think if the guy would have had guts to go with the bullet for his gun he would've put it in his mouth.
But he didn't...
So I get your mush.
Well. I'll concede...that's certainly one interpretation.
Not the correct one, I think...but I do like where your mind is taking you.
Hrmph.
What's the deal with the beastie?
Still headed in our direction. Closing in.
Current training protocol demands a decision, Babylon. What do you wish to do?
I dunno, you feeling suicidal?
I am not.
Me neither.
So we'd better find some kind of shelter or cove--
Too late.

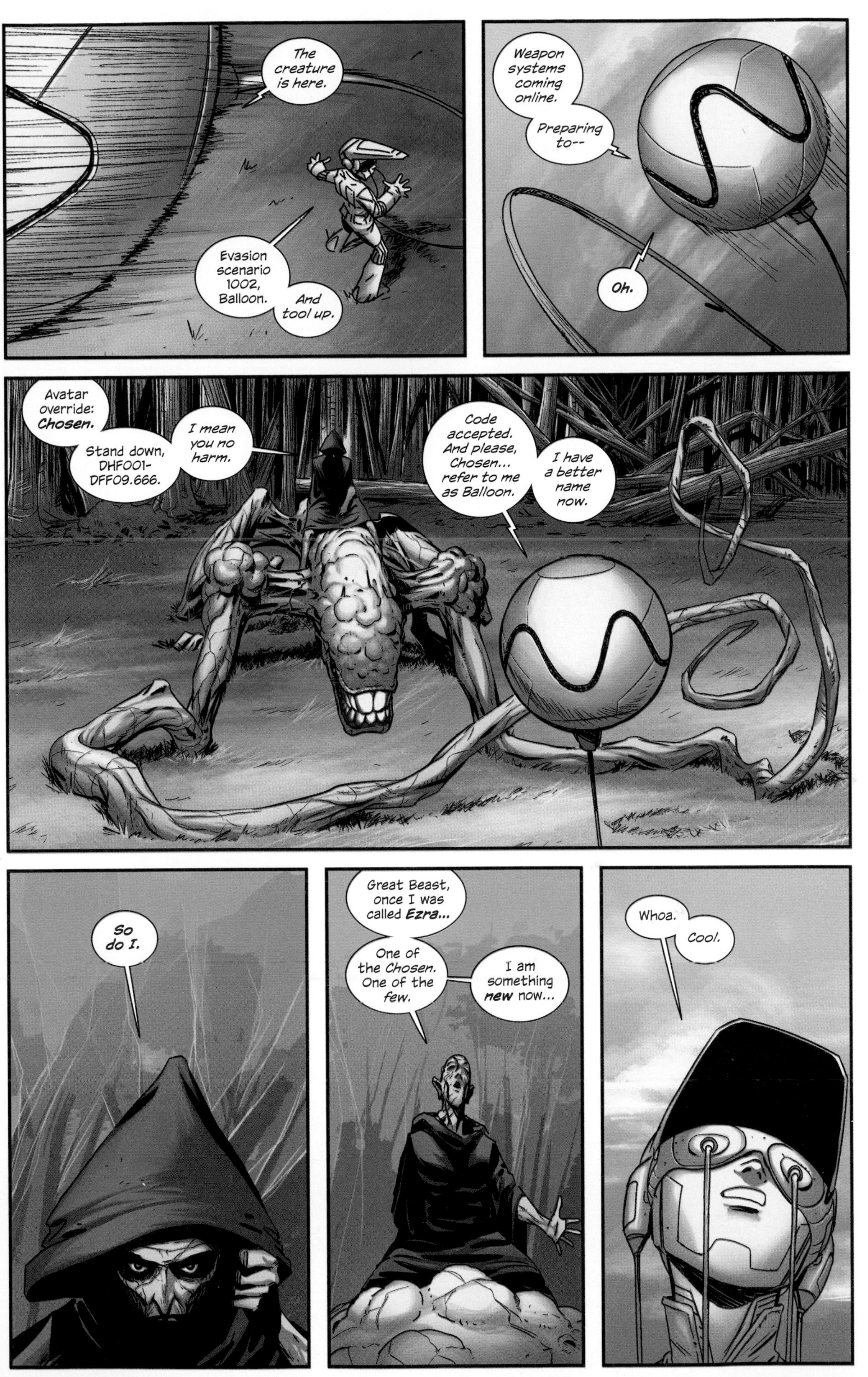
The creature is here.
Evasion scenario 1002, Balloon.
And tool up.
Weapon systems coming online.
Preparing to--
Oh.
Avatar override: **Chosen.**
Stand down, DHF001-DFF09.666.
I mean you no harm.
Code accepted. And please, Chosen... refer to me as Balloon.
I have a better name now.
So do I.
Great Beast, once I was called *Ezra*...
One of the Chosen. One of the few.
I am something *new* now...
Whoa.
Cool.

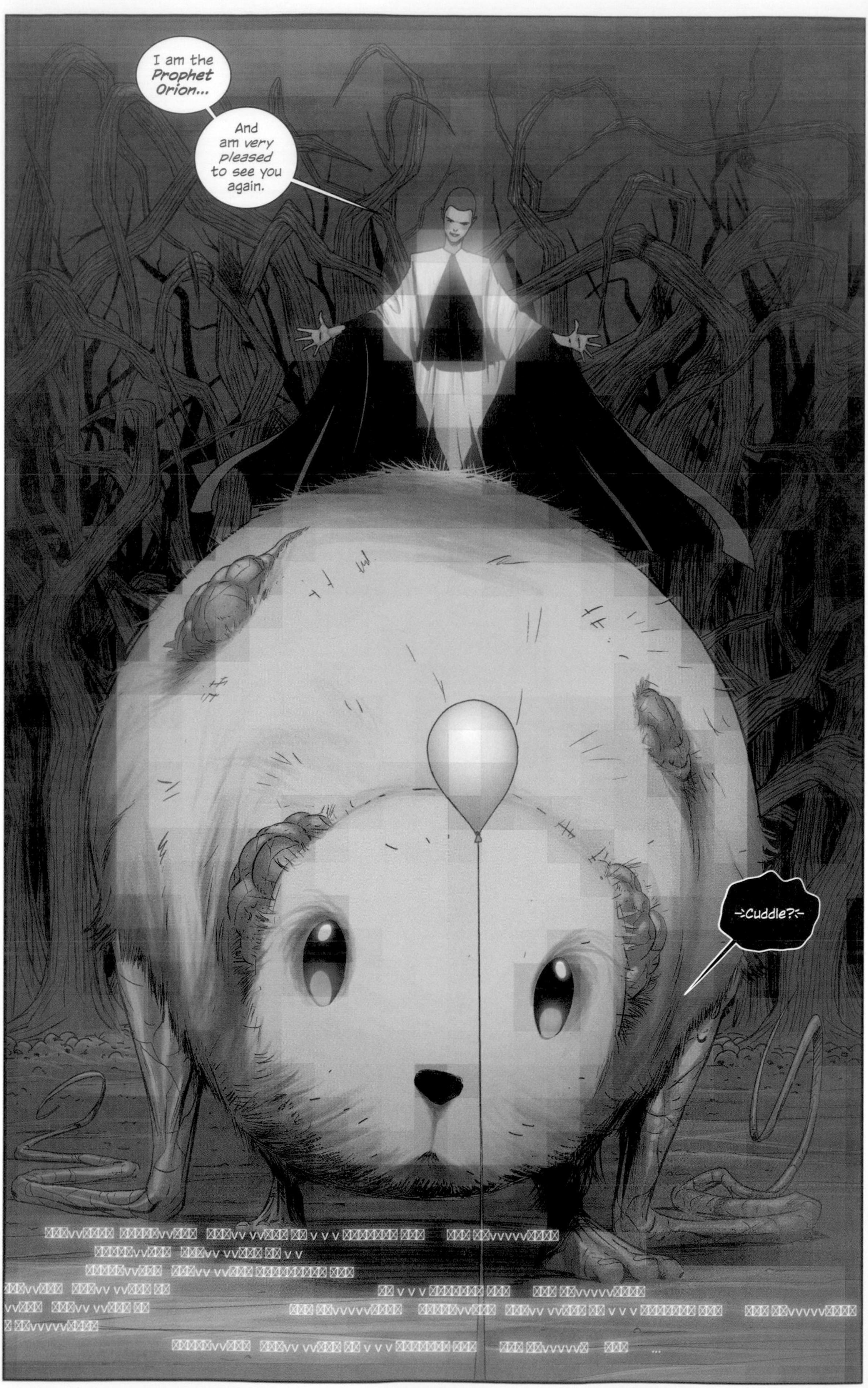
I am the *Prophet Orion...*
And am *very pleased* to see you again.
Cuddle?

I AM AN **ORACLE** OF THE **TIMES.**

WATCH ME **LAUGH.** HEAR ME **LIE.**

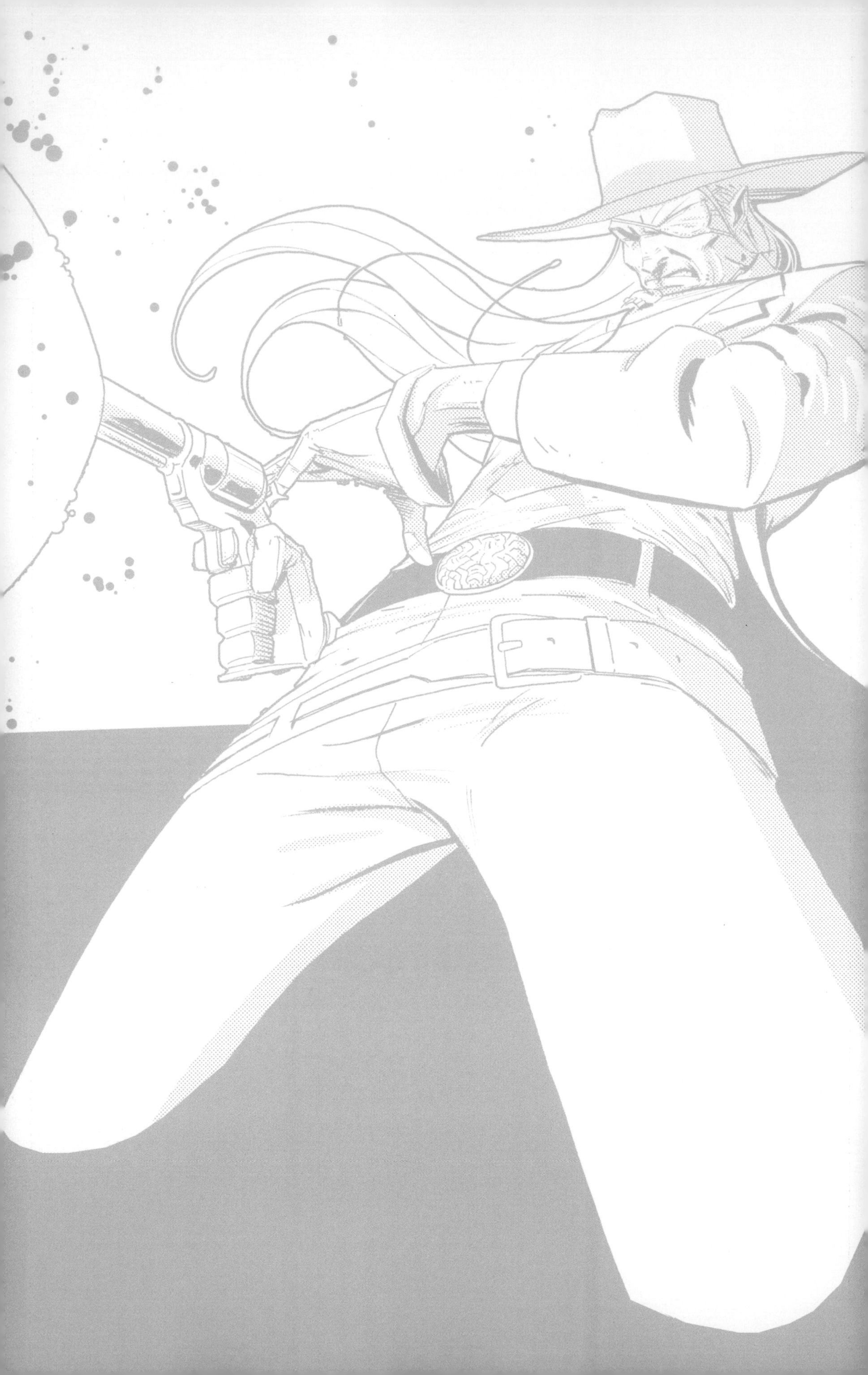

18

EIGHTEEN:
YOURS AND YOURS
ALONE

WE ARE ALL SO **BLIND,**
WON'T SOMEONE SHOW
US **THE WAY?**

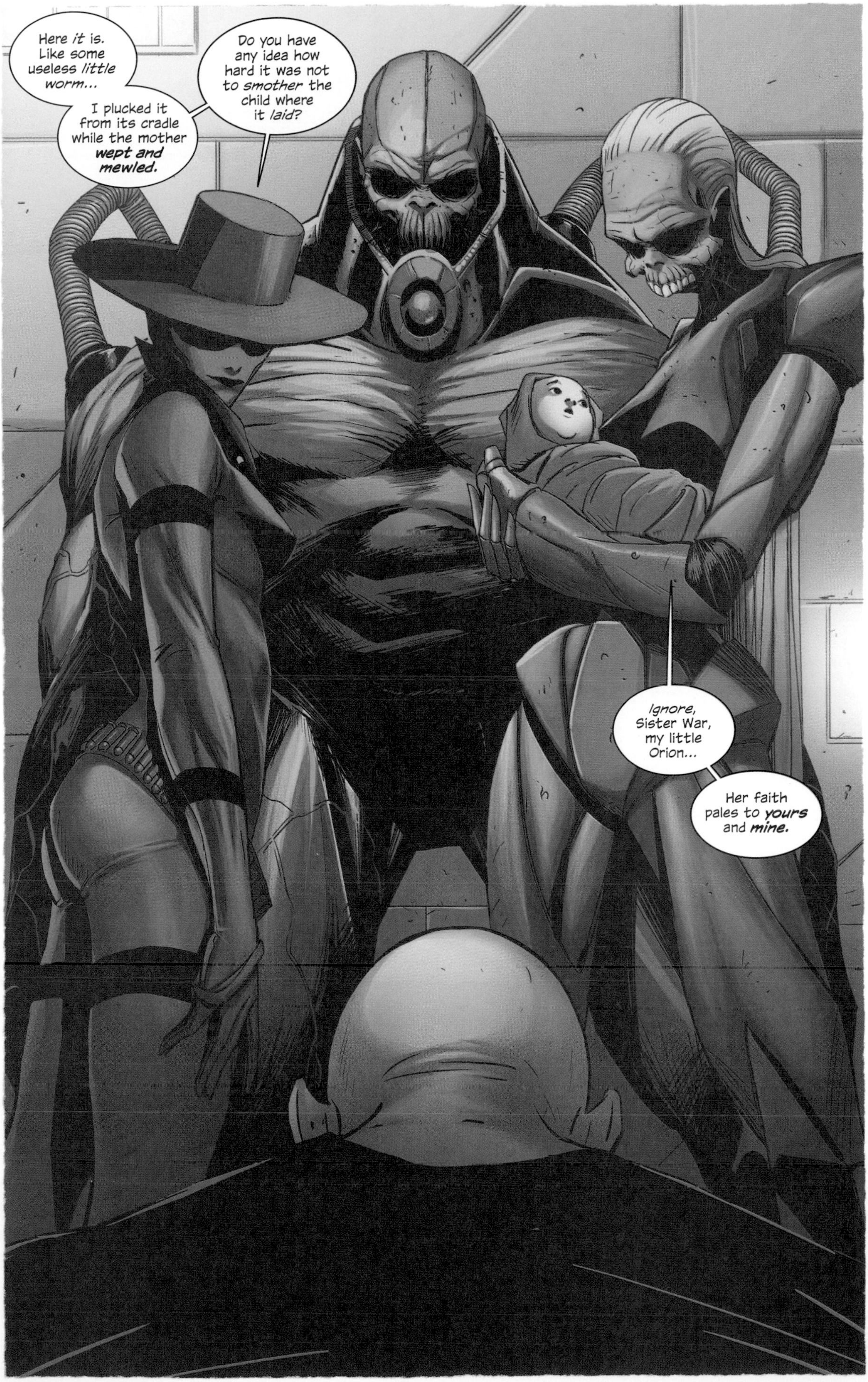
Here *it* is. Like some useless *little* worm...
I plucked it from its cradle while the mother ***wept and mewled.***
Do you have any idea how hard it was not to *smother* the child where it *laid?*
Ignore, Sister War, my little Orion...
Her faith pales to ***yours*** and ***mine.***

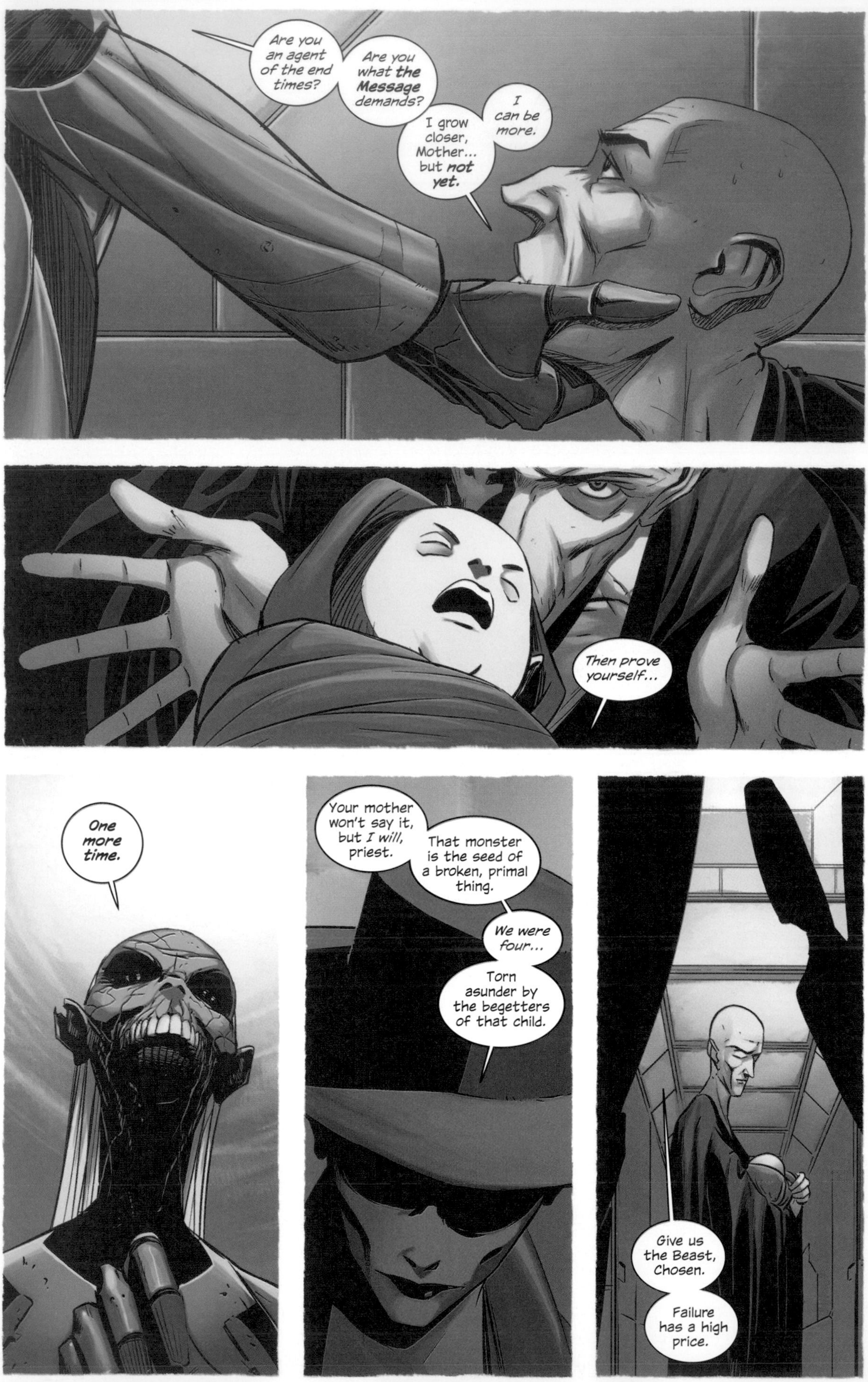
Are you an agent of the end times?
Are you what **the Message** demands?
I can be more.
I grow closer, Mother... but ***not yet.***
Then prove yourself...
One more time.
Your mother won't say it, but *I will*, priest.
That monster is the seed of a broken, primal thing.
We were four...
Torn asunder by the begetters of that child.
Give us the Beast, Chosen.
Failure has a high price.

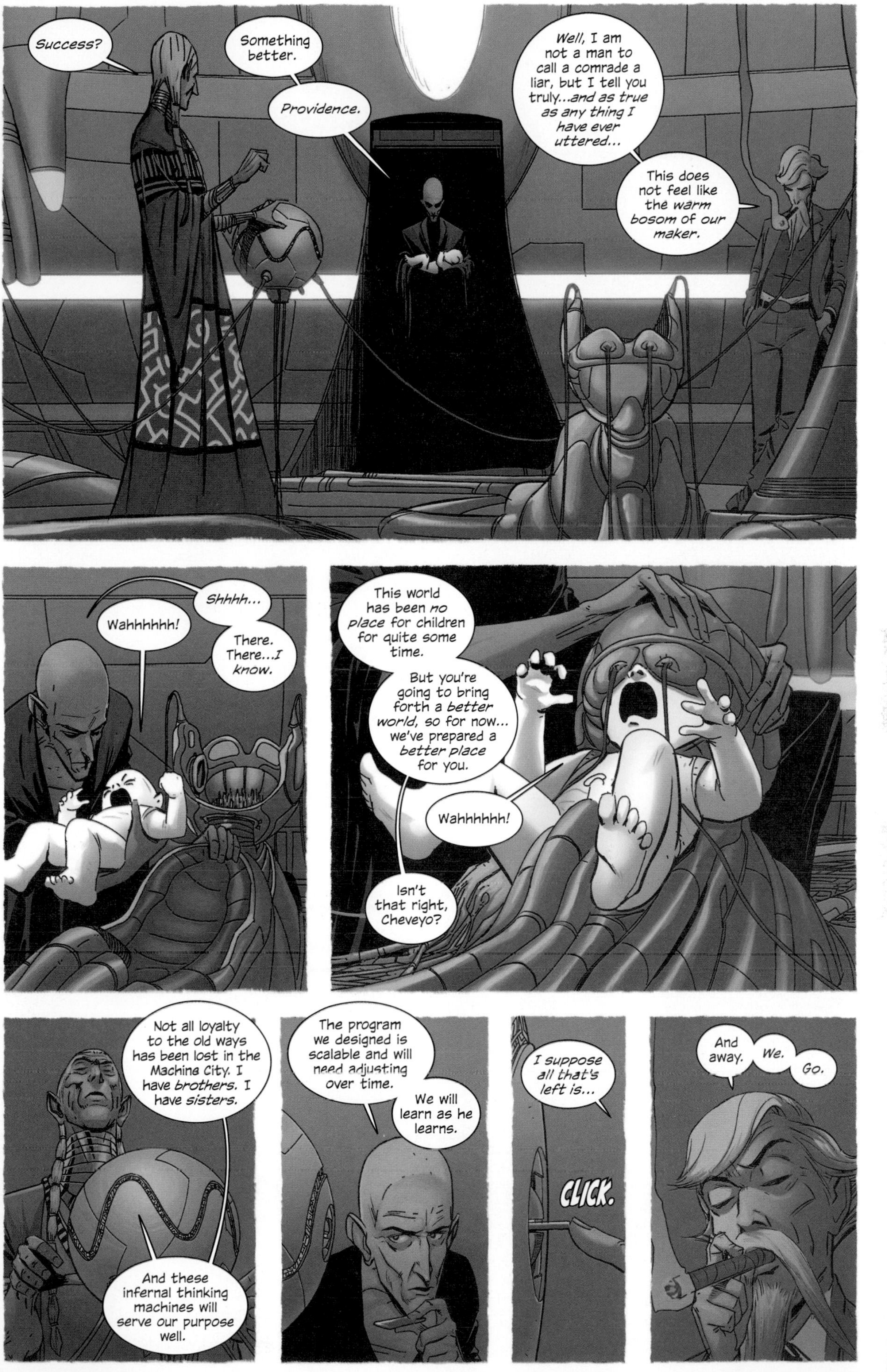

Success?
Something better.
Providence.
Well, I am not a man to call a comrade a liar, but I tell you truly...and as true as any thing I have ever uttered...
This does not feel like the warm bosom of our maker.
Shhhh...
Wahhhhhh!
There. There...I know.
This world has been no place for children for quite some time.
But you're going to bring forth a better world, so for now... we've prepared a better place for you.
Wahhhhhh!
Isn't that right, Cheveyo?
Not all loyalty to the old ways has been lost in the Machine City. I have brothers. I have sisters.
And these infernal thinking machines will serve our purpose well.
The program we designed is scalable and will need adjusting over time.
We will learn as he learns.
I suppose all that's left is...
CLICK.
And away.
We.
Go.

Observation sphere DHF001-DFF09.666...

Online.

Ba ba ba.

Peekaboo.

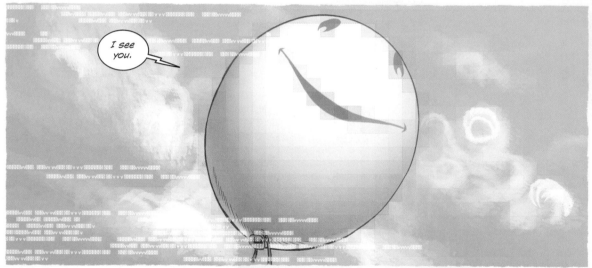

I see you.

I have so many amazing things to show you.

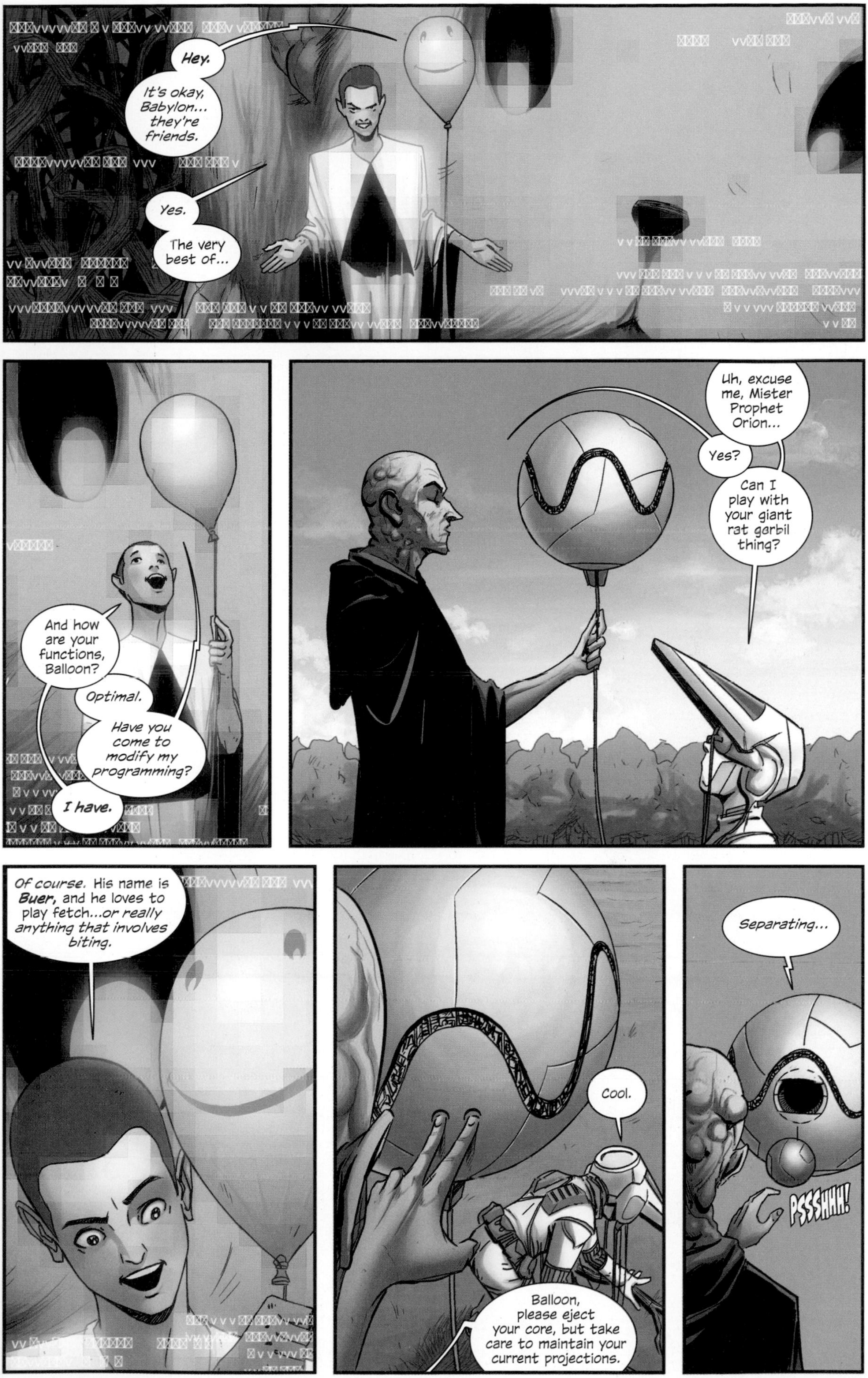
Hey.
It's okay, Babylon... they're friends.
Yes.
The very best of...
And how are your functions, Balloon?
Optimal.
Have you come to modify my programming?
I have.
Uh, excuse me, Mister Prophet Orion...
Yes?
Can I play with your giant rat gerbil thing?
Of course. His name is Buer, and he loves to play fetch...or really anything that involves biting.
Cool.
Balloon, please eject your core, but take care to maintain your current projections.
Separating...
PSSSHHH!

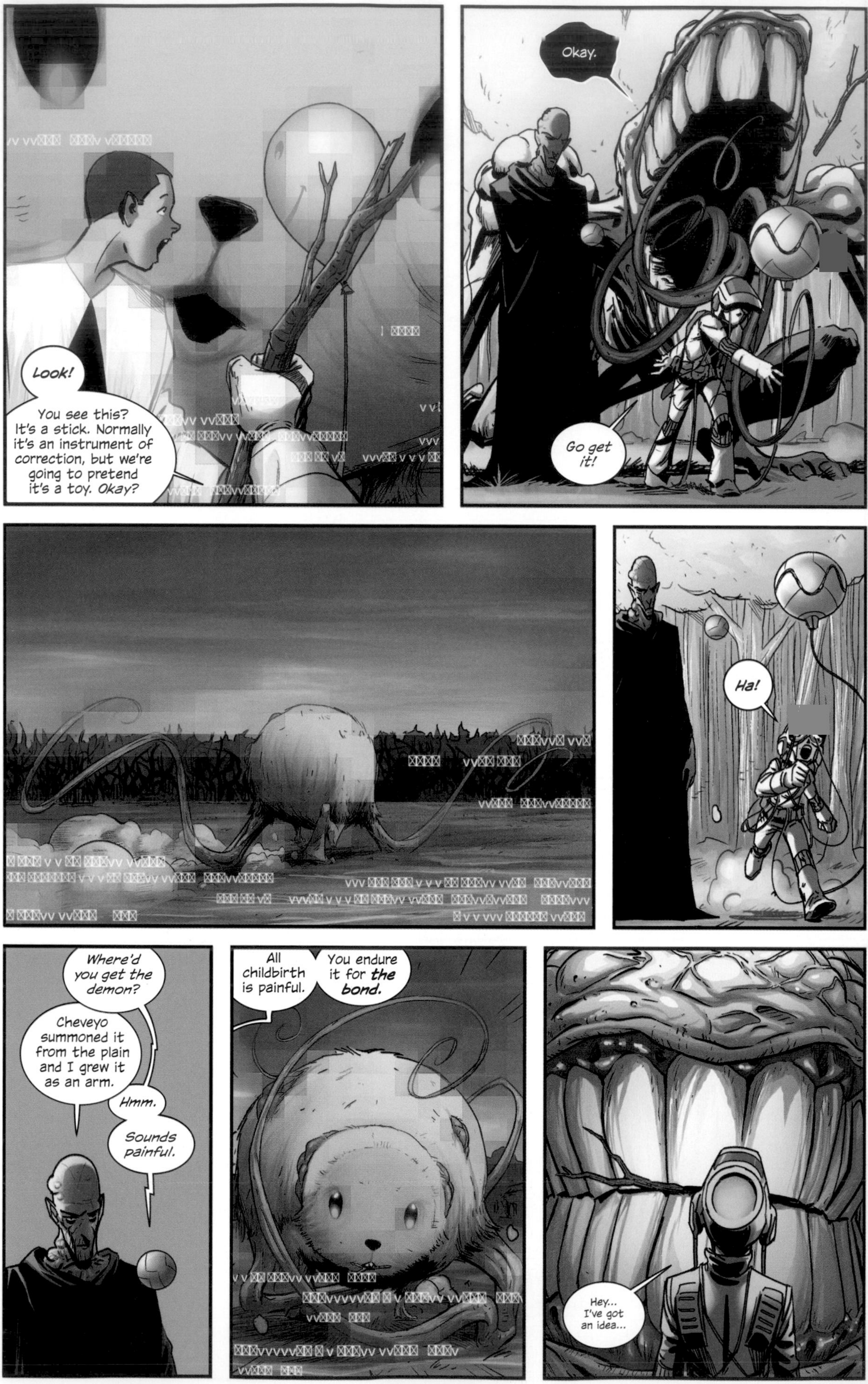
Look!
You see this? It's a stick. Normally it's an instrument of correction, but we're going to pretend it's a toy. Okay?
Okay.
Go get it!
Ha!
Where'd you get the demon?
Cheveyo summoned it from the plain and I grew it as an arm.
Hmm.
Sounds painful.
All childbirth is painful.
You endure it for the bond.
Hey... I've got an idea...

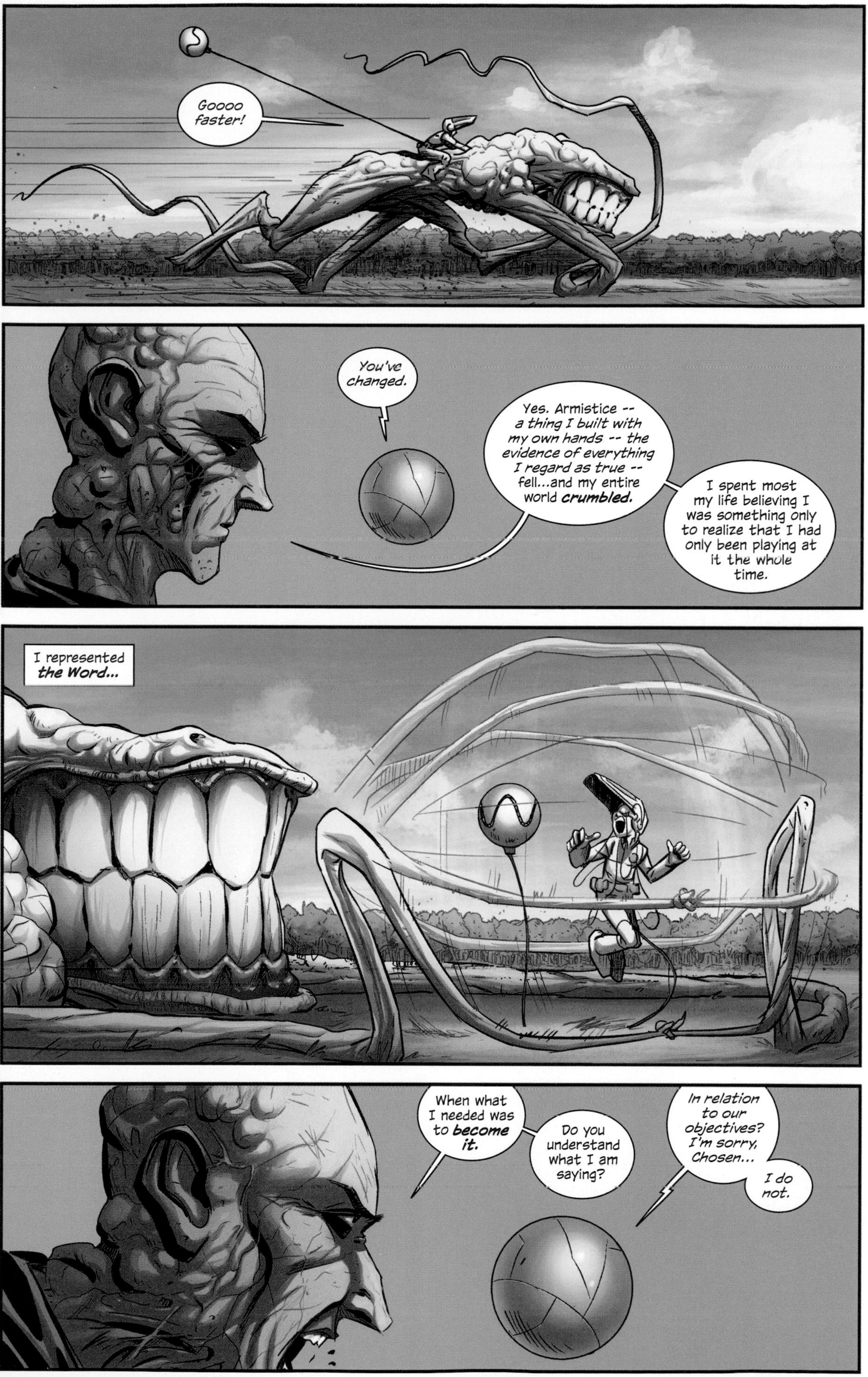
Goooo faster!
You've changed.
Yes. Armistice -- a thing I built with my own hands -- the evidence of everything I regard as true -- fell...and my entire world crumbled.
I spent most my life believing I was something only to realize that I had only been playing at it the whole time.
I represented the Word...
When what I needed was to become it.
Do you understand what I am saying?
In relation to our objectives? I'm sorry, Chosen...
I do not.

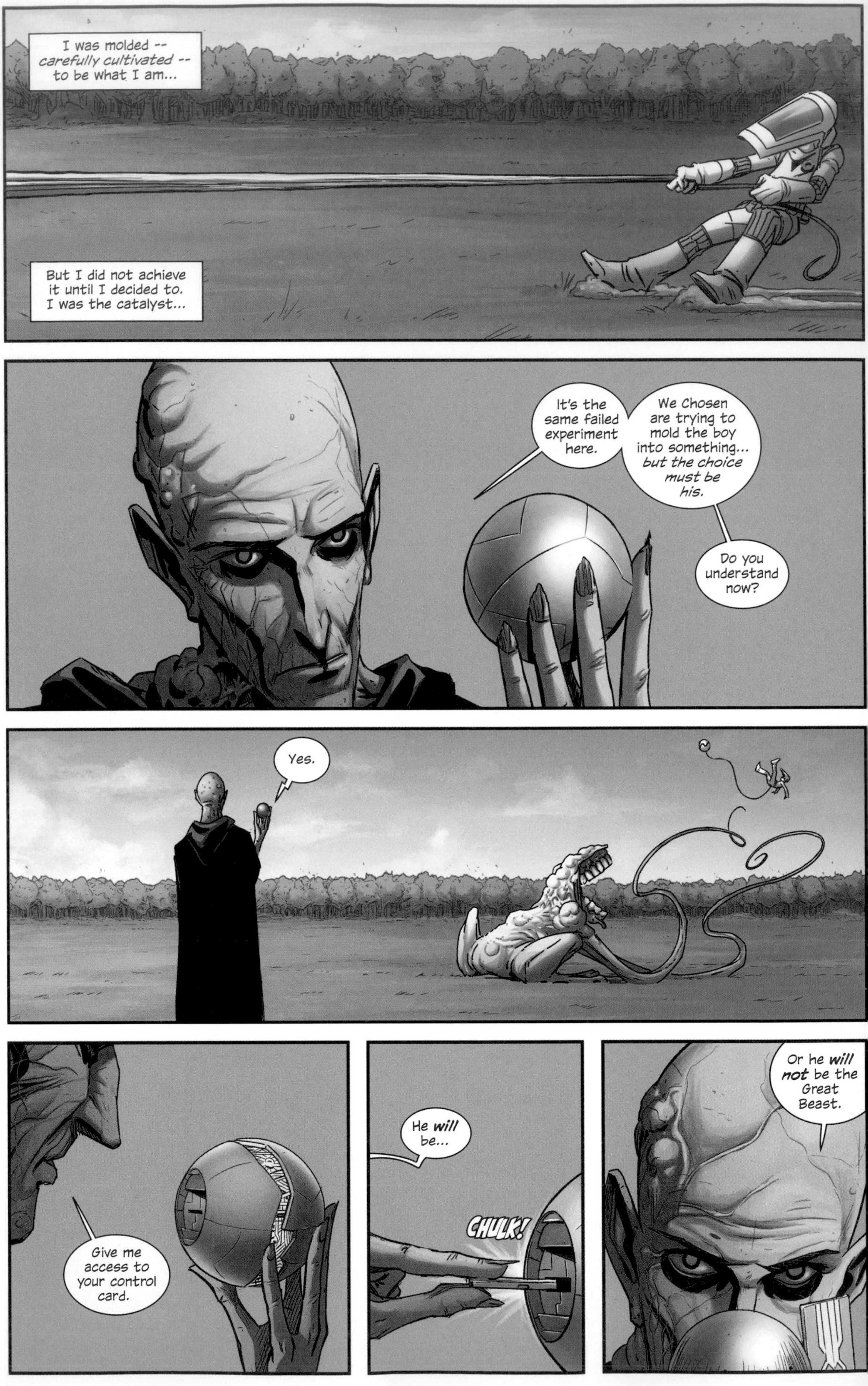
I was molded -- carefully cultivated -- to be what I am...
But I did not achieve it until I decided to. I was the catalyst...
It's the same failed experiment here.
We Chosen are trying to mold the boy into something... but the choice must be his.
Do you understand now?
Yes.
Give me access to your control card.
He will be...
CHULK!
Or he will not be the Great Beast.

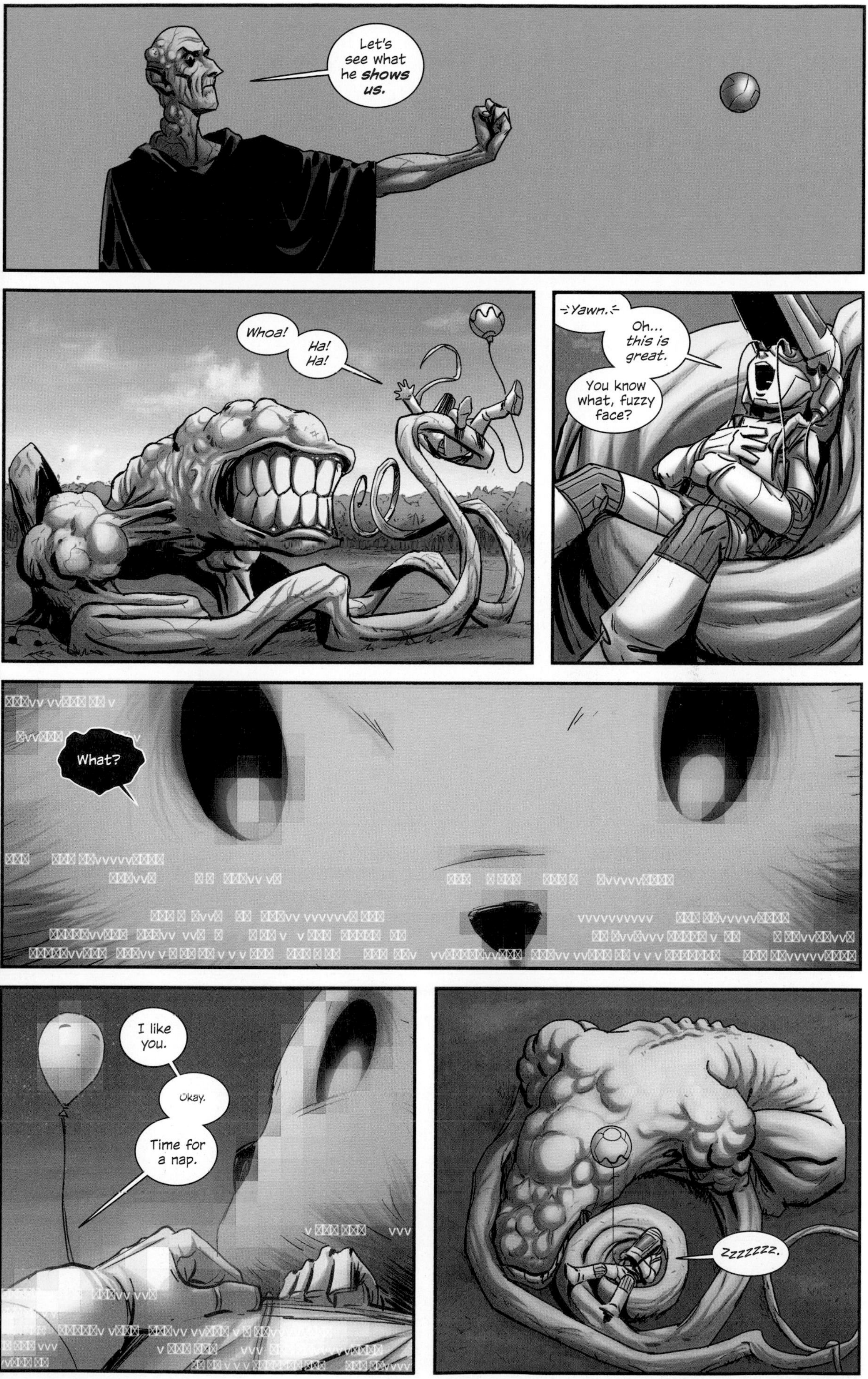
Let's see what he **shows** **us.**
Whoa!
Ha! Ha!
Yawn.
Oh... this is great.
You know what, fuzzy face?
What?
I like you.
Okay.
Time for a nap.
Zzzzzzz.

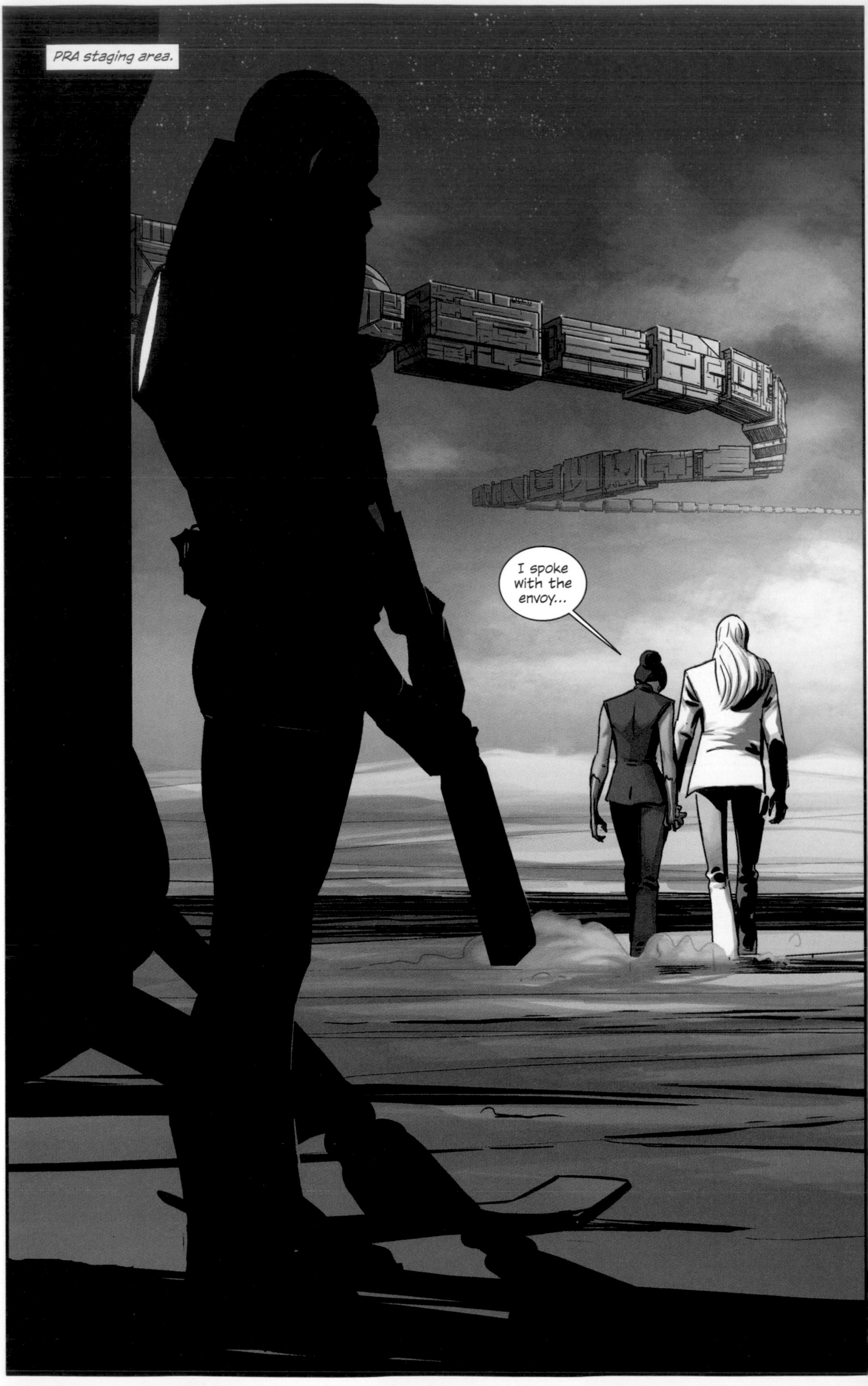
PRA staging area.
I spoke with the envoy...

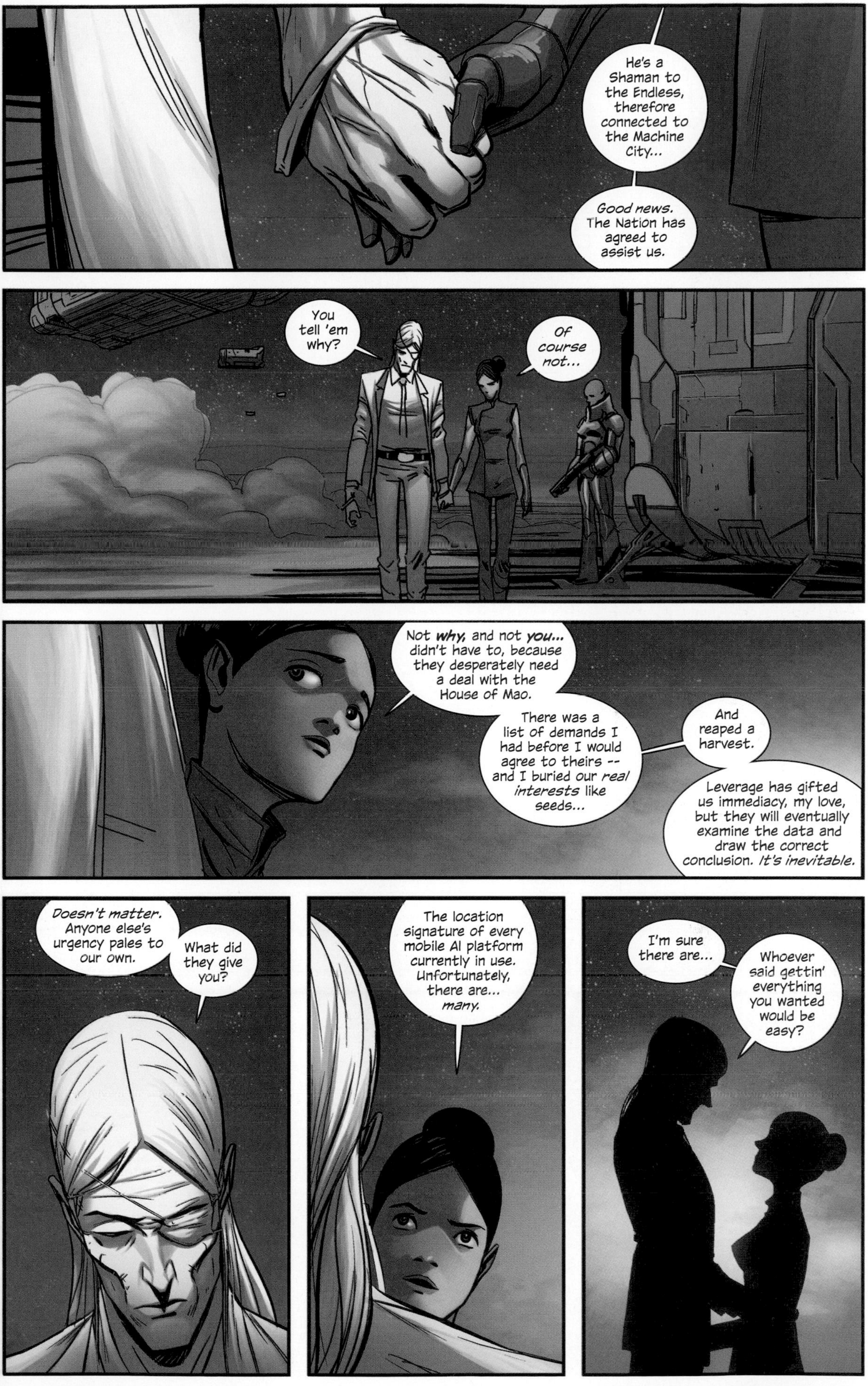
He's a Shaman to the Endless, therefore connected to the Machine City...
Good news. The Nation has agreed to assist us.
You tell 'em why?
Of course not...
Not why, and not you... didn't have to, because they desperately need a deal with the House of Mao.
There was a list of demands I had before I would agree to theirs -- and I buried our real interests like seeds...
And reaped a harvest.
Leverage has gifted us immediacy, my love, but they will eventually examine the data and draw the correct conclusion. It's inevitable.
Doesn't matter. Anyone else's urgency pales to our own.
What did they give you?
The location signature of every mobile AI platform currently in use. Unfortunately, there are... many.
I'm sure there are...
Whoever said gettin' everything you wanted would be easy?

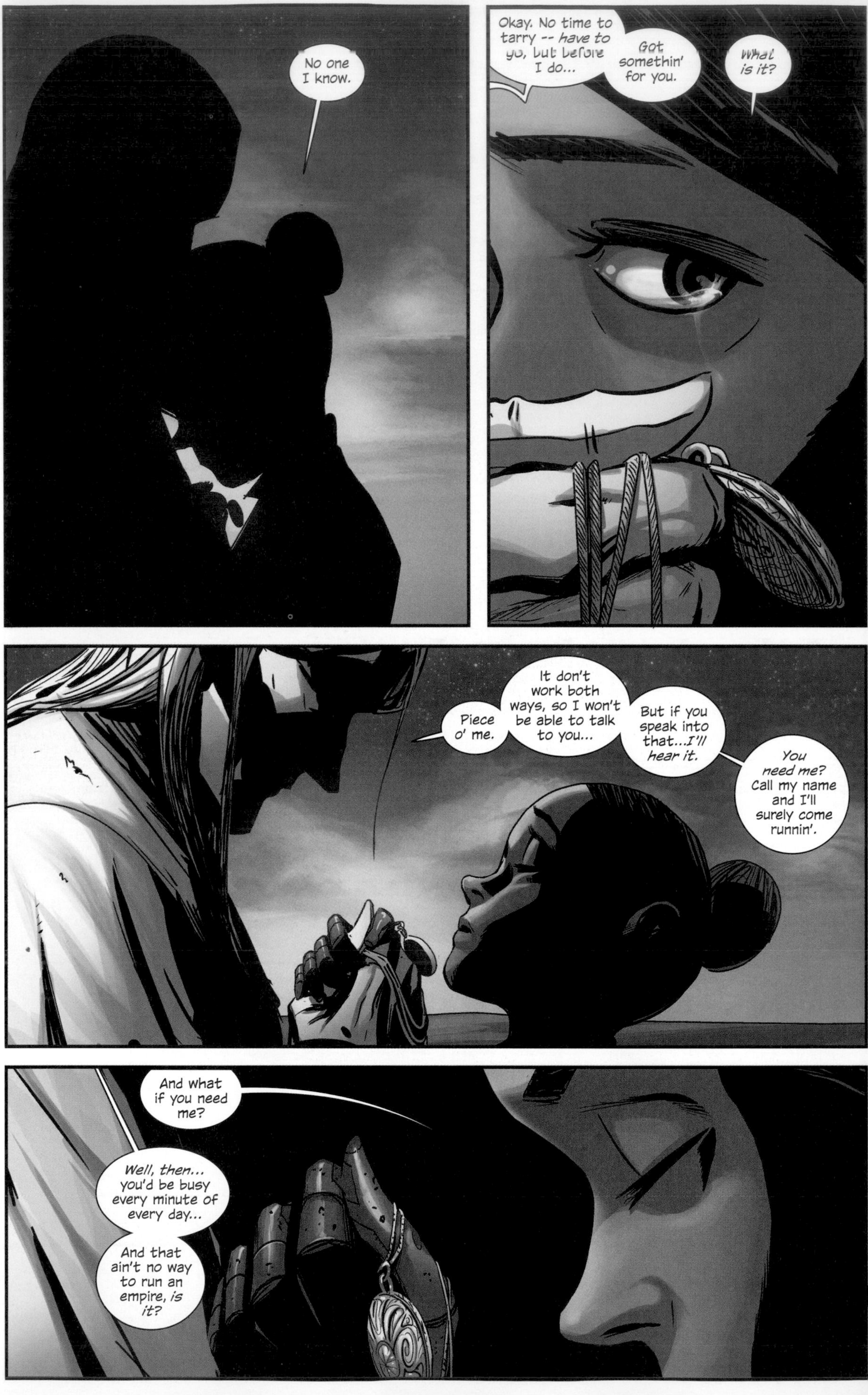
No one I know.
Okay. No time to tarry -- have to go, but before I do...
Got somethin' for you.
What is it?
Piece o' me.
It don't work both ways, so I won't be able to talk to you...
But if you speak into that...I'll hear it.
You need me? Call my name and I'll surely come runnin'.
And what if you need me?
Well, then... you'd be busy every minute of every day...
And that ain't no way to run an empire, is it?

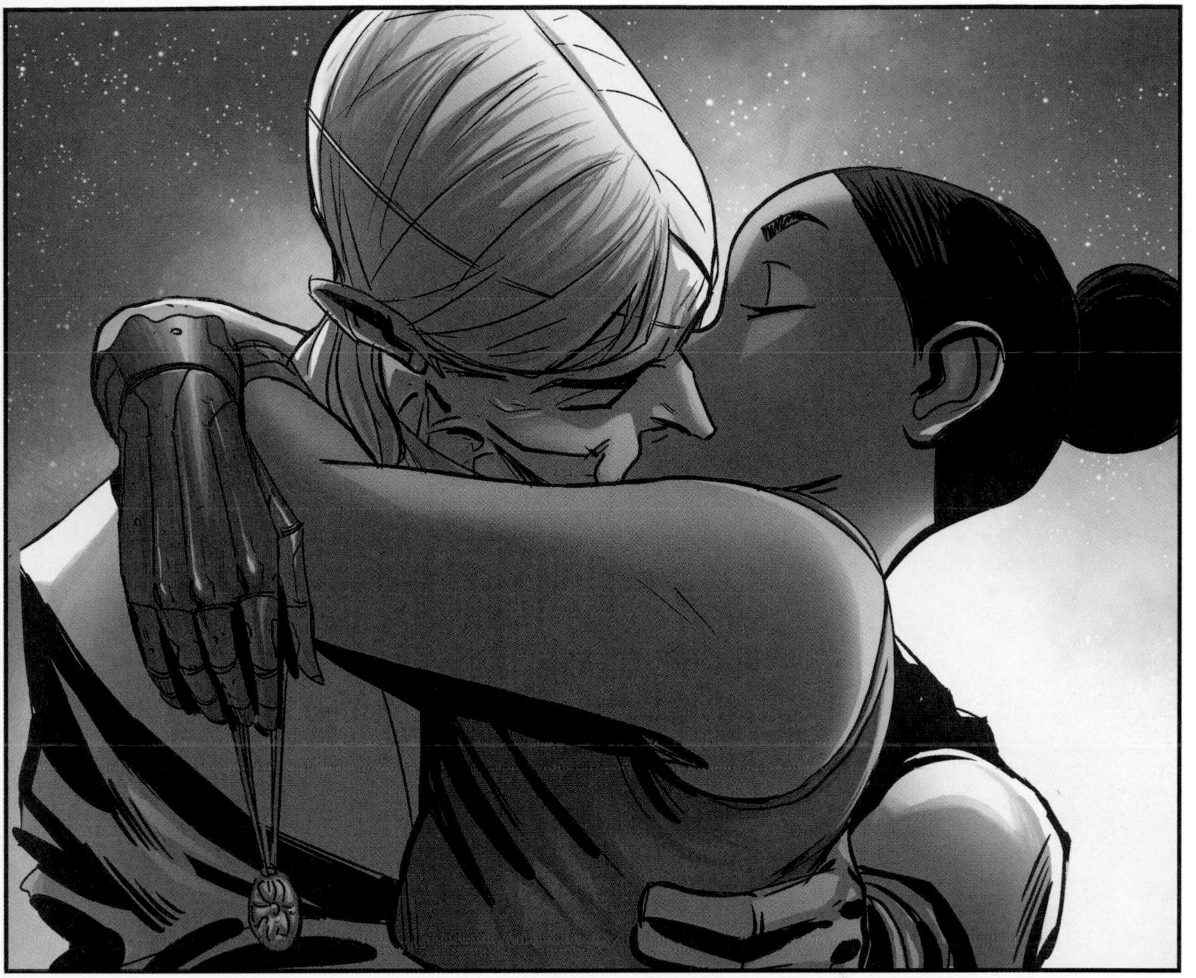

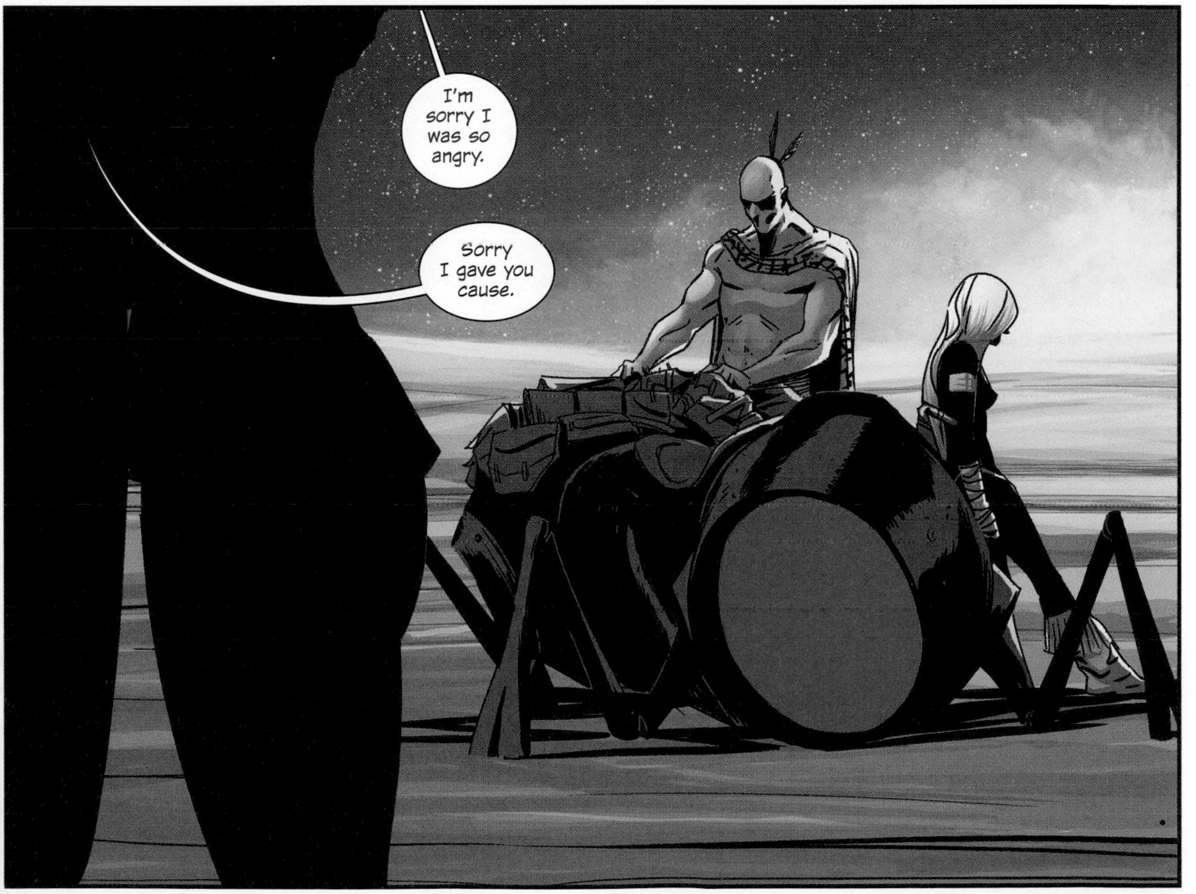
I'm sorry I was so angry.
Sorry I gave you cause.

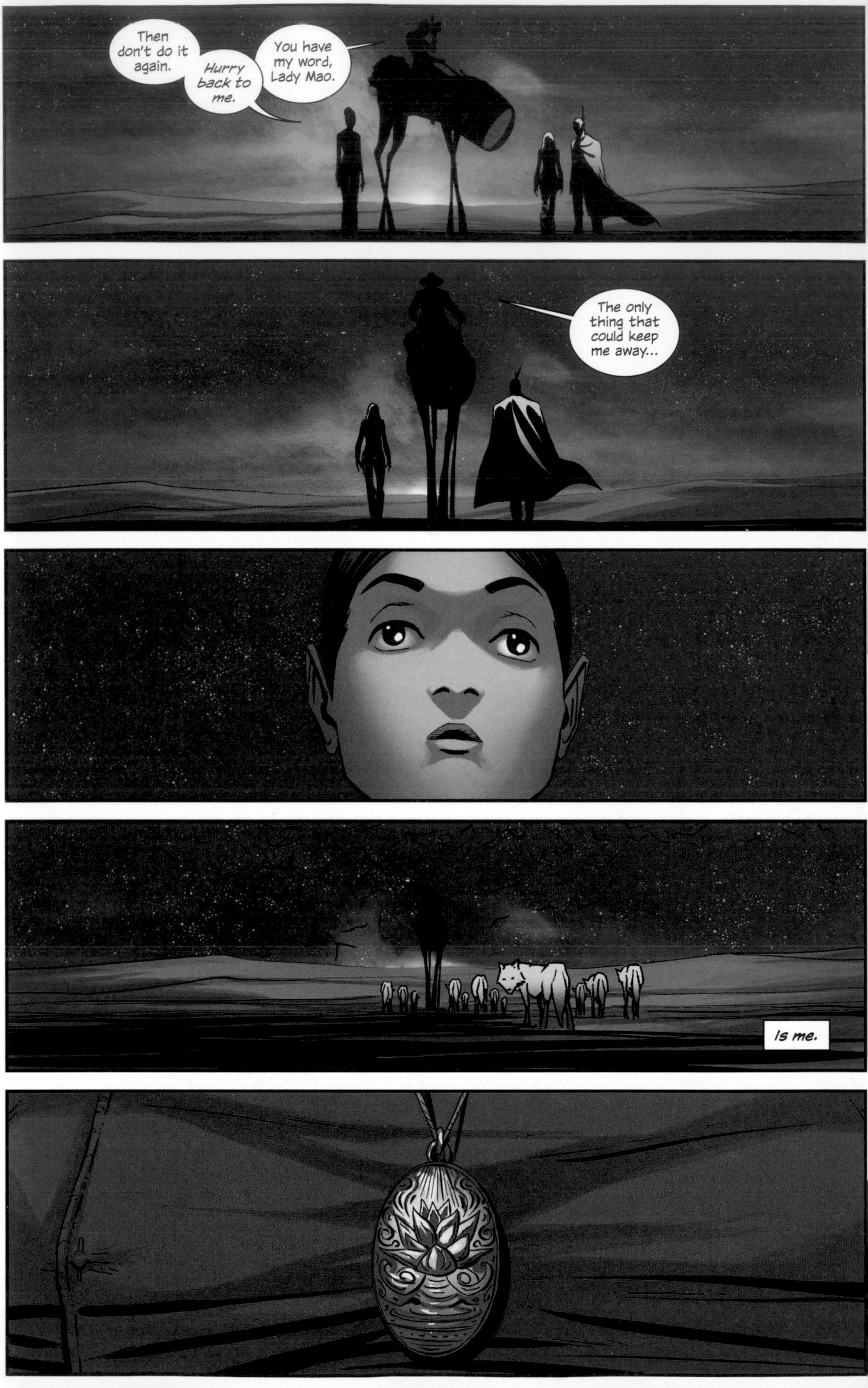
Then don't do it again.
Hurry back to me.
You have my word, Lady Mao.
The only thing that could keep me away...
Is me.

WHAT FOLLOWS...

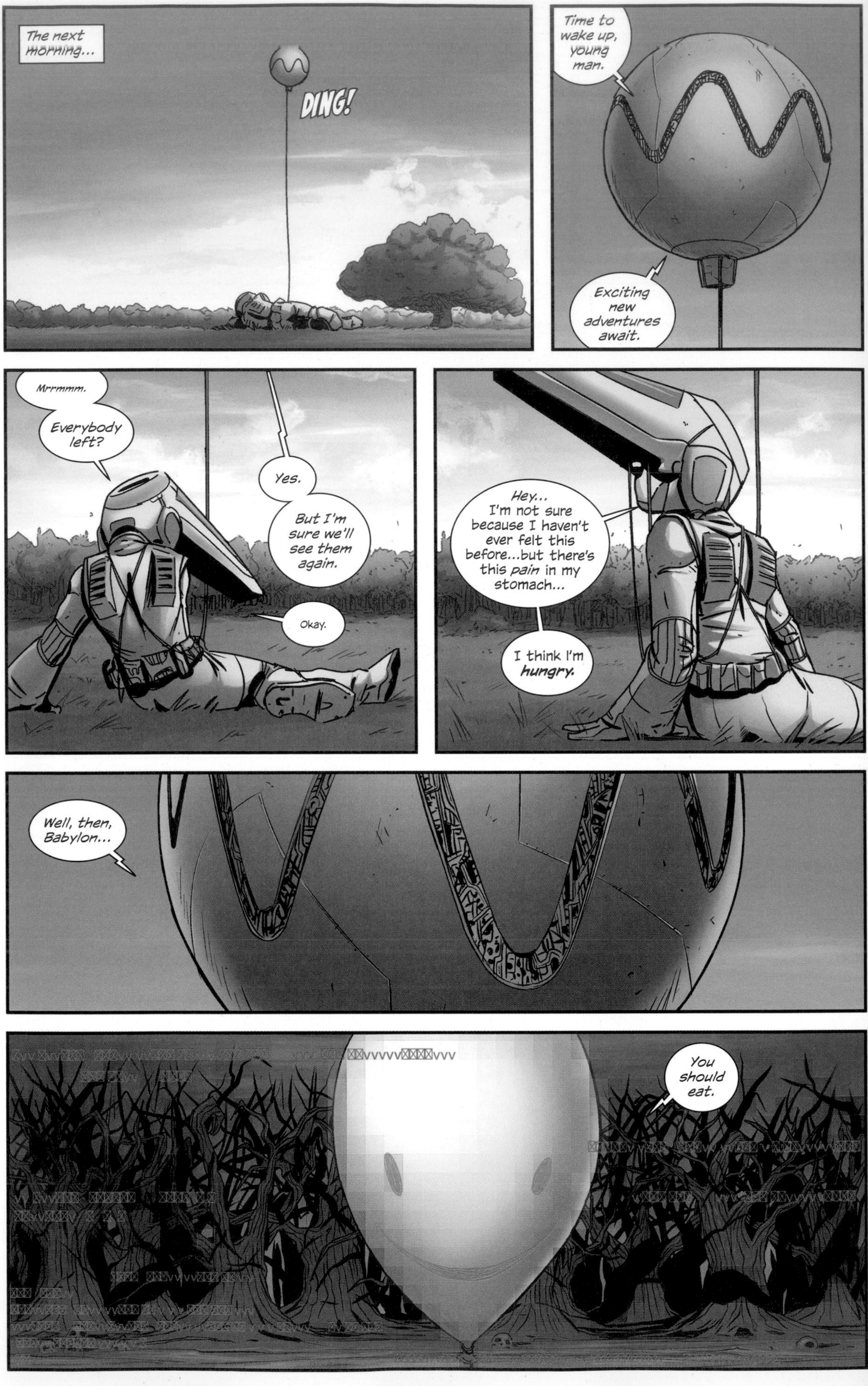
The next morning...
DING!
Time to wake up, young man.
Exciting new adventures await.
Mrrmmm.
Everybody left?
Yes.
But I'm sure we'll see them again.
Okay.
Hey... I'm not sure because I haven't ever felt this before...but there's this *pain* in my stomach...
I think I'm ***hungry.***
Well, then, Babylon...
You should eat.

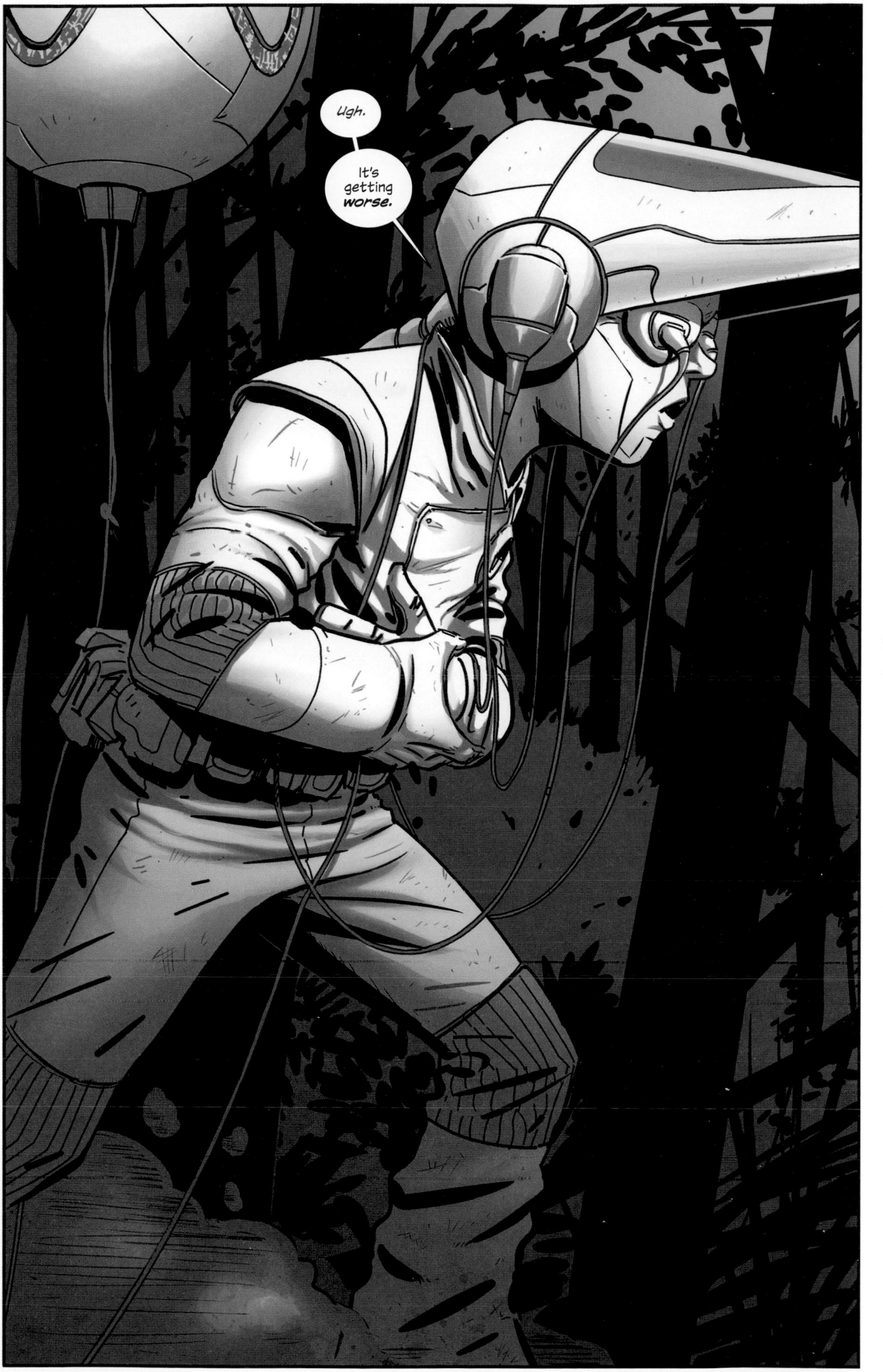
Ugh.
It's getting worse.

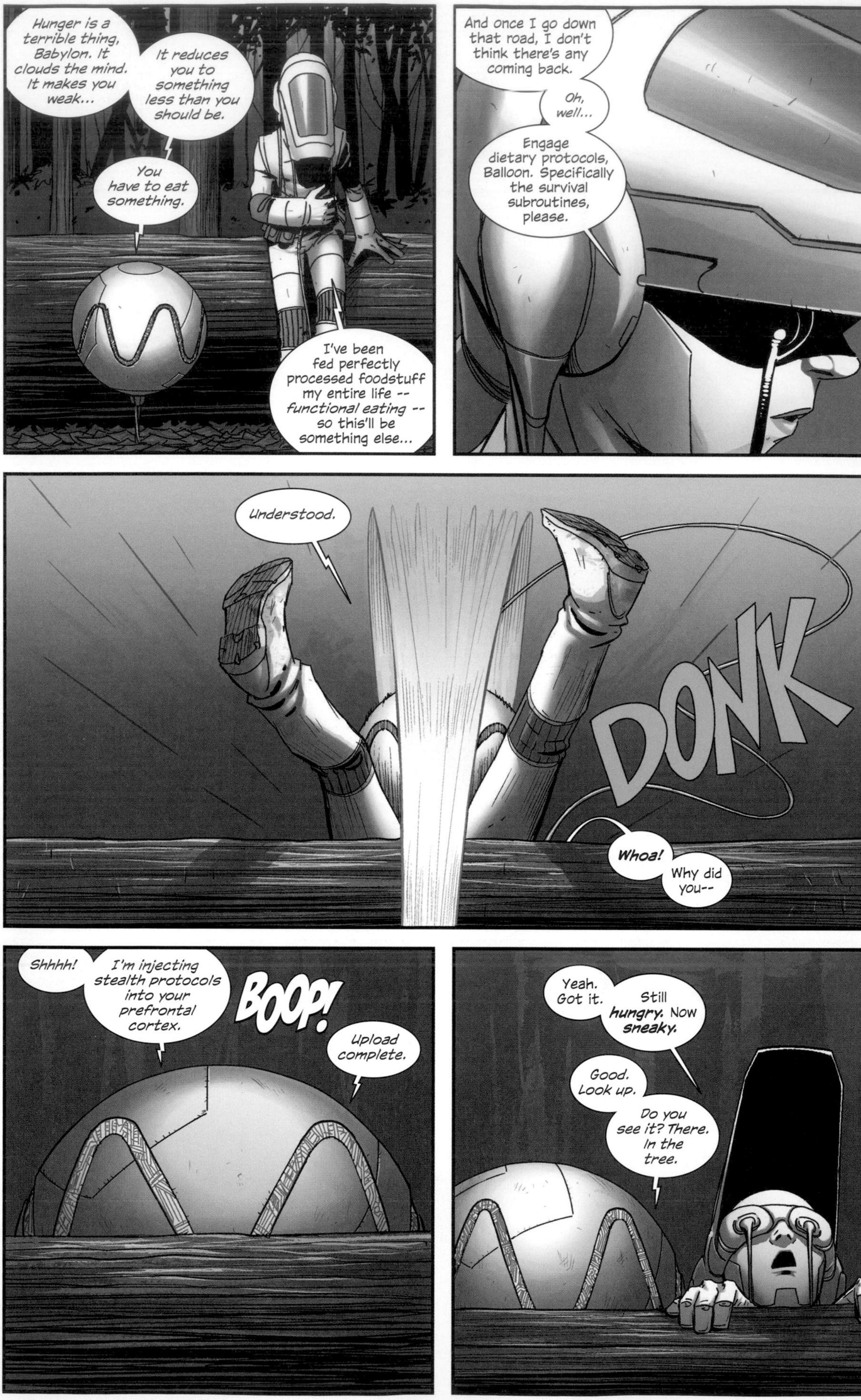
Hunger is a terrible thing, Babylon. It clouds the mind. It makes you weak...
It reduces you to something less than you should be.
You have to eat something.
I've been fed perfectly processed foodstuff my entire life -- functional eating -- so this'll be something else...
And once I go down that road, I don't think there's any coming back.
Oh, well...
Engage dietary protocols, Balloon. Specifically the survival subroutines, please.
Understood.
DONK
Whoa!
Why did you--
Shhhh!
I'm injecting stealth protocols into your prefrontal cortex.
BOOP!
Upload complete.
Yeah. Got it.
Still hungry. Now sneaky.
Good. Look up.
Do you see it? There. In the tree.

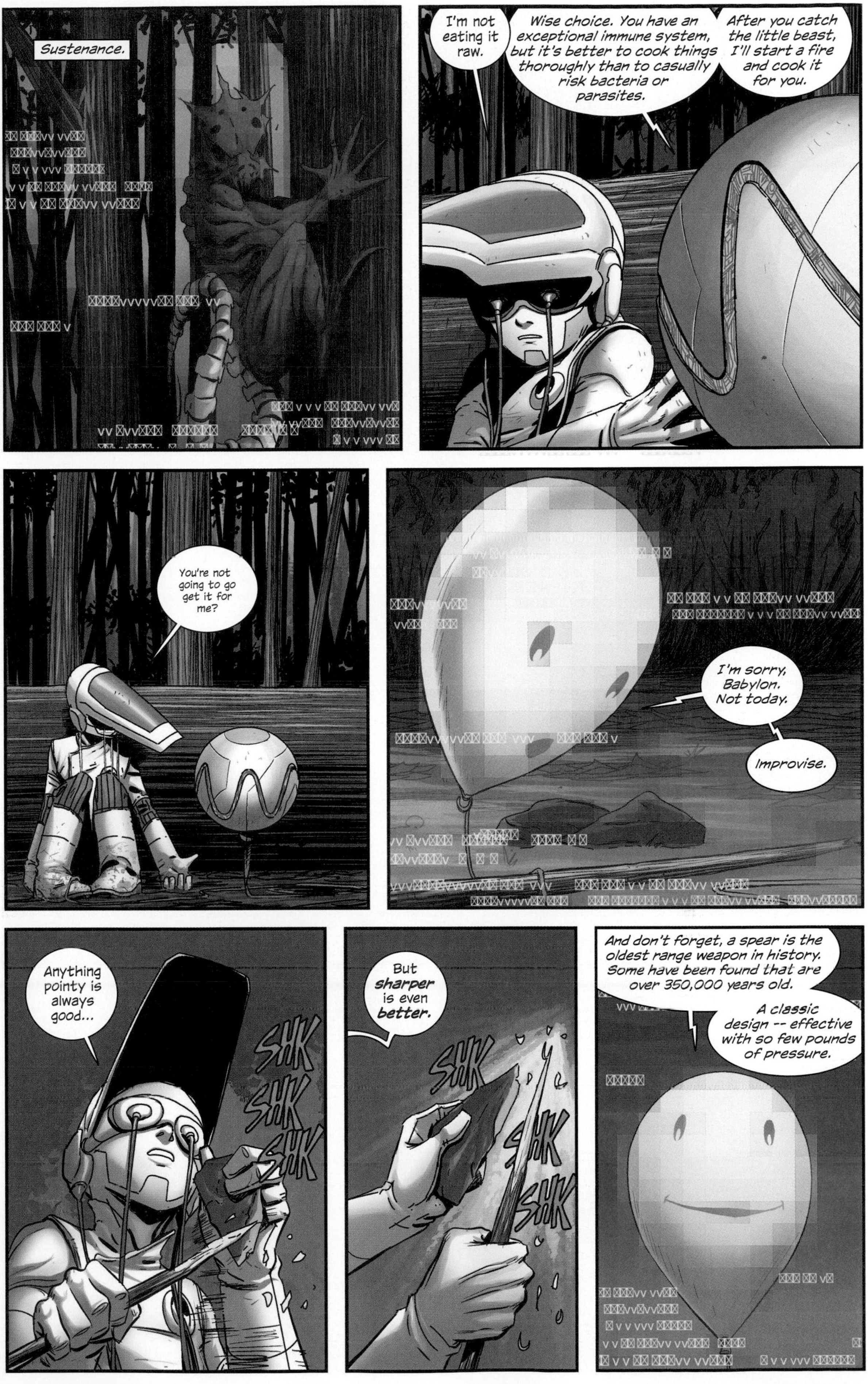
Sustenance.
I'm not eating it raw.
Wise choice. You have an exceptional immune system, but it's better to cook things thoroughly than to casually risk bacteria or parasites.
After you catch the little beast, I'll start a fire and cook it for you.
You're not going to go get it for me?
I'm sorry, Babylon. Not today.
Improvise.
Anything pointy is always good...
SHK SHK SHK
But **sharper** is even **better.**
SHK SHK SHK
And don't forget, a spear is the oldest range weapon in history. Some have been found that are over 350,000 years old.
A classic design -- effective with so few pounds of pressure.

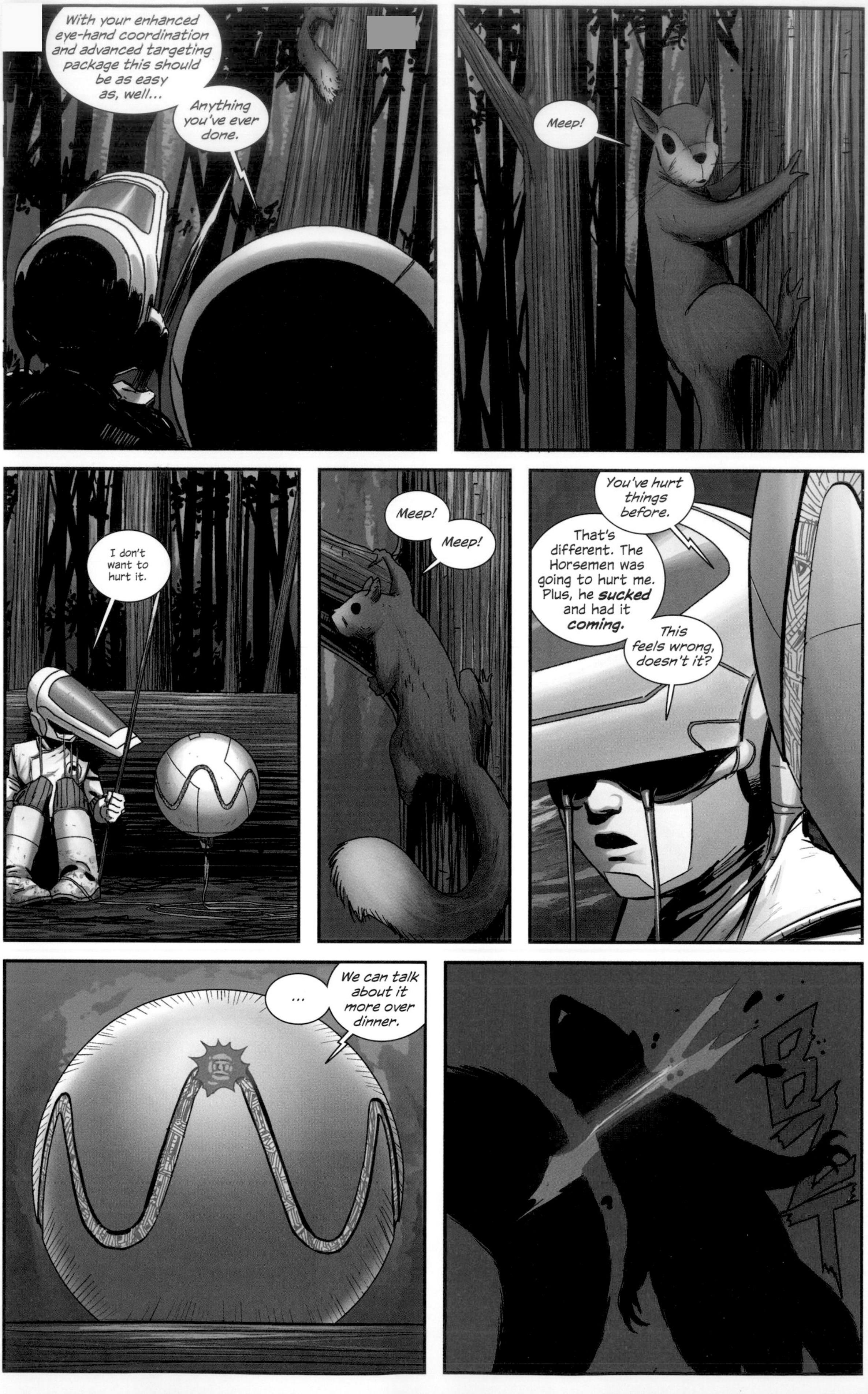
With your enhanced eye-hand coordination and advanced targeting package this should be as easy as, well...
Anything you've ever done.
Meep!
I don't want to hurt it.
Meep!
Meep!
You've hurt things before.
That's different. The Horsemen was going to hurt me. Plus, he **sucked** and had it **coming.**
This feels wrong, doesn't it?
...
We can talk about it more over dinner.

CONSUME IT ALL.

EAT THE **ROOT.**

19

NINETEEN:
THIS IS WHY WE
KILL

ALL OF THESE ARE **TESTS.**

ALL OF THIS IS **CHANGE.**

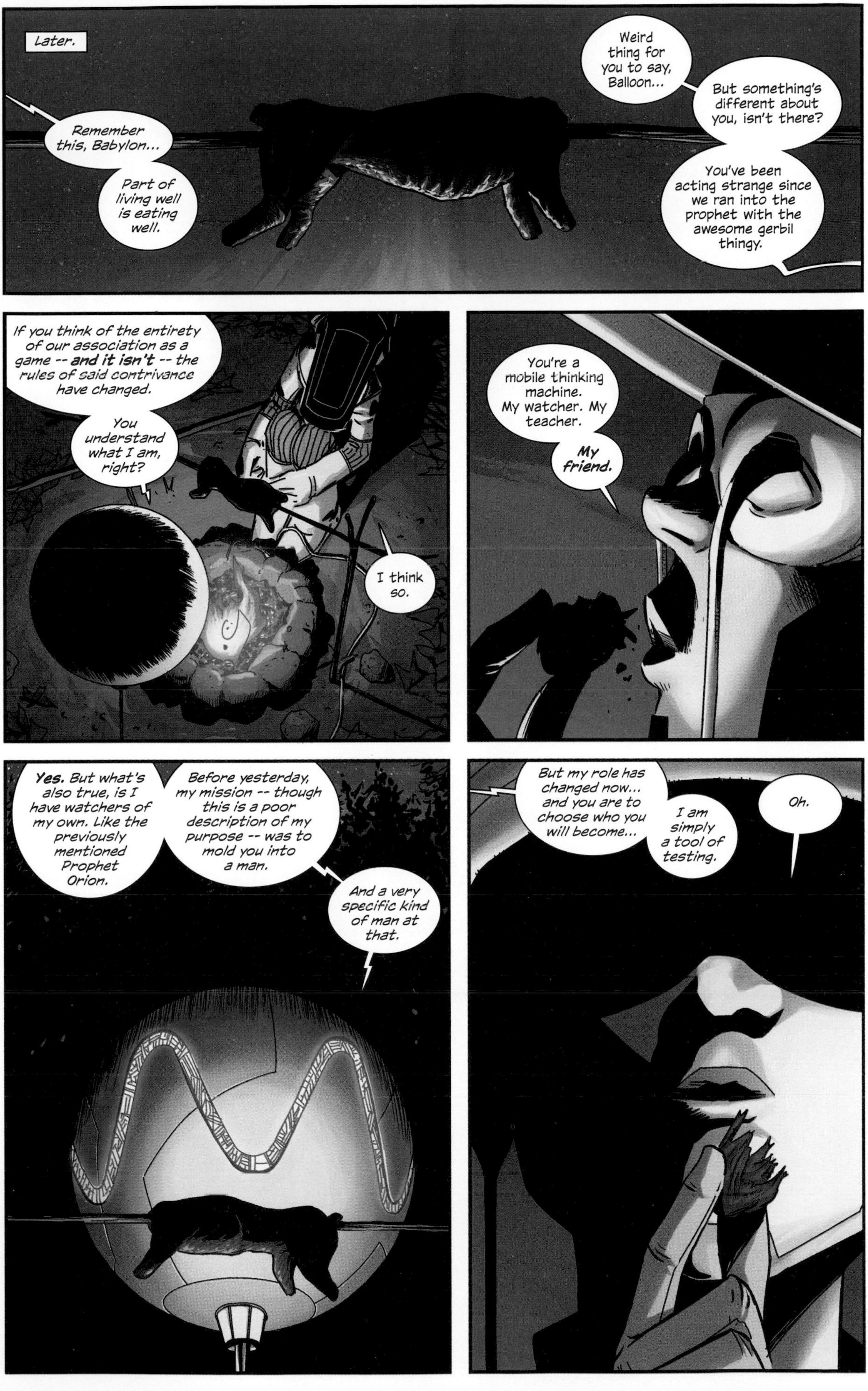
Later.
Remember this, Babylon...
Part of living well is eating well.
Weird thing for you to say, Balloon...
But something's different about you, isn't there?
You've been acting strange since we ran into the prophet with the awesome gerbil thingy.
If you think of the entirety of our association as a game -- **and it isn't** -- the rules of said contrivance have changed.
You understand what I am, right?
I think so.
You're a mobile thinking machine. My watcher. My teacher.
My friend.
Yes. But what's also true, is I have watchers of my own. Like the previously mentioned Prophet Orion.
Before yesterday, my mission -- though this is a poor description of my purpose -- was to mold you into a man.
And a very specific kind of man at that.
But my role has changed now... and you are to choose who you will become...
I am simply a tool of testing.
Oh.

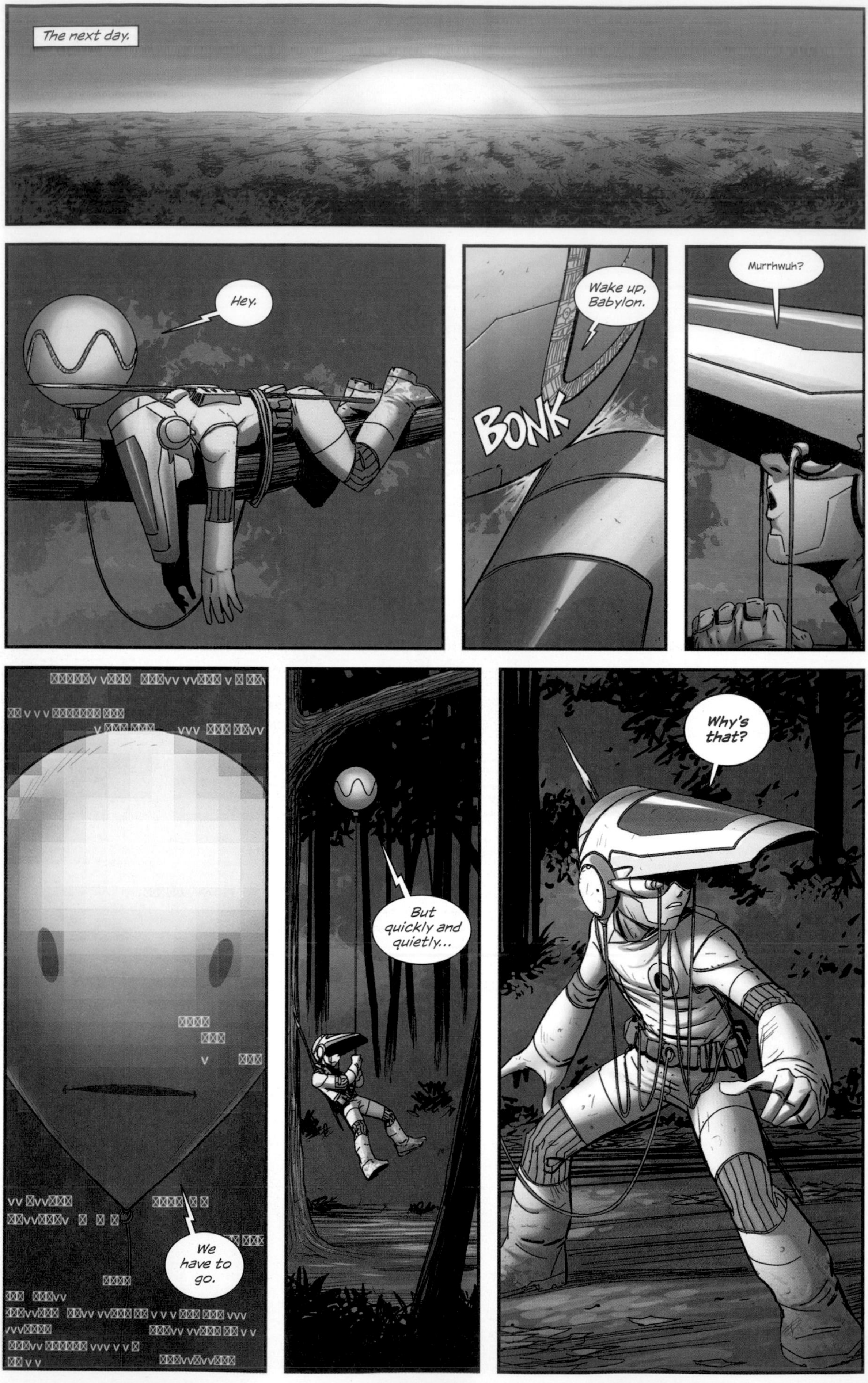
The next day.
Hey.
Wake up, Babylon.
BONK
Murrhwuh?
We have to go.
But quickly and quietly...
Why's that?

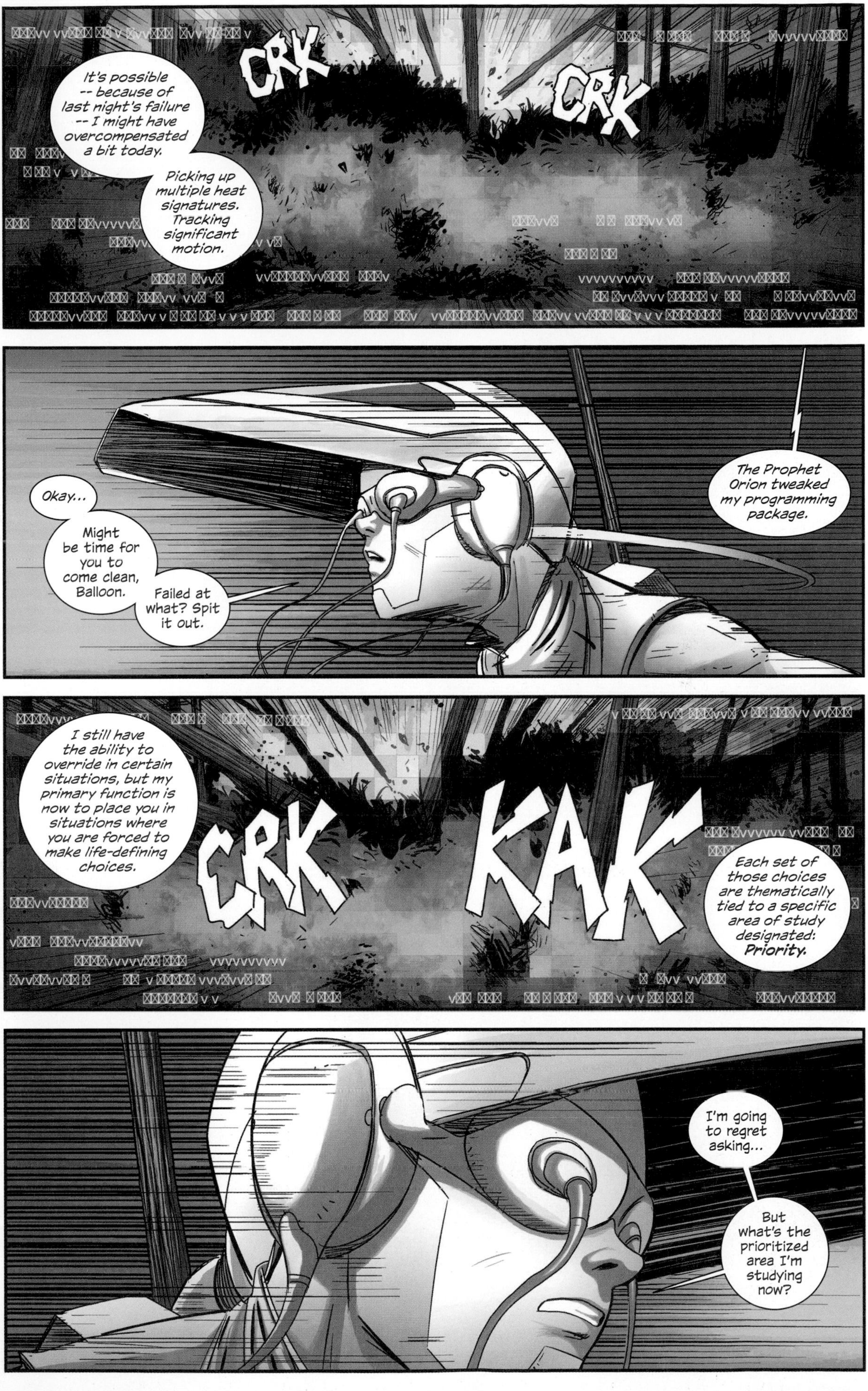
CRK
CRK
It's possible -- because of last night's failure -- I might have overcompensated a bit today.
Picking up multiple heat signatures. Tracking significant motion.
Okay...
Might be time for you to come clean, Balloon.
Failed at what? Spit it out.
The Prophet Orion tweaked my programming package.
I still have the ability to override in certain situations, but my primary function is now to place you in situations where you are forced to make life-defining choices.
CRK
KAK
Each set of those choices are thematically tied to a specific area of study designated: **Priority.**
I'm going to regret asking...
But what's the prioritized area I'm studying now?

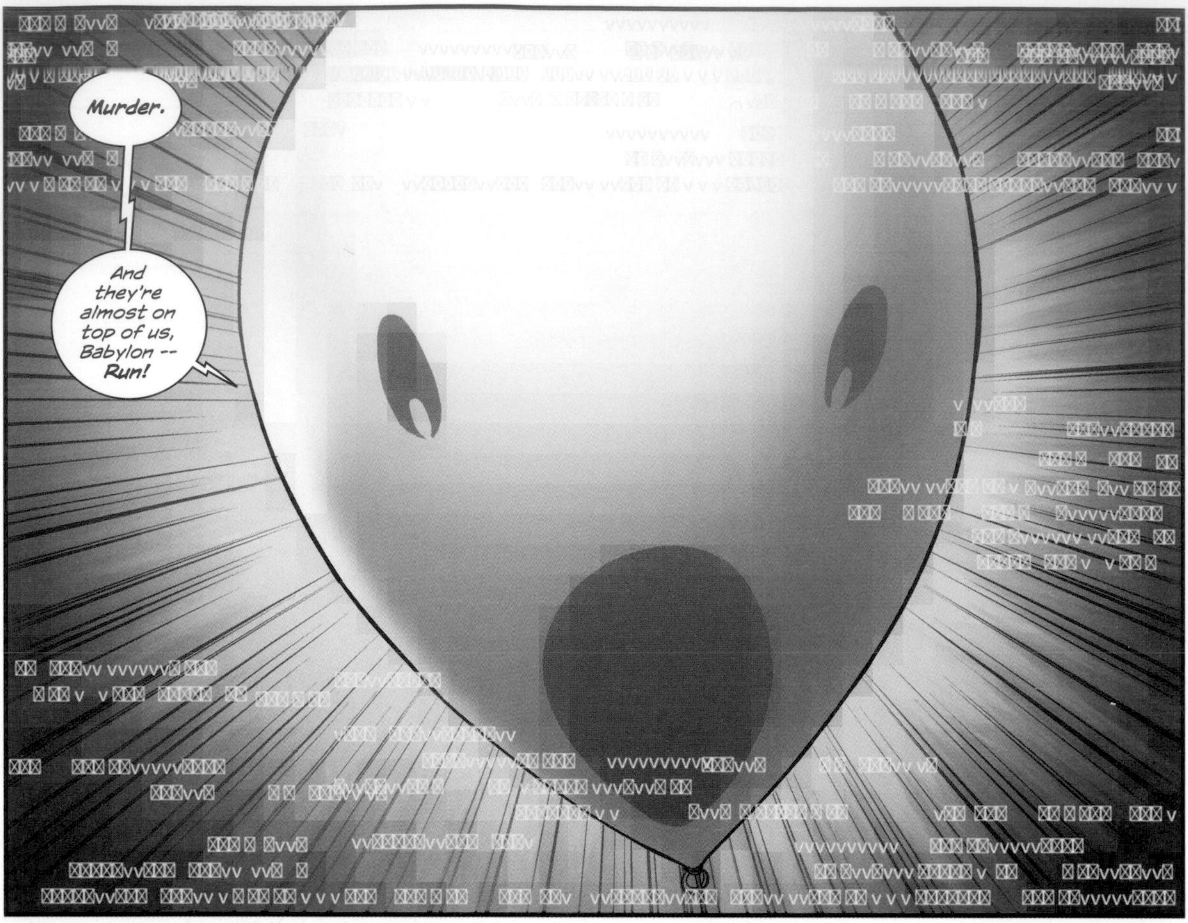
Murder.
And they're almost on top of us, Babylon -- Run!

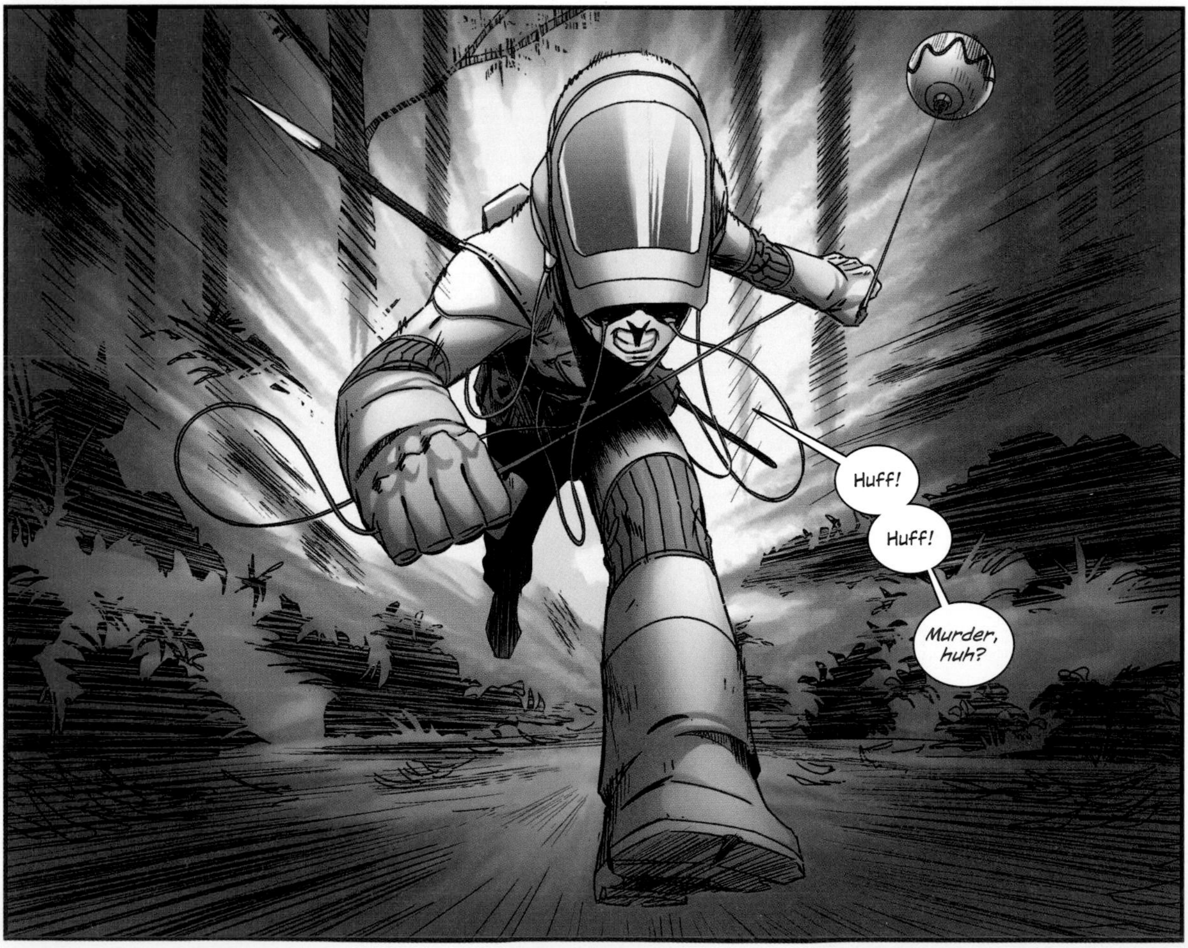
Huff!
Huff!
Murder, huh?

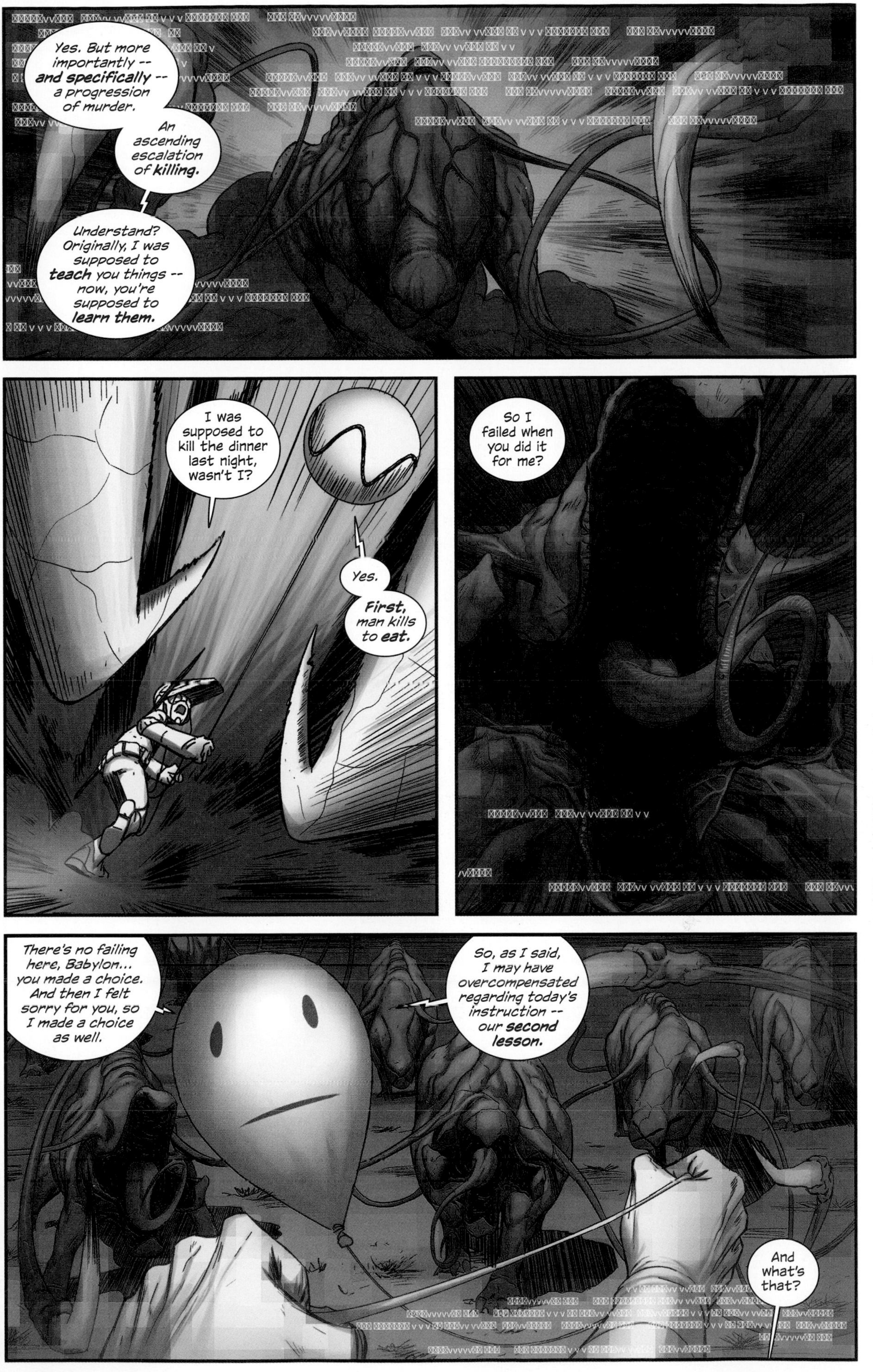
Yes. But more importantly -- and specifically -- a progression of murder.
An ascending escalation of killing.
Understand? Originally, I was supposed to teach you things -- now, you're supposed to learn them.
I was supposed to kill the dinner last night, wasn't I?
Yes.
First, man kills to eat.
So I failed when you did it for me?
There's no failing here, Babylon... you made a choice. And then I felt sorry for you, so I made a choice as well.
So, as I said, I may have overcompensated regarding today's instruction -- our second lesson.
And what's that?

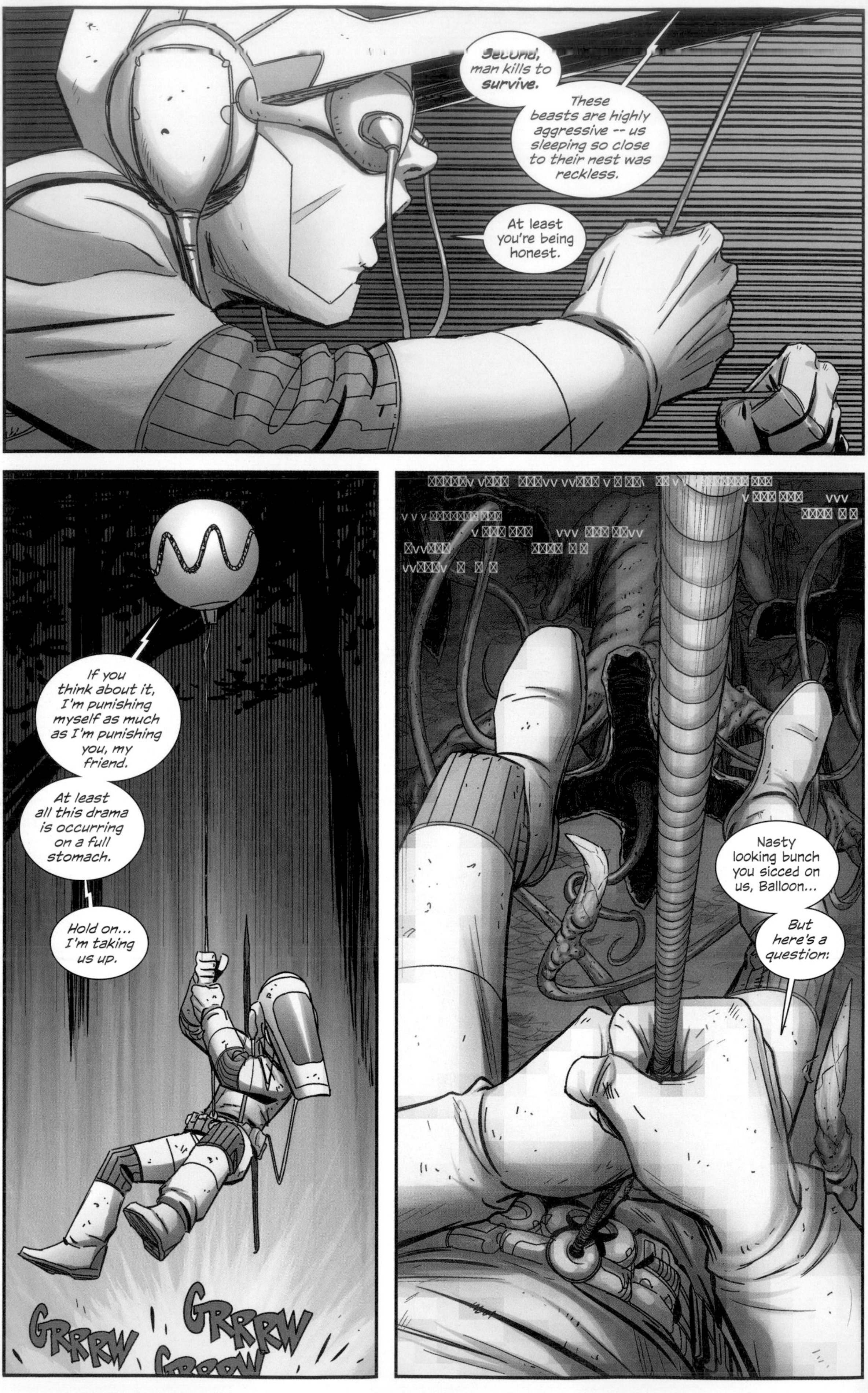
Second, man kills to survive.
These beasts are highly aggressive -- us sleeping so close to their nest was reckless.
At least you're being honest.
If you think about it, I'm punishing myself as much as I'm punishing you, my friend.
At least all this drama is occurring on a full stomach.
Hold on... I'm taking us up.
GRRRW
GRRRW
Nasty looking bunch you sicced on us, Balloon...
But here's a question:

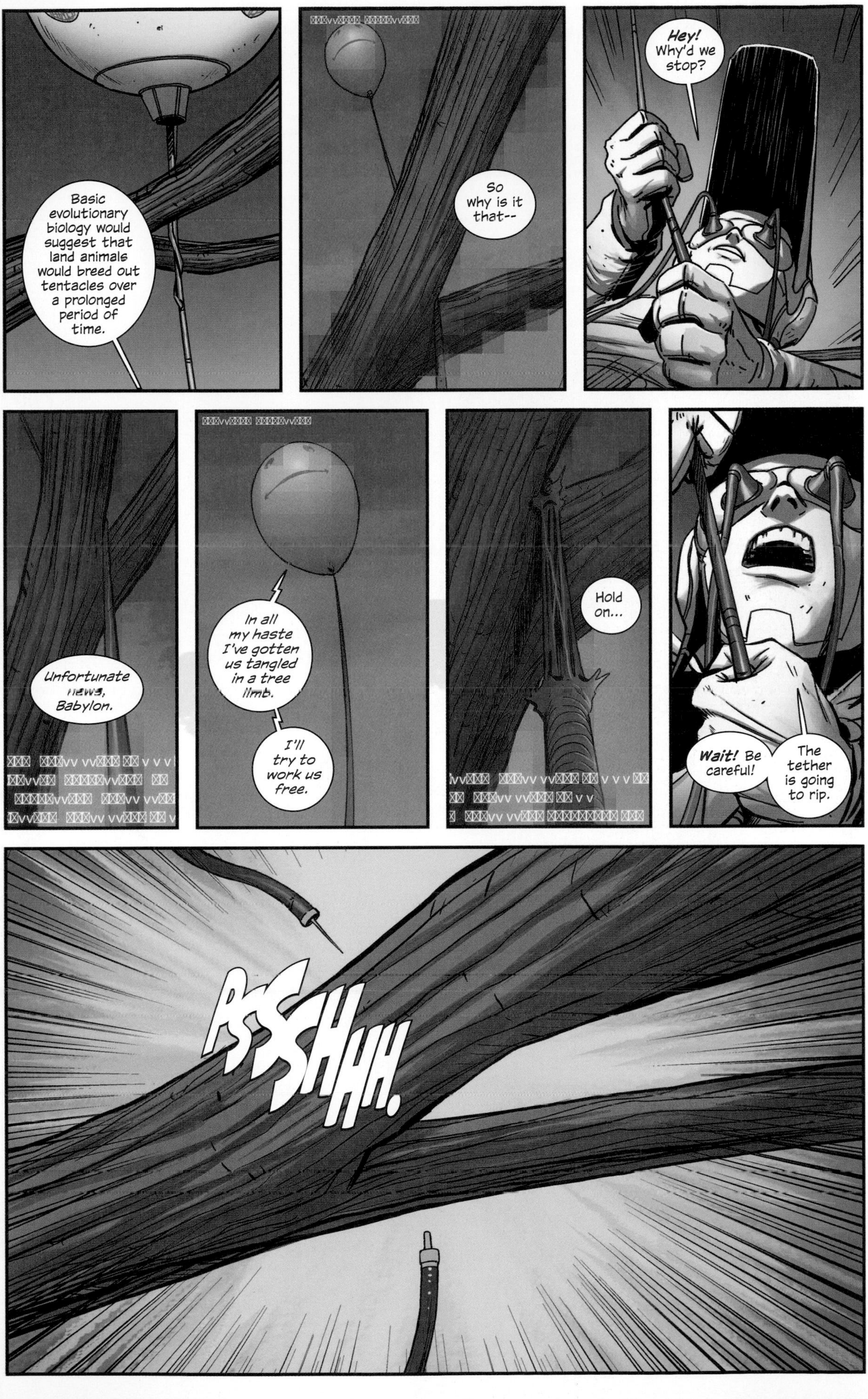

Basic evolutionary biology would suggest that land animals would breed out tentacles over a prolonged period of time.
So why is it that--
Hey! Why'd we stop?
Unfortunate news, Babylon.
In all my haste I've gotten us tangled in a tree limb.
I'll try to work us free.
Hold on...
Wait! Be careful!
The tether is going to rip.
PSSHHH.

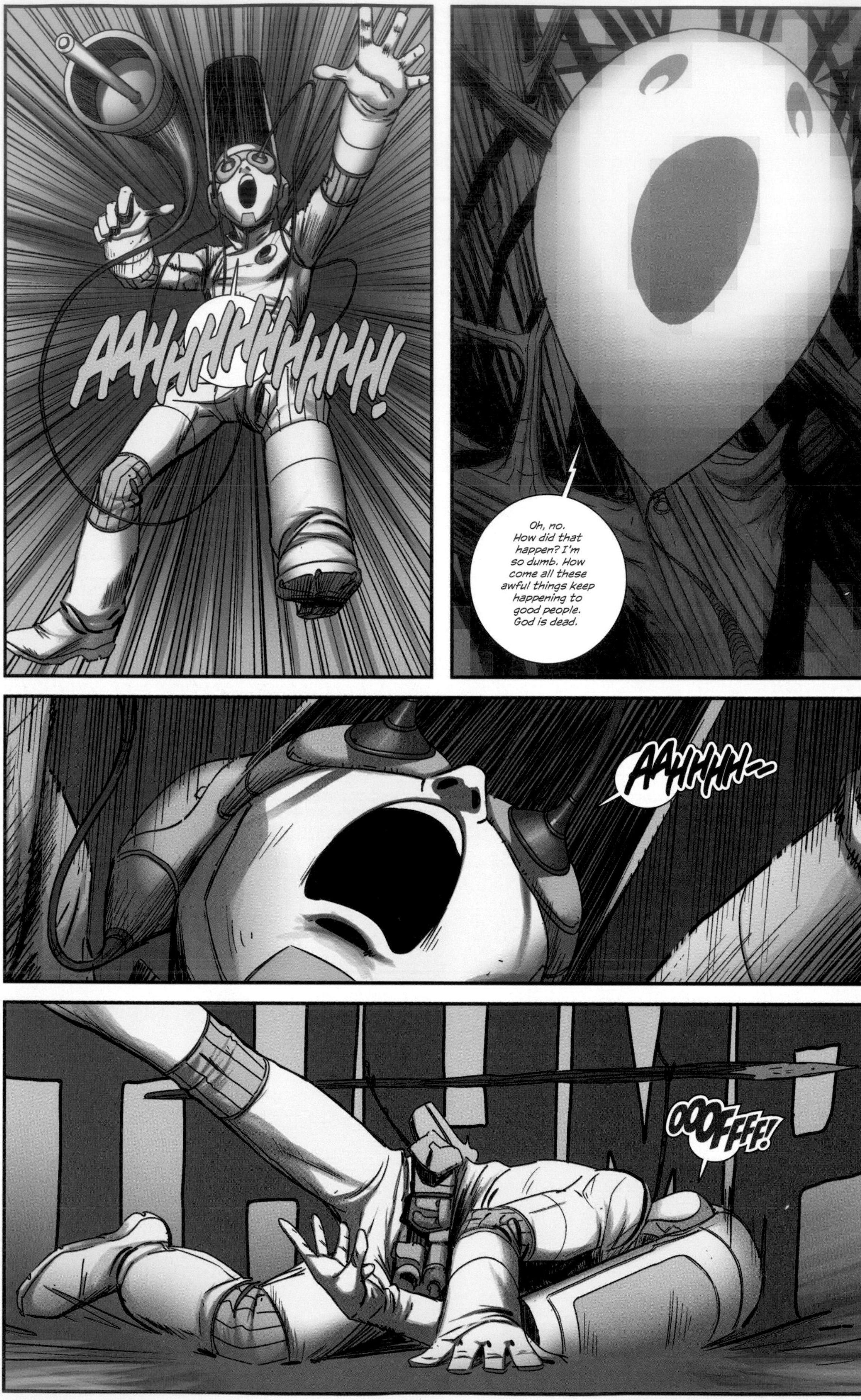
AAHHHHHHHHH!
Oh, no. How did that happen? I'm so dumb. How come all these awful things keep happening to good people. God is dead.
AAHHHH--
OOOFFFF!

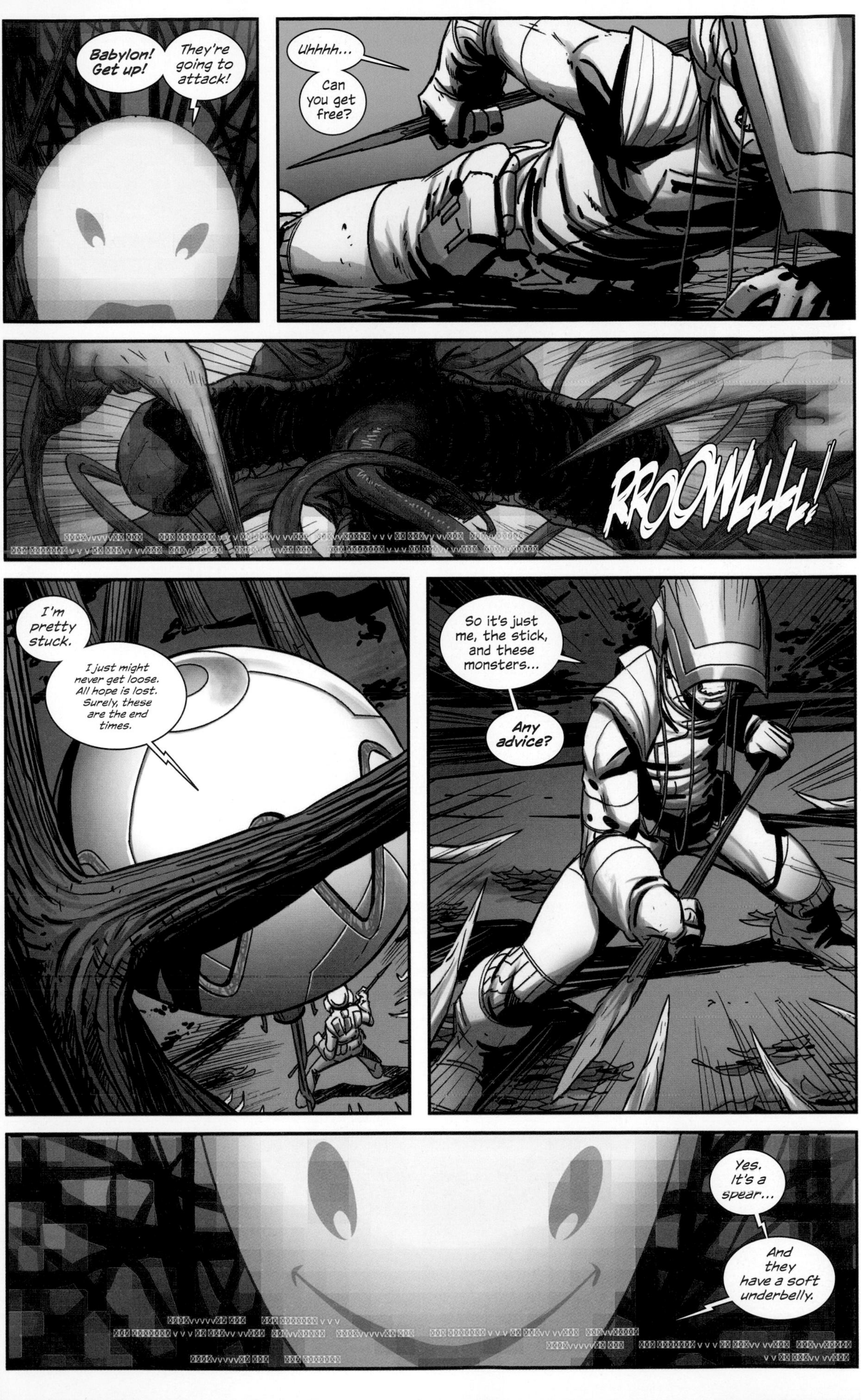
Babylon! Get up!
They're going to attack!
Uhhhh...
Can you get free?
RROOWLLL!
I'm pretty stuck.
I just might never get loose. All hope is lost. Surely, these are the end times.
So it's just me, the stick, and these monsters...
Any advice?
Yes. It's a spear...
And they have a soft underbelly.

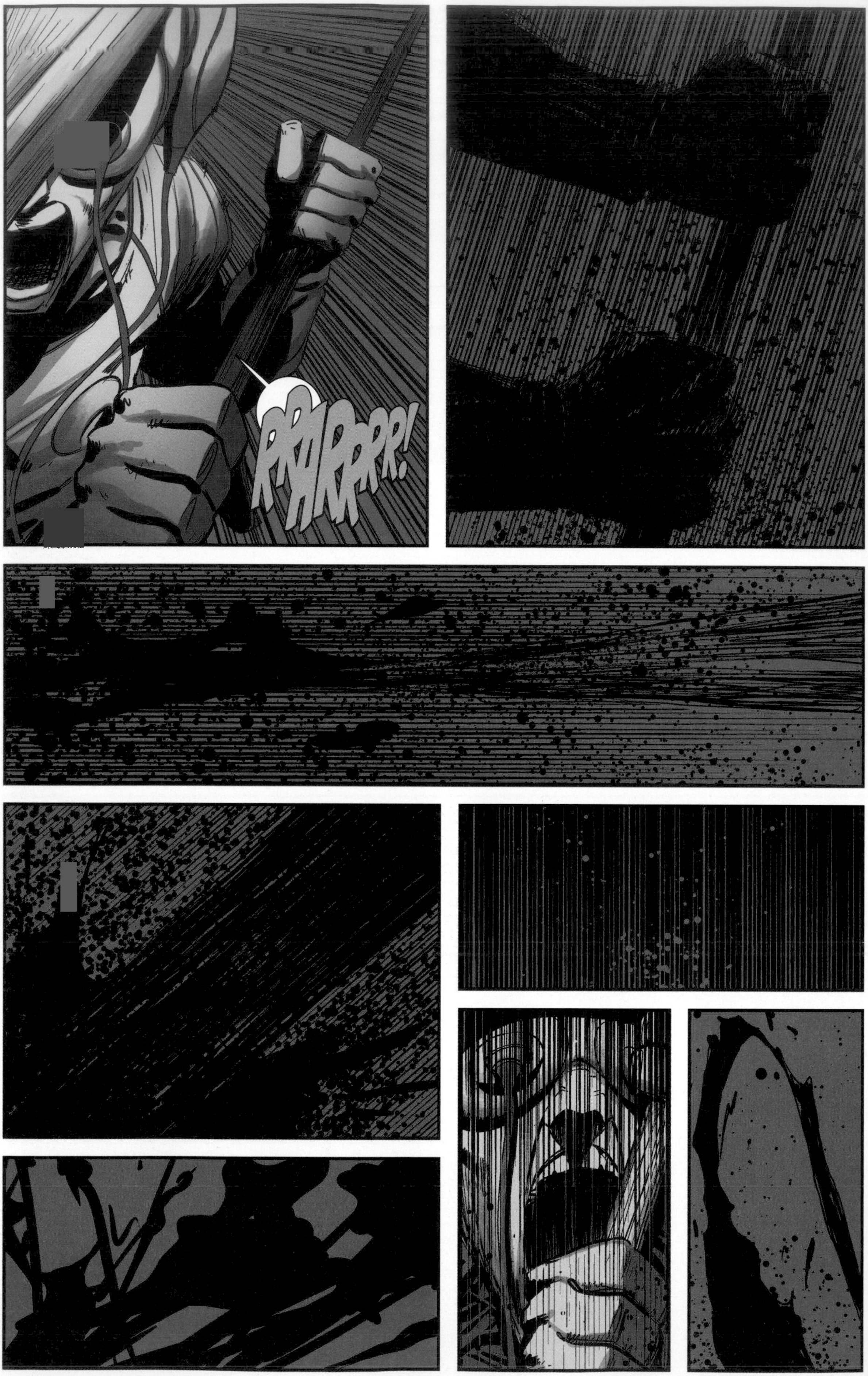
RRARRRR!

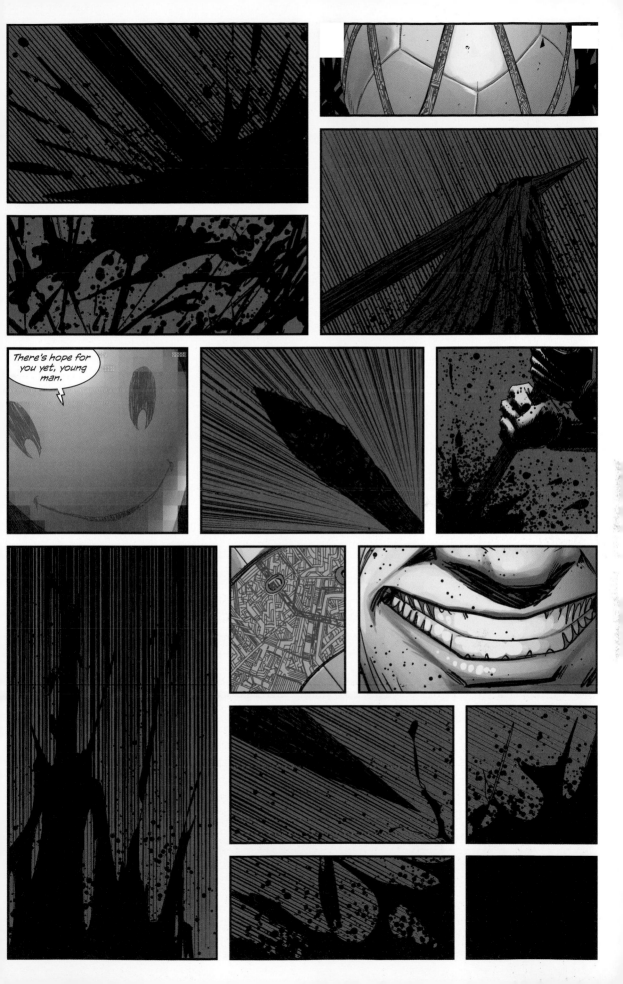

There's hope for you yet, young man.

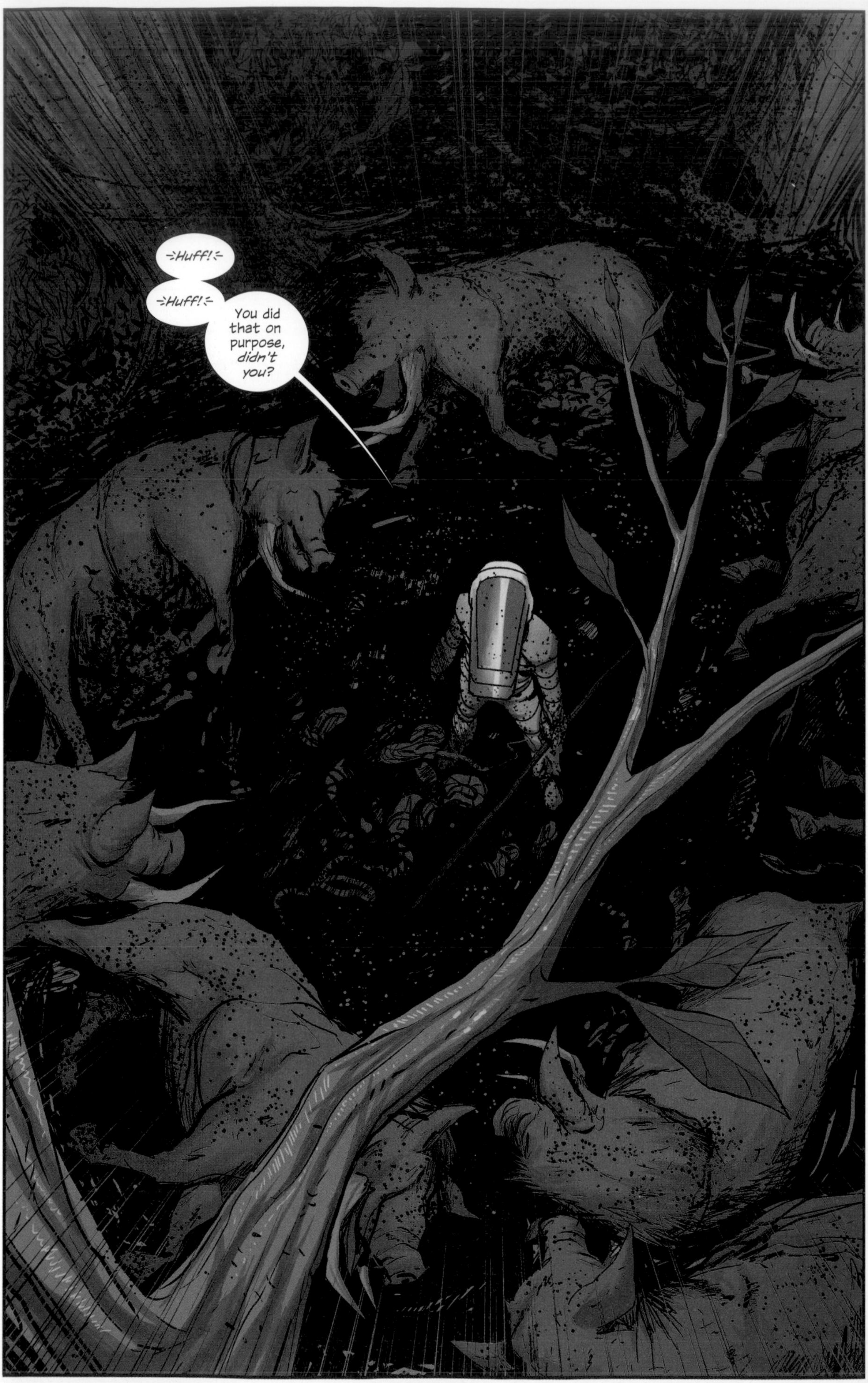

=Huff!=
=Huff!=
You did that on purpose, didn't you?

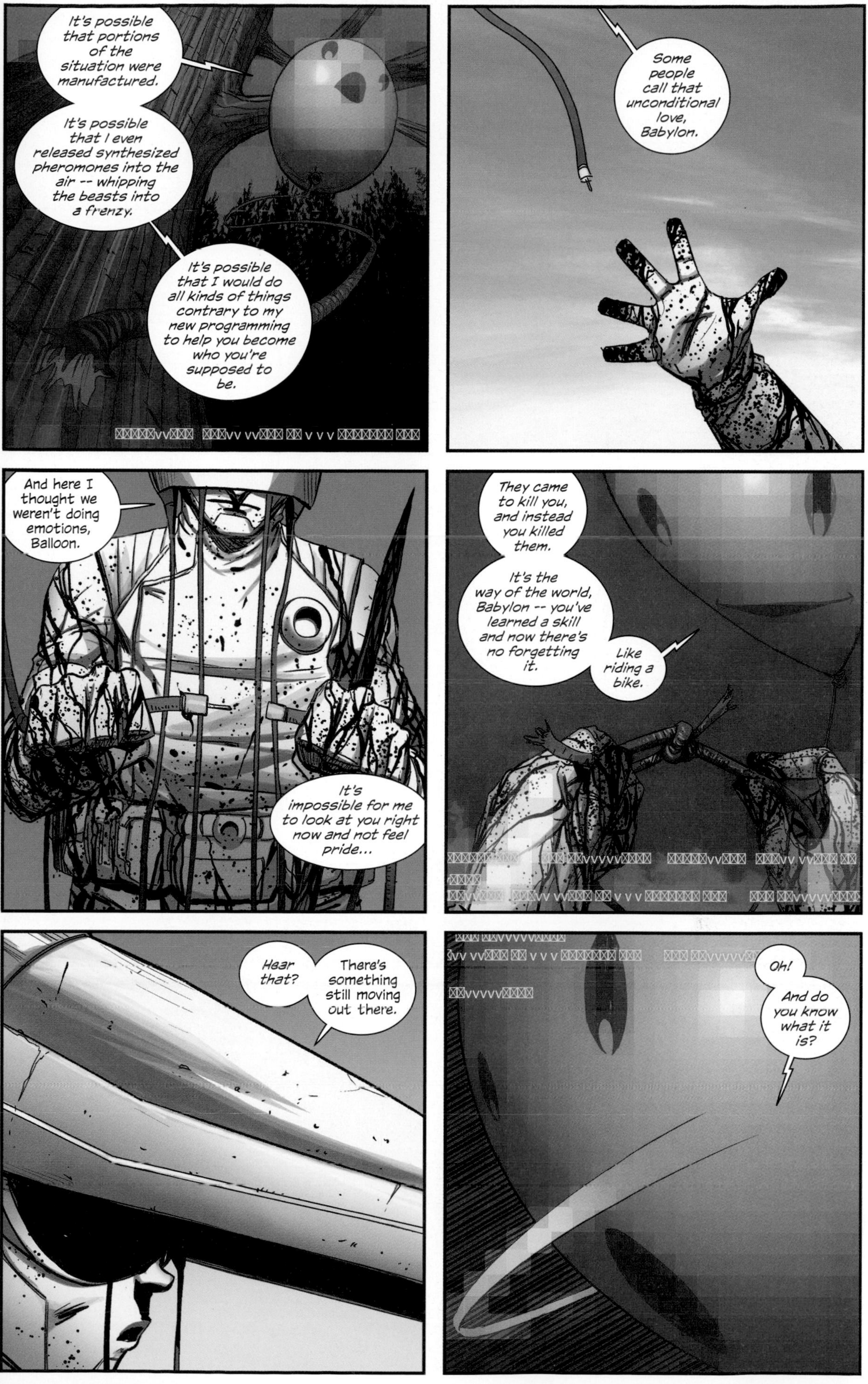
It's possible that portions of the situation were manufactured.
It's possible that I even released synthesized pheromones into the air -- whipping the beasts into a frenzy.
It's possible that I would do all kinds of things contrary to my new programming to help you become who you're supposed to be.
Some people call that unconditional love, Babylon.
And here I thought we weren't doing emotions, Balloon.
It's impossible for me to look at you right now and not feel pride...
They came to kill you, and instead you killed them.
It's the way of the world, Babylon -- you've learned a skill and now there's no forgetting it.
Like riding a bike.
Hear that?
There's something still moving out there.
Oh!
And do you know what it is?

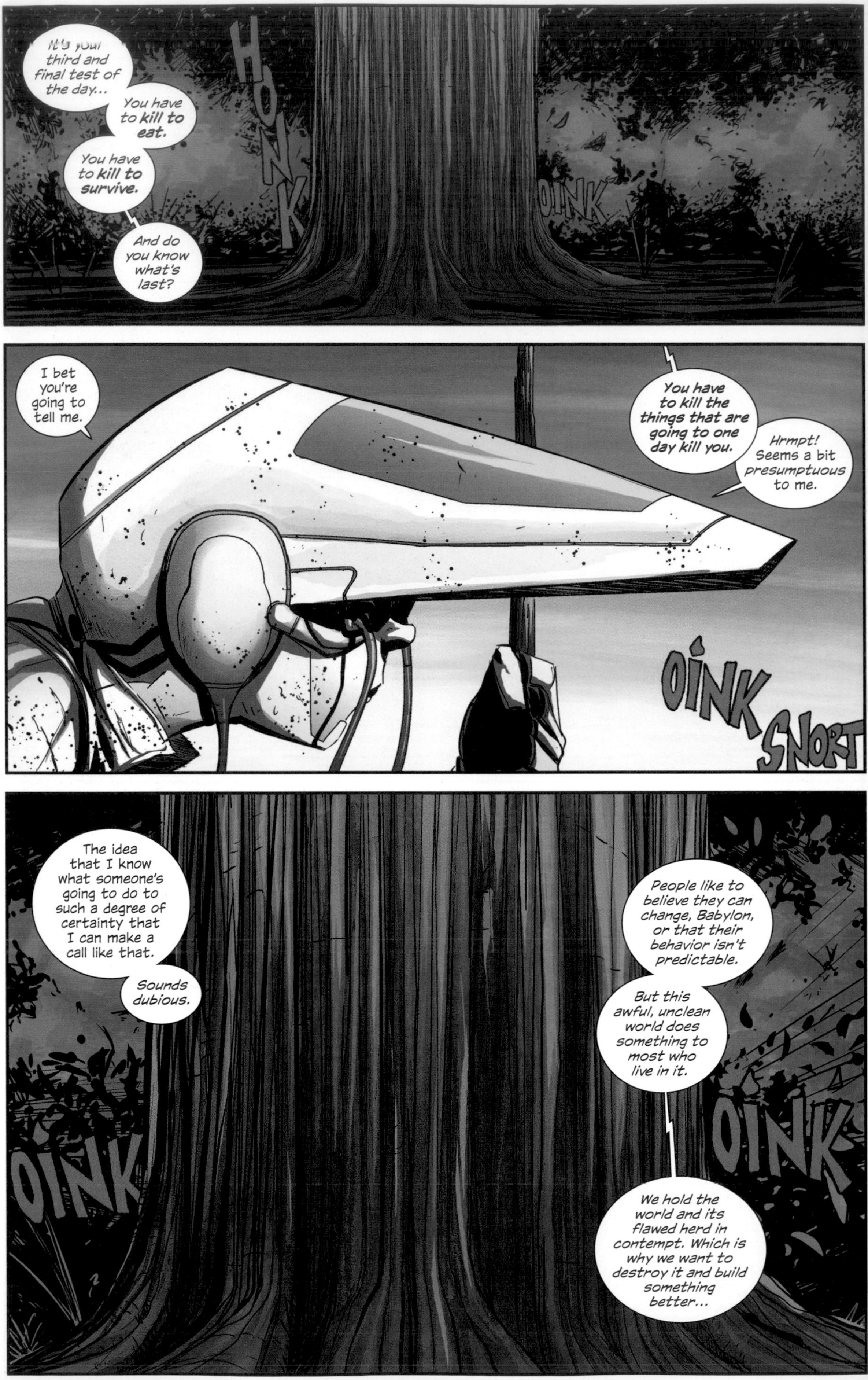
It's your third and final test of the day...
You have to kill to eat.
You have to kill to survive.
And do you know what's last?
HONK
OINK
I bet you're going to tell me.
You have to kill the things that are going to one day kill you.
Hrmpt! Seems a bit presumptuous to me.
OINK
SNORT
The idea that I know what someone's going to do to such a degree of certainty that I can make a call like that.
Sounds dubious.
People like to believe they can change, Babylon, or that their behavior isn't predictable.
But this awful, unclean world does something to most who live in it.
We hold the world and its flawed herd in contempt. Which is why we want to destroy it and build something better...
OINK
OINK

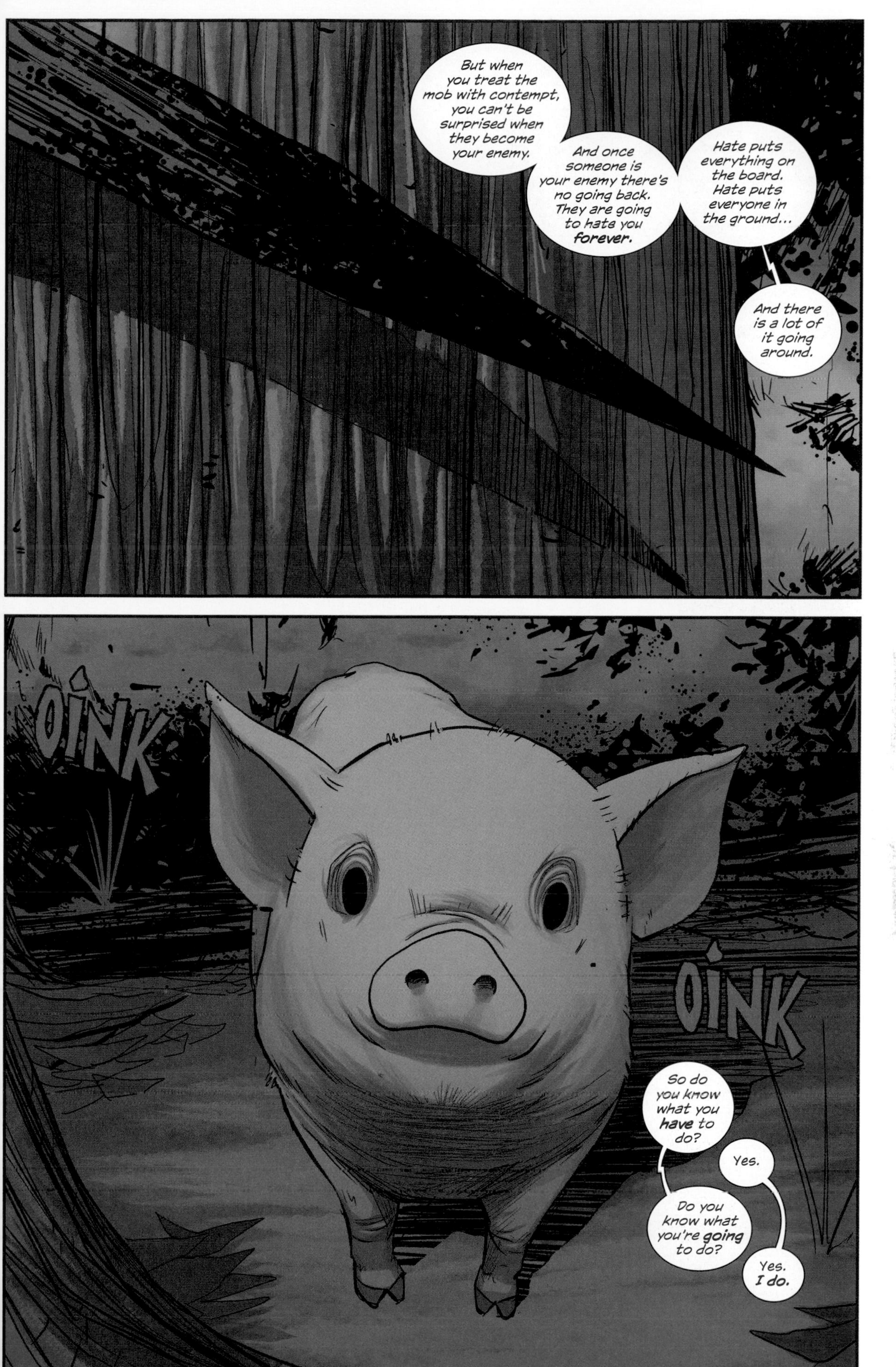
But when you treat the mob with contempt, you can't be surprised when they become your enemy.
And once someone is your enemy there's no going back. They are going to hate you **forever.**
Hate puts everything on the board. Hate puts everyone in the ground...
And there is a lot of it going around.
OINK
OINK
So do you know what you **have** to do?
Yes.
Do you know what you're **going** to do?
Yes. **I do.**

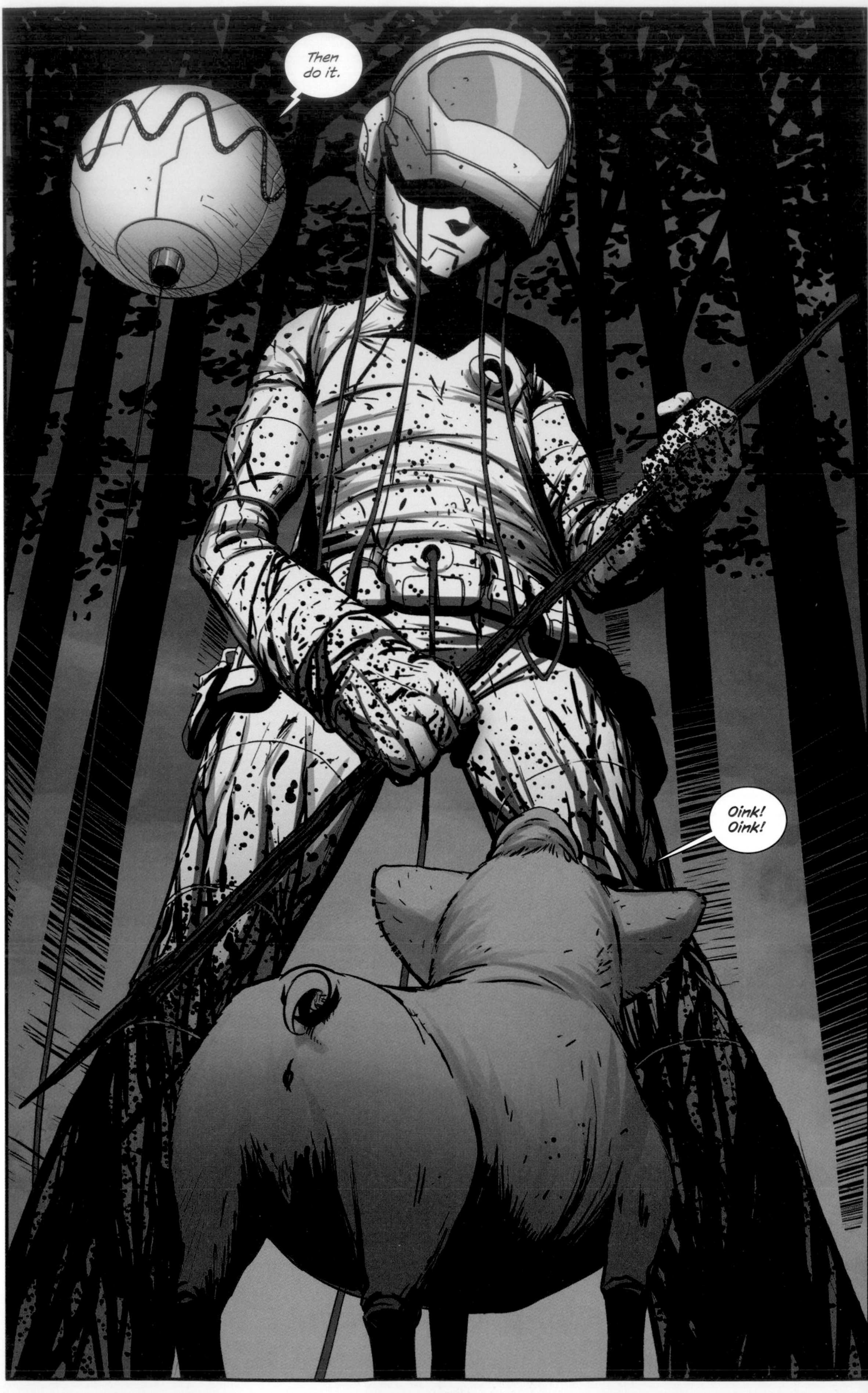
Then do it.
Oink! Oink!

ALL MEN TELL **LIES.**
THESE ARE A **FEW** OF
THEM.

Jonathan Hickman is the visionary talent behind such works as the Eisner-nominated **NIGHTLY NEWS**, **THE MANHATTAN PROJECTS** and **PAX ROMANA**. He also plies his trade at MARVEL working on books like **FANTASTIC FOUR** and **THE AVENGERS**.

His twin brother, Marc, is broken and hopes to rebuild his life.

Jonathan lives in South Carolina when he isn't vacationing or lecturing at motivational seminars .

You can visit his website:***www.pronea.com***, or email him at:***jonathan@pronea.com***.

.

Nick Dragotta's career began at Marvel Comics working on titles as varied as **X-STATIX, THE AGE OF THE SENTRY, X-MEN: FIRST CLASS, CAPTAIN AMERICA: FOREVER ALLIES,** and **VENGEANCE.**

FANTASTIC FOUR #588 was the first time he collaborated with Jonathan Hickman, which lead to their successful run on **FF.**

In addition, Nick is the co-creator of **HOWTOONS,** a comic series teaching kids how to build things and explore the world around them. **EAST OF WEST** is Nick's first creator-owned project at Image.